THE JEWEL THIEF

THE JEWEL THIEF

Jeannie Mobley

VIKING

VIKING

An imprint of Penguin Random House LLC, New York

First published in the United States of America by Viking,
an imprint of Penguin Random House LLC, 2020

Copyright © 2020 by Jeannie Mobley

Visit us online at penguinrandomhouse.com

LIBRARY OF CONGRESS CATALOGING-IN-PUBLICATION DATA IS AVAILABLE
ISBN 9781984837417

Printed in the USA

10   9   8   7   6   5   4   3   2   1

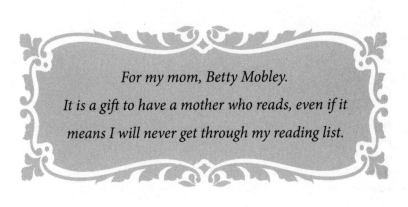

For my mom, Betty Mobley.
It is a gift to have a mother who reads, even if it
means I will never get through my reading list.

THE
JEWEL
THIEF

ONE

Louvre Palace, April 25, 1673

I kneel, gritting my teeth against the pain of my cracked ribs and blistered hand. The hard, cold edge of the marble step bites into my knees as the king's glare forces me down against it. Such cruel irony. I am exactly *where* I'd planned to be on this day, kneeling before the glory of Louis XIV, but so very far from the victory I'd envisioned. I should be here with my father, beauty beyond imagining in hand. Instead, I am chained and beaten, a delicious spectacle for this heartless court, and Papa—well, who knows exactly where Papa is. I pray to the Virgin and every saint in heaven that he is finishing our grand project and not lying in a drunken stupor somewhere, rendering all our hard work and sacrifice in vain.

"Juliette Pitau." The king's voice draws me out of my prayer. He rolls my name slowly across his tongue as he might an old wine, deciding if there is any sweetness to it, or if it has soured to vinegar.

I raise my eyes to his gleaming presence. Louis XIV is all that he claims to be—the living sun—ablaze with the fire of his own vanity. Black-clad ministers orbit him, their muted coats and manners only sharpening his brilliance. When they glance my way, they register cold indifference to colder disdain, but I don't care. The king alone matters. He alone will sanction death, and how much pain I will endure before it comes.

He alone is the one I must defy.

I clench my teeth and dare a glance at his face. A mistake, I realize too late. He snares my eyes with his own and I cannot look away. Knowing I am pinned, he smiles and leans back in his gilded chair, luxuriating in his power to hold me dangling, poised to fall the moment he wills it. He stretches out one silk-hosed leg, allowing the court to admire his strong, curving calf, his shapely ankle, and, of course, his stylish, well-heeled shoe with its preposterously large bow.

"Juliette Pitau," he says again, his voice languid like a cat lazily stretching, flexing its claws. "I am waiting for an answer."

I swallow and draw a breath. I have prepared an answer, though I know it is not the one he wants. I force out the trembling words. "I confess to all charges, Your Majesty. I alone am guilty."

His smirk tightens ever so slightly. "It seems to me, Mademoiselle Pitau, that you are at the center of a large conspiracy."

My heart contracts with fear and my words tumble out too

quickly. "No, Your Majesty. The others are innocent. They had no knowledge—"

"*Where is my diamond, Juliette?*" My name cracks like a whip on his tongue.

I swallow again as desperation flares through my body. Doubtless, the king can hear it in the quiver of my voice. But this is my only chance. "You will have it, Your Majesty. If you will only give us two days! All we have done is for your glory. You will shine like the sun, I assure you!"

His eyebrows raise in their exquisite arch, his control tucked neatly back into place. "Do I not shine like the sun already?" He shifts, letting the gold embroidery on his velvet robes catch the light. Rubies and diamonds flash from every finger.

"You are *le Roi-Soleil*," I reply, obediently. The Sun King, resplendent in his jewels and power. "The day you came into power is the day the sun rose on all of France."

Amusement ripples across his features, and I realize I have slipped into a trap. Like a cat, he will play with me for a time before the fatal blow.

"And your father?" Louis asks. "Did the sun rise on him too?"

I grit my teeth again. What answer does he expect me to make? The mouse never knows the rules of the cat's game, except, perhaps, that it can't win. All I can think is to repeat a warning I should have heeded a year ago. "If you are the sun, Your Majesty, my father is Icarus."

"Ah, Icarus, who flew too close to the sun in his waxen wings and fell. Do you expect my pity, mademoiselle?"

A single tear falls down my cheek before I can stop it. "My father believed he was doing your bidding, Your Majesty." It's what I should have said before.

"And was that your intent too? To do my bidding?"

I lower my gaze to the enormous bows on his shoes, hoping humility will lend credence to my answer. "Yes, Your Majesty."

"Then tell me *where the diamond is!*" he demands, slamming a fist on the arm of his chair. The assembled ministers jump, puppets on a single string.

I jump too. Pain explodes along my ribs where I was kicked mercilessly the night before. My hand jerks instinctively toward my side, but the chains that bind my hands deny me that comfort.

"Spain, perhaps? Were you working for Charles of Spain?" the king asks, pulling my attention back.

"Our work has been for you and no other, Your Majesty," I assure him, though my mouth is nearly too dry to speak.

"Then why do you defy me?"

Choosing words wisely has never been my talent, but I struggle forward. "The diamond is not ready, Your Majesty. Give my father two more days and you will have it. I swear on the Virgin Birth, I am telling the truth."

"You will forgive me if I have little confidence in your claims of truth," he says.

I raise my eyes to his again. Such boldness could cost me dearly, but he must see my sincerity. "If you will grant us the time, I will confess all and the diamond will be returned more glorious than you can imagine."

His lip curls in an arrogant smile. "You underestimate my imagination, mademoiselle."

I smile back, dangerously matching his arrogance, knowing I do not. "Two days, Your Majesty. Please."

"And if I do not grant you that time?"

"Then I will tell you nothing and your diamond will be lost." The words are out before I can stop them, but even as I speak, I know I have gone too far. If stealing the diamond didn't solidify my fate, my impudence surely will.

The king throws back his head and laughs so hard it sets the long black ringlets of his wig bouncing. His ministers try to join in, but they cannot seem to muster more than a nervous tittering.

As for me, I must clench every muscle in my aching body to remain still.

"I have no need of your bargains, mademoiselle," the king says when his mirth has died away at last. "Monsieur Colbert, have the charges read. She is wasting my time."

"Yes, Your Majesty," Jean-Baptiste Colbert says with a reproachful glance at me. I have known him since childhood, when his frequent visits to Papa's workshop were accompanied with bonbons for my brother and me, but his loyalty to Louis makes him now as cold as the rest. He turns and nods to a clerk, who steps forward from the shadows, breaking my heart all over again.

How could they be so cruel as to give this job to René? Dear, kind, gentle René. Of everyone I have hurt he deserves it the least. I squeeze my eyes shut and bite my lip to hold back the sob that rises in my throat, but his voice, hard and indifferent, tears a deep gash in my defiance, and I cannot hold my anguish.

"Juliette Pitau, you are herewith charged in the court of His Majesty King Louis XIV of France with consorting with Jews, conspiracy with known traitors, theft from the treasury of France, and high treason against the king."

The room falls silent when he has finished. Hot tears slide down my cheeks.

At last, the king speaks. "You do not deny these charges?"

"I deny treason, Your Majesty. Of the rest, I am guilty."

The king stands. "Take her away."

The guards who brought me and forced me to my knees now grip my arms and haul me upright again. I lift my head at last and wince to find myself eye-to-eye with Louis, who rises from his gilded throne to get the last word.

He steps forward, and tilts my face upward to his with a painful grip on my jaw. The large ruby on his finger, a stone that I myself polished for his pleasure, bites into my throat. His breath is hot and foul on my face.

"Be assured, Juliette Pitau. Before you die, you *will* tell me what you have done with my diamond."

Two

What you have done with my diamond. I almost laugh at his choice of words. There is so much more to that answer than simply the question of where it is. That is a story that might redeem me if I were allowed to tell it. More likely, I will be taken to the rack, where my answers will be necessarily brief. I shudder, and the rising laughter curdles into something bitter.

The king releases my chin and turns away. The guards yank me toward the door, but I refuse to be dragged away moaning and begging for mercy, so I find my feet, stiffen my back, and raise my head to glare around me at the dozens of gawking faces, eager for fresh gossip. Most of them are strangers—bored gentlemen twirling their wide mustaches, curious ladies fluttering fans—all indulging in the brief entertainment of a craftsman's daughter's condemnation. No doubt my defiance made it better sport for them. Gave them something to talk about in their salons this evening.

The few faces I recognize are no more comfort than the strangers. Suzanne du Plessis-Bellière looks wary, but she needn't be. She has survived greater scandals than any that may arise here. Master and Madame Valin glow in triumph at my demise. They have never made a secret of their spite. I glare back and pray they will be rewarded for their role in this by the fires of hell.

André stands beside them, in a brocade coat far too fine for his status, his chestnut hair arranged in curls on his shoulders instead of pulled back in a practical ponytail as befits a craftsman. Apparently, he has profited nicely from all of this. I flinch despite myself when our eyes meet. I search his smooth face for something—anything—of his feelings. I have known André longer than any of them, and yet his expression is empty of kindness or sympathy or regret. Perhaps he feels none.

The guards pull me away, out of the room and down unadorned corridors meant only for servants and undesirables such as myself. At last they step out into the blinding sunlight of a small courtyard. I gulp down a few breaths of fresh air while I have the chance, before being stuffed into the black-shuttered carriage that will return me to my prison cell at the Bastille. It is a small mercy that, since the king is trying to avoid scandal, I am spared the open cart that exposes most prisoners to public ridicule.

Many of the cells in the Bastille are quite fine, intended as they are for the king's enemies of noble rank. I, however, am only worthy of a small chamber of bare stone with one tiny window set high on the wall to let in the mere suggestion of light and air. The only furnishing is a single narrow cot covered with a worn woolen blanket, and a broken pisspot, its dried-up contents spread across the floor in the corner. The room is dark and reeks of suffering.

I retreat to the cot, toss aside the blanket, which is crawling with fleas, and curl myself into the corner, hugging my knees to my chest. Alone at last, I let the tremors rise from the cold dread at my core.

There will be torture—Louis has assured me of that. Will it be the rack? Hot pincers under my skin? Fear writhes like maggots inside me. I should have fawned and complimented and begged the king for mercy; perhaps then he would have granted me a quick end. Too late, my mind scrabbles for some way out, some way to once again twist ruin to opportunity, but this time, there are no further chances, I am as impotent as a rat in a cage, facing only a black, hopeless ending. My squirming gut gets the better of me, and I bend over and heave the dregs of bile from my empty stomach onto the floor.

To come so close only to end in such failure. My cause had been noble: to save Papa, save our Jewish friends, resurrect beauty out of the wreckage of my father's despair. Instead, I have destroyed it all. If Papa is the classical Icarus flying too near the sun in his waxen wings, I am Daedalus, who crafted those wings and launched him on his fatal flight. I bury my head in my arms in a futile effort to ward off black despair.

When I hear a key in the lock, I sit up and I try to pull myself together. I expect the torturer, but it is not some faceless, shirtless brute from the bowels of the dungeon. It is Monsieur Colbert and René, still in their neat court dress, looking out of place in the filthy cell.

I scramble to my feet, carefully keeping my eyes away from René. Having him see me like this, my muslin dress torn and streaked with blood, my hair in a wild tangle, and my face bruised and tearstained, is a needless humiliation. Neither of us deserves this indignity, but all I can do is pretend it away and focus hard on Colbert. I curtsy before him, and his eyebrows arch.

"A bit late to find your manners, mademoiselle. More grace and less pride would have served you well before the king."

"*Oui*, monsieur," I agree humbly, though this is hardly a revelation. Now, however, is not the time to offer insolence, not when this might be my last chance to beg for mercy.

Stepping aside from the doorway, he snaps his fingers, and a bevy of servants scramble in. They set a table and chair in the middle of the room. I watch in confusion as they arrange a stack of papers and all that is needed to write—quills, penknife, pounce pot, and inkwell—on the table. Out of the corner of my eye, I can see René pressed against the wall beside the door, as if I am a poisonous serpent and he means to keep as far from me as possible in the close, entrapping space. Try as I might to pretend indifference, my rebellious eyes seek him out. He is dressed as usual in the unadorned coat and breeches of fine black wool, befitting his station as a clerk, but I think him the most beautiful thing in Louis's court. His smooth brown hair is tied back simply with a black ribbon. It looks so soft in the dim light that my fingers tingle with the urge to touch it. His high brow and warm, honeyed eyes usually give his face an openness I find endearing. Now, however, anger has chiseled those features into a stony mask. Knowing that I am to blame for this transformation gouges me with guilt, and I wrench my eyes back to Colbert.

The last servant sets a jug of wine and a cup on the table and hurries out of the cell, closing the door behind him. Only then does Colbert speak.

"I do not know, mademoiselle, why the king did not pronounce a sentence this morning. You certainly gave him ample reason to condemn you."

I stare, blinking, like a rabbit pulled from its warren. Stunned. I assumed, with my admission of guilt, that my fate was sealed. Hope floods through me at what the table, the papers, and the quills might mean.

"I thought it was to be . . ." My words trail off, unwilling to suggest the unthinkable.

"You play a dangerous game," Colbert says, his tone cautionary. "You are very lucky the king is in a merciful mood. His Majesty has granted you one day to tell all before he pronounces your sentence. One day to make your confession and to produce the diamond that you claim now carries the sun within it."

"He has agreed to my bargain?" A way forward opens before me, only to be slammed shut by Colbert.

"He agrees to nothing!" he snaps. "Are you so stupid that you think you can bargain with the king before the whole court? Make deals with him for mercy in exchange for his own stolen property?"

I bite my lip. Of course, the king could not appear so weak.

"Make no mistake, no bargain has been struck," Colbert continues. "Louis may end this little arrangement at any time he desires. You have piqued his curiosity. Perhaps it was in calling your father Icarus. The king likes a good tale, after all, and at the moment, yours might amuse him. And your accomplices will hardly smuggle the stone out of Paris now—every way is watched and every wagon searched."

"The Blue will not be smuggled out," I assure him. "It only wants polishing and a setting fit for a king."

"Then why not reveal its whereabouts now?" Colbert asks.

His question is sincere, his tone almost imploring, and temptation tugs at me to tell him. But for any of us to earn the king's pardon, the stone must be perfection, and I must have the chance to prove that the others are innocent, even if I am not.

"Many months of hard work and great skill have gone into the stone, monsieur. It should go to the king a finished masterpiece. After all, the Blue is the work of two masters," I say, hoping he understands. "Truly, it will far exceed the king's expectations."

Colbert considers me for a long moment while my eyes plead with him. Finally, he sighs and, with the flick of his hand, signals to René, who has remained beside the door. Still silent and scowling, René steps forward, pulls out the chair, and seats himself. He picks up the penknife and begins sharpening the quills one at a time.

"You have one day, Juliette," Colbert says. "As your hand is unfit for writing, my assistant, René, will take down your words. The king has been gentle with you so far, but he does not have to be."

I try to flex my burned hand, which, even if I survive, might never write again. He has a strange idea of gentle, but I say nothing.

Colbert does not notice. He picks up a quill and considers it, running his fingers along its smooth white length.

"Do you see this feather, mademoiselle?" he says after a moment. "It is not wax. It will not melt in the sun. It holds within it the power of flight. Of freedom. Remember that, if you wish to save yourself. You must tell all, truthfully, and with respect. *Comprenez-vous?*"

"*Oui*, monsieur."

He sets the quill back on the table and straightens his velvet coat with a crisp tug at its embroidered lapels. "I have other matters to attend to. The affairs of state do not wait on the whims of a foolish girl." He nods once to René, then turns abruptly and is out the door, which is sealed and locked behind him.

I wait in silence until the lock clangs shut, then I let out my breath and turn to René. It is a blessed relief to have a friend at last, even a friend who is angry with me. Not that I can blame him. I owe him an apology after our last meeting, and my arrest must have put him in an uncomfortable position at court. Yet I am surprised at the set of his jaw and his complete refusal to look at me. He sharpens a quill, then uncorks the inkpot, moving in a measured, methodical way, as if I am not even in the room. As if I am not even alive, which, come tomorrow, may very well be the case.

I know I must swallow my pride and apologize if I am going to set things right between us, so I clear my throat and speak.

"René, I am sorry."

The granite contours of his face shift but don't soften. He says nothing.

"I am sorry," I repeat, more insistent this time. "I do not blame you for what happened when—"

His eyes narrow. "Perhaps, mademoiselle, I blame you," he says, anger clipping each word.

I wince at this unexpected jab. My apology could have been more humble, but this retort seems unfair.

"I never meant to hurt you," I assure him, hoping to explain. "You know I'd been dealt a terrible blow when we last met."

"You think this is about our last meeting?" At last he looks at me, and I am forced back by the blaze of his eyes.

A new fear grips my heart, and I can't breathe. What if this is no mere quarrel between us? What if I have lost his love for good?

"To think I imagined myself in love," he sneers, unmoved by the horror that must show openly on my face. He rises from his seat and stalks away from me.

"René—"

"You're not capable of love. Everything between us was a lie!" He turns back to glare at me, challenging me to defend myself, but I am so appalled by the injustice of his accusation that I can only gape at him. Even my silence seems to offend him, and he begins pacing the cell like a trapped beast.

I feel trapped too, as if there is not enough air in the room for the two of us. I push down my rising panic.

"René, I don't know what you've heard," I begin, trying to keep my voice steady, "but—"

"Damn it, Juliette! I've heard it all!" He slams his fist against the wall, and I shrink back. "I know about the other men—about your long history of seductions to get what you want."

"What are you talking about?" This is a version of me I'm sure he's never met, as I am not aware of it myself.

"I was there yesterday for André's full testimony. Imagine what a fool I felt."

"André. Of course." My indignation rises to full boil. I hardly dare imagine the lies André is spreading with that treacherous serpent's tongue of his. "And I suppose he's cast himself as an innocent victim in this whole affair? One of my hapless conquests?"

A stricken look floods across René's face. Apparently, that is exactly what André has said. My hands go to my hips.

"Honestly, René, how can you believe André?"

"Madame du Plessis-Bellière has given an account too," he says.

This brings me up short. André has condemned me with lies, but Suzanne du Plessis-Bellière might have condemned me with the truth. No wonder René thinks the worst of me. I shudder. If I have poisoned his sweet heart into something hard and bitter, perhaps I deserve the punishment that awaits me. And yet my motives were always pure. I cling to that solid fact amid the flotsam of my once-glorious plans.

"Just hear my side of the story," I beg.

He gives a sharp, cynical laugh. "I have no choice, do I? My penance for falling into your web is to record your confession." He takes his seat again and dips the quill in the ink. "If it were up to me, the king would have condemned you and been done with it."

His words wound me, as he intends. If they are true, the king's pardon would hardly matter, but I am not willing to believe them so easily. I plant my hands firmly on the table and lean over it, bringing us face-to-face.

"Look me in the eye and tell me you mean that," I demand.

He glances at me, then quickly away. It is enough. I have seen the wounded love still within him, and I know what I must do. My confession must acquit me with the king, but more than that, it must reach deep into René's injured heart and rekindle the affection there. And yet some of what I must tell the king will surely hurt René more deeply.

So, this is my choice, then: to strive to save myself and in so doing lose René, or strive for his forgiveness and forsake my life? I close my eyes for a moment to quiet my pounding heart and gather in the chaos of my thoughts. I have faced the impossible before and overcome it.

The king only wants to know where the diamond is and how I managed to steal it from under his nose. But if I am going to win back René's love, I must tell more. I must relive all the tragedy and heartbreak that brought me here. It would be so much easier to just tell the king what he wants to know, but the king's pardon without René's forgiveness? Life without love is not enough.

Strengthened by this conviction, I start at the beginning.

THREE

The day of Cardinal Mazarin's funeral, my life changed forever. Many people's lives changed when he died, not least of all Mazarin's. Of course, King Louis would say that when Mazarin died, the sun rose in the court of France. With his death, Louis claimed his inheritance, which included more than just the crown. It included the cardinal's famous diamonds, eighteen seemingly miraculous stones that glittered with an internal fire, unlike any other diamonds in the world. Possessing those stones kindled a new fire in young Louis's heart.

"You are meant to be confessing your crimes, mademoiselle," René interrupts impatiently, "not recounting the history of France. Mazarin died more than a decade ago."

"But that is the day it all began," I insist. "If I don't start there—"

"I am only here to record your confession. Tell me how you stole the diamond, and nothing more."

I don't want to argue, so I simply continue where I left off. "Papa had been an ordinary gem-cutter before that day, with our apartments over his workshop and Maman taking commissions and selling fine trinkets from a counter in the front. That morning, with Mazarin barely in his tomb, soldiers came to Papa's workshop and took him to the king. I was only six, but I remember that day vividly."

"No doubt," René mutters. He is turning the quill idly in his hand and not writing anything down. "Even then you were calculating how you might rise in the world."

On the contrary—I was terrified. Imagine how you would feel to see the king's men come for your beloved father. I cried, and Maman paced the floor until he returned an hour later, his eyes ablaze with excitement. He strode directly to the table, and there, on its bare surface, he tipped out a velvet bag. Three raw amethysts clattered to the tabletop.

Maman looked at him, her gaze full of question and hope.

"His Excellency the Cardinal has left his jewels to the crown," Papa said.

"His diamonds?!" Maman exclaimed, her eyebrows raising. I had heard the Mazarin diamonds excitedly discussed on more than one occasion. When master gem-cutters dined together, the mystery of their rare brilliance was often the topic of debate.

"I've seen them, Marie!" Papa said, his eyes themselves glinting like diamonds. "They let me examine them. It is as I have always speculated. They are diamonds, like any other. But the cut! *Mon Dieu*, Marie! It is the cut that gives them that sparkle—that brilliance."

My mother looked down at the three large, uncut stones on the table. "And these?" she asked.

Papa picked up one of the stones, rolling it between his fingers, examining how the light caught and shifted on it. "He wants to outshine Mazarin. He wants to outshine all the world, and I daresay he will, Marie. He is challenging every master gem-cutter in Paris to cut him stones that will outshine the Mazarins. From the result, he will select his crown jeweler."

Maman drew in a sharp gasp of air. "Can you do it, Jean? Can anyone?"

Papa's smile widened. "I have seen them, Marie. I have touched them. Mark my words, I will make young Louis shine like the sun!"

And of course, he did just that, at least with those first stones. When he was appointed as crown jeweler, our lives changed forever. We moved to the royal jeweler's workshop and apartments in the Manufacture Royale des Meubles de la Couronne on the Left Bank. It was very grand, but it was the king's property—all of it. We were—are—entirely dependent on the favor of the king. You accuse me, René, of striving for glory, but striving to see Papa succeed was not ambition. Our home, our lives—everything depended on it.

I was on the cusp of womanhood seven years later, in 1668, when Jean-Baptiste Tavernier returned from India, brightening a gray Paris winter with silks and gems and tales of adventure. Across the Seine in the Marais district, the salons of the nobility buzzed with his stories of forbidden delights and wealth beyond imagining. But for me, the real excitement began when the king invited Tavernier to appear—along with his rumored hoard—at the Louvre Palace. Tavernier's audience before the king foretold great glory for us. He was rumored to have brought back hundreds of precious stones, and so we were invited to the spectacle.

Maman had fine new gowns made for both of us for the occasion. She needed a new gown to adjust to her changed figure since giving birth to my brother Georges just a year before, the first of her many pregnancies since my birth to bring forth a healthy child. She chose patterned, dove-gray wool for her gown that disguised her gradually thickening waistline and elegantly contrasted with her dark eyes and hair. As for me, Papa's position had earned our family wealth and prestige over the past seven years, and Maman was determined to capitalize on his position to make a good marriage for me when the time came.

"They will see you as the fine bud you are and know you will blossom into a lovely wife for a lucky gentleman's son," Maman said, smiling approvingly as the seamstress fitted me in rosy silk, creamy lace, and boning that rendered me nearly too stiff to move. "It's never too soon to be seen."

I had no objection to my mother's schemes on my behalf, but I was still a child at heart. I wasn't thinking about gentlemen's sons, but of Tavernier's stories of tigers and elephants, powerful rajas and golden palaces. I was eager, too, to see his rumored hoard. The diamond mines of India were said to produce miraculously colored stones the size of small dogs.

As we arrived at the palace, my heart fluttered like a caged bird, trapped in the stiff bodice of my gown. Maman and Papa walked in front, and baby Georges had been left at home with a nurse, so I was free to crane my neck to gawk at the glories of the palace without Maman's reproach.

The Louvre offered every pleasure to the eye with its high marble columns, painted ceilings, and polished floors, but what I remember most was the light. The way it flowed in through the windows and transformed the very air into something glorious. The way it livened the gilded plaster scrollwork along the walls, brightened the king's ancestors where they looked down with cool arrogance from a dozen portraits. Everything was grander and mightier in that golden light, as if light itself had been bent to the service of the king.

"Isn't it gorgeous, Juliette!" said André, my father's apprentice, who walked beside me. While I had been brought along to be seen by prospective husbands, André had come to assist Papa in evaluating Tavernier's gems. André had only been with Papa for about a year, and I still knew more about diamonds than he did. Maman, however, insisted I be seen as an elegant young lady, and that meant refraining from menial work.

The king's great audience chamber was already overcrowded and noisy when we entered, a crush of vibrant silks and rich damasks, a hundred voices clamoring in boast and gossip. I had felt proud and elegant to don the first properly grown-up gown I'd owned, but now, as I looked around at the real ladies of court, their hair wrapped in strands of pearls, their throats sparkling with gemstones, their cunning use of powder, rouge, and lace leading the eye downward toward the treasures barely concealed by plunging necklines, I felt like a plain child of the streets. I shifted closer to Papa and slid my hand into his.

"Juliette, *mon petit bijou*, you are not shy, are you?" he said.

I shook my head, but clutched his hand a little tighter. I tried a deep, steadying breath, but the air was thick with perfume and the musk of unwashed bodies and it made me a little dizzy.

He bent to speak into my ear. "These are the finest people in the world, *ma chérie*. There is nothing here to be afraid of!"

"*Mais oui*, Papa," I said, and forced myself to let go of his hand.

Maman straightened the bow in my curls and smiled at me. "Nothing at all to fear, Juliette," she repeated. "You look beautiful."

A man in the uniform of the *garde du corps*, the king's personal guard, approached us, and Papa turned to him, all business.

"Monsieur Pitau, I am instructed to escort you to His Majesty," the guard said.

Papa nodded, and we made our way forward through the crowd, following the bobbing plume on the musketeer's hat.

That was the first time I saw His Majesty Louis XIV up close. He was seated on his gilded chair on the dais at the head of the room, draped in flowing robes of blue and gold velvet. His red stockings were gartered with blue ribbons. His black curls tumbled around his shoulders, and a froth of Flemish lace adorned his throat. A massive gold sunburst set with the largest Mazarin diamond flashed upon his breast. At first, I was besotted by his genteel beauty, but when he turned his keen black eyes on my father I shrank back. It was like the sun breaking free from the clouds—a fierce, bright, cunning sun, filled with power. André felt it too, and our hands found each other of their own accord as we straightened to attention.

Papa swept into a deep bow, Maman dropping into an elegant curtsy beside him. André and I hurried to follow suit.

"Rise, Pitau," the king commanded. "This shall, I hope, be a great day for both of us." His lips curled at the prospect.

"God willing, Your Majesty," Papa replied.

"I see you have brought your family to witness the spectacle of Monsieur Tavernier."

"You were most gracious, Your Majesty, to extend the invitation to them. My apprentice, André, will assist me should the occasion require it," Papa said.

The king glanced at André and Maman. Then his eyes raked my frame from head to toe. In a mere instant, the king's gaze seemed to have stripped me naked, and my cheeks flamed.

"How old are you, Mademoiselle Pitau?" the king asked, a crinkle by his eyes betraying his amusement at my embarrassment.

"Thirteen, Your Majesty." My voice came out in a tiny squeak.

"Thirteen," the king mused. "A tender age." He had been king for nine years by the time he was thirteen, but I said nothing.

"Juliette is eager to hear tales of the Orient, Your Majesty," Papa said.

Louis looked back at me, grinning. "And tell me, would you like to travel to India, my little mouse?"

My cheeks flamed still hotter. I could feel the eyes of the court watching, enjoying this exchange. Maman's eyes were on me too, demanding a ladylike reply. I swallowed again to steady my voice. "I should like to see its wonders, Your Majesty, but perhaps not its dangers."

The king laughed. "You have raised a wise daughter, Monsieur Pitau."

Papa beamed at me. "She is my little jewel," he said.

"Your family may observe from over there, where your boy will be on hand should you require him," the king said with a vague wave of his hand, as if he had suddenly grown bored with the conversation. "You are to stay here at my side, to advise me, Jean Pitau."

"As you wish, Your Majesty," Papa said, bowing again.

Maman, André, and I moved to the side, Maman glowing with pride.

"You did well, Juliette," she said when we were out of earshot of the king. "You caught the king's eye, and I daresay that caught the eyes of the court."

I smiled, glad to have pleased her, though my knees still trembled from the encounter. A moment later, however, my attention was turned from the king as a flutter went through the crowd. Monsieur Tavernier had arrived.

He approached, a spectacle to behold. A cloak of tiger skin trailed down his back, and a turban of patterned silk, embellished with a bright blue jewel and a nodding peacock feather, swathed his head. He wore curious, curling-toed slippers of red leather, stitched all around with iridescent threads. The man glowed with the spoils of adventure, and I admired every inch of him, at least until I glanced at Louis and saw his disapproval. It was folly to shine too brightly in the presence of the Sun King.

Tavernier began tales of danger and adventure in the steaming jungles and vast deserts of India, but just as my imagination soared to that distant land, the king interrupted.

"Your hoard, Tavernier," he said. "Show us your treasure."

Tavernier nodded politely. He unfurled a velvet cloth on the king's table and tipped up a leather pouch. The crowd strained forward for a better view as hundreds of diamonds tumbled onto the velvet, glinting in the rays of sunlight that fell through the high windows of the Louvre. Tavernier spread the stones with a casual sweep of his hand, as if they were no more than kernels of wheat in the market. Even as a jeweler's daughter, I had never seen anything like it. I could scarcely draw breath. If Louis bought even a small fraction of the stones, Papa would have work to keep him for a lifetime—and a chance to craft the greatest jewels in Europe. Louis would indeed shine like the sun, and my father would be the man to make him do so.

But to my astonishment, Tavernier was not finished. He took a second bag from his belt and, reaching inside, plucked out three more diamonds, each increasing in size. Robin's egg. Quail's egg. Chicken's egg. With each, my heart pounded harder in my chest, until I thought it might burst through. The last was larger than anything the king possessed, even the famous Mazarin diamonds, though the uncut stones were not so bright.

Then Tavernier reached one more time into his bag and with deliberate slowness and a sly smile drew out the last stone.

The Tavernier Violet.

He did not lay it on the dark cloth with the others. He held it up into the light. It was deep and blue, and as big as an outstretched palm, and the air around it shuddered with the collective gasp from a hundred astonished mouths.

Perhaps God was watching, or perhaps the devil himself, because just then, the clouds parted and the sun rained in through the clerestory windows. A shaft of light broke over the stone and scattered into azure beams that danced and shimmered in the air like church light. One ray, turned by the stone's natural cleavage, shone upon the breast of the king, piercing the Mazarin diamond and casting it momentarily blue.

The sheer beauty stopped my heart for an instant. When it beat again, it was quickened with a glorious dream. Already, I was afire with pride, knowing Papa would be the one to make that vision a reality. To transform the dark, uneven stone that Tavernier held aloft into a glittering jewel on the king's breast. A jewel worthy of Louis, the greatest king in the world, to be crafted by Papa, the greatest gem-cutter.

If I had turned to Papa, I might have seen his pursed lips and furrowed brow, or even the naked fear in his eyes. I might have realized that while all the court beheld a vision of triumph, Papa was seeing his own downfall.

Three years passed. Papa polished and shaped the many small diamonds the king had acquired from Tavernier. The king's new passion for coats rather than capes created a great demand for diamond-set buttons and trim. The fact that the stones weren't afire with brilliance like the Mazarins was, as far as anyone at court knew, the fault of the diamonds, and not of the gem-cutter who fashioned them. Papa, of course, knew otherwise. Because with the abundance of diamonds from Tavernier's hoard came confirmation of what Papa had known in his heart for some time, but had shared with no one: try as he might, he could not entirely replicate the success he'd had cutting amethysts on much harder diamonds.

While Papa worked the small stones, the Violet was kept as a curiosity, not to be set in a jewel or an ornament but to be brought out and handed around whenever Louis wished to impress visitors with its unique color and enormous size of nearly 115 carats.

And yet, though it did inspire awe, its size was not enough to please the king. On the contrary, it rankled Louis that the Violet refused to shine. While the Mazarin diamonds danced in the light, the Tavernier brooded in shadow. Fire burned at the heart of the Mazarins, but the Tavernier harbored the mysterious depths known only to drowning men. The Mazarins filled the court with joy, but when Tavernier's Violet came out on its velvet pillow, the room fell silent and solemn, as if to gaze into its heart was to contemplate mortality itself.

Yet, though it did not shine at court, it burned in the king's dreams. And the dreams of a Sun King burn hot indeed. Which is why, after three years of dreaming, Louis called upon Papa to put fire into the heart of the Violet.

FOUR

I come now to one of the few parts of my story that soothes my aching heart like a balm of sweetest honey. Thinking of that night, I dare, for the first time since starting my narration, to close the space between René and me in this dreary cell. His clothes give off a spicy, perfumed scent reminiscent of court, but without the underlying stink of politics. I breathe it in and am reminded of all that I am fighting for.

"You were there the day Papa was called back to court, René. It was a great feast to celebrate some political victory for the king. My mother thought we were invited because Papa's jeweled scepter in the king's hand awed his rivals into submission. Looking back, I think it was because Louis was feeling generous in his new glory—wanting to shine for the whole world."

"A feeling you would know," René mutters.

I pretend not to hear. "How glorious the king's banquet room was! Beneath vast chandeliers glittering with crystal and hundreds of wax candles, a long, U-shaped table was laid with the finest linen and china. The king's guests milled around the room—lords and ladies so colorfully arrayed that a peacock would have seemed bland in their company."

I pause, giving René a sidelong glance and a smile as I think how to butter my next words. "Imagine my delight when, as the crowd began to take their places at the long table, the handsomest young man in the room approached and bowed before my father."

"Leave me out of it," René grumbles, and I can see he's still too hardened against me for such flattery. And yet my words are true, and it just might be that if I continue on, the account of that splendid night will begin to dissolve the hard shell on his heart.

"Whatever you feel toward me now, René, don't reject the pleasure you felt then," I say.

"It gives you pleasure, remembering how cruelly you used me?"

I refuse to rise to this bait. He can be stubborn in his conviction, but so can I. I press on, made bold by his defiance.

"I recognized you at once when you greeted Papa," I say. "You see, I had seen you before, shadowing Colbert on his visits to the workshop, accounts book in hand. I had never spoken to you before that night, but I had admired your eyes, and the way you wore your hair, simply tied back instead of the ostentatious curls flaunted by so many young gentlemen." I reach out and hesitantly touch that rich brown hair now, and am encouraged when he does not slap me away.

"I had even admired your hands," I say, looking to where he writes out the confession on which my survival depends. Such a heavy task for his elegant, fine-boned fingers. "But you had never been as handsome as you were that night. You had given up your usual drab clerk's garb for blue velvet breeches and a waistcoat of gray silk. You wore silver buttons on your coat, and your eyes glowed with welcome and good humor. When you rose from your bow and spoke, I was feeling like the luckiest girl in all of Paris."

"Monsieur Colbert sends his greetings and asks me to accompany you and your family to your seats," you said to my father, with a smile toward me that felt like a sunburst in my heart.

"How very kind," Papa said. "May I present my wife, Marie, and my daughter, Juliette." My brother, Georges, of course, was still too young to attend such an event with us.

You bowed again before us and introduced yourself, your eyes dancing with pleasure, and oh, René, how my heart leapt.

We were seated far down the table, nowhere near the king, but I didn't mind. Especially not when you took the seat beside me. Soon the courses of food began to arrive: basted pheasant, calf's liver, and oysters to start, followed by soups of every hue— chestnut and cream, bisque of shellfish, beef madrilene. After the soup came platters of whole fish on beds of smoked eels, then courses of glazed duck and hares stuffed with truffles.

"What do you think of the king's table?" you asked me, as the plates were cleared and new ones set before us in preparation for the twelfth course. I shifted in my seat, my corset stays straining, though we were not yet to dessert.

"I have never seen so much fine food," I said. We had always eaten well, but I had never sat through more than six courses before. We'd been at table for nearly two hours, and yet servants were now carrying in entire haunches of roast venison, studded with cloves of garlic.

You laughed, not in ridicule, but in agreement. "It is overwhelming, is it not? My first feast at the palace lasted nearly five hours—and I had filled up by the third course, not expecting another fifteen to come. I thought I would burst."

"I'm near to bursting," I admitted, realizing only after I'd spoken that my words might not befit a lady. I was glad Maman was seated on the other side of Papa where she could not hear.

"So, you have not always been here at the palace?" I asked, trying to move past my faux pas.

"My father sent me to work with Colbert three years ago, when I turned fifteen."

"Three years?" I said, calculating quickly in my head. "That is when I first came to the palace too. When Monsieur Tavernier presented his hoard to the king."

Your face lit with a smile. "I had only been here a few months then. Tavernier's visit was so anticipated that Colbert let us all off our tasks so we might attend. I had been terribly homesick until then, and the spectacle was very welcome."

"It was a spectacle," I agreed.

You laughed again, an easy, unaffected laugh that made a lightness rise up inside me.

"In truth, I didn't see a thing," you said. "I wasn't very tall then, and I was in the back of the crowd with some gentleman's velvet cape flapping in my face. All I saw of Tavernier that day was the feather in his cap—a ridiculously long peacock feather—bobbing around above everyone's head."

"It wasn't a cap, but a turban," I said, smiling at the memory. As a child of thirteen, I had thought it very elegant, but in hearing his description, I could see how ridiculous it had been, a Frenchman dressed up like a raja when he was not even a gentleman.

"I saw plenty of his riches after that day, though," you continued. "Colbert set me to the task of cataloging every stone for the crown's records. It was dazzling at first, but by the time we finished, I didn't care if I ever saw another diamond again. But I suppose you have seen far more than I."

"Perhaps," I said, "but I never tire of them."

"I should think not. All I did with Tavernier's hoard was count and weigh the raw stones. Your father turns those drab bits of rock into diamonds."

"They are diamonds all along," I reminded you, though I beamed with pride at your words. "His job is to find the beauty in them."

You gave me a flirtatious glance, and under the table, your leg shifted to brush against mine. "Your father has a great talent for creating things of beauty."

My cheeks flushed and my heart skipped a beat. I did not shift my leg away.

We talked on, speaking of Papa's work and your work for Colbert while course after course continued to arrive. Conversations around us turned to philosophy and politics, but we were cocooned in our own small pleasures, our legs still touching, our hands brushing "accidentally" against each other as we reached for food or for our glasses. In no time at all, the evening slipped away, and the clock was striking midnight.

The king wiped his mustache on the corner of the tablecloth, slipped a boiled egg into his pocket for later, and turned away from the table. He spoke a few words into the ear of Monsieur Colbert, then offered his elbow to the queen, and they retired from the chamber. This brought an abrupt end to the long feast.

At a nod from Colbert, you scrambled to your feet. "It was a pleasure to meet you, mademoiselle," you said with a small bow, before hurrying to your master.

I watched you go with disappointment, then followed Papa and Maman as we joined the stream of guests leaving the hall. But as we neared the door, we heard you calling to Papa. I blushed, thinking you were coming to declare your desire to court me, but when you reached us at last, you spoke in a formal tone, quite different from our light banter at the table.

"Monsieur Pitau, the king requires a word with you," you said, not even glancing my way.

The hopes my family had shared before the feast, which I had forgotten in your company, returned to my heart. Perhaps a great honor would be bestowed on Papa after all.

Papa turned to us. "You may wait for me in the carriage," he said, but you smiled at my mother and again at me.

"It is a cold night, and the carriage will not be comfortable. Many people attend the king's toilette. Your family may come along."

We were led to the king's bedchamber, where Louis was making ready for bed before a crowd of observers, as if watching the king put on his nightshirt was the greatest entertainment Paris had to offer. The crowd hovered on one side of a gilded balustrade. On the other side sat the king, cushioned on red velvet, his feet upon a tasseled stool. Attendants, themselves of high noble rank, assisted him out of his jewels and lace, while others pulled back the brocade curtains and turned down the embroidered coverlet on the king's massive bed. A few feet away, a dozen or more advisers stood at attention, having been summoned for a final question or task from the king. At least as many ladies and gentlemen hovered near the door in hushed reverence. They were there at the king's invitation for the honor of watching. I watched too, though my stomach squirmed at the thought of all those eyes watching me prepare for bed.

"Monsieur Pitau," the king called as we entered. He waved Papa forward to stand opposite him behind the balustrade. Maman and I held our position near the door.

"You have been my crown jeweler for a decade now, and yet you continue to amaze me," the king said, holding up the golden starburst that had just been removed from his coat.

"It is an honor to serve you, Your Majesty," Papa replied with a bow.

"That is why I have decided to entrust you with the greatest treasure of the French crown," the king said. He snapped his fingers and Colbert stepped forward from beside the bed, a pretty rosewood box in his hands. A fleur-de-lis of white oak and gold adorned the polished lid.

The crowd leaned forward with excited, expectant eyes. The box was known to them. Just as everything Louis did inspired a fashion, this box, which had been brought out to display his great treasure many times, had inspired all the ladies of court to commission such fine boxes for their jewels. Papa knew what lay within it as well. He flinched as Colbert bowed beside the king and Louis took the box into his hands.

Two words shuddered through the air, whispered from a score of awestruck lips as Louis lifted the lid to reveal the huge, dark stone, inky black on a cushion of crimson velvet: "Le Violet!"

My breath caught in my throat. The Violet at last. The commission above all others. I remembered again the vision of the Mazarin cast in blue upon the king's breast—the image of what the Violet would look like when Papa transformed it. My blood sang through my veins.

Louis returned the box to Colbert, who carried it to where Papa waited.

"Make it shine, Pitau," said the king. "Fill it with light, like the Mazarins!"

Papa did not reach for the box. In fact, he took an involuntary step away from it, as if repulsed.

"Your Majesty," he said, a tremor breaking his words. He

swallowed and began again. "I must remind you, if I were to cut the Tavernier in the Mazarin style, a great deal of stone will be lost. Too much stone."

"I'm sure you can find a way," said the king.

"But, Your Majesty—" Papa said again, the desperation like a knife's edge at his throat.

"Look at it, Pitau. Look!" Louis interrupted. "What do you see?"

Papa looked down into the diamond. He said nothing, but his shoulders drooped.

"What good is it to me if it does not shine? If it does not pierce my rivals with its beauty?" Louis demanded. The court murmured their agreement.

"No good at all, Your Majesty," Papa said, his voice flat with defeat.

"Make it brilliant, Pitau. Capture the sun in its heart and I will grant you a title. Imagine, monsieur, the life you could give your wife. The marriage you could secure for your daughter." He looked past Papa to us, and I lowered my eyes quickly, but not before his eyes passed over me and his lips curled in admiration.

"She is a lovely little gem herself, is she not? Imagine her as a gentleman's wife."

I heard Maman gasp, but I could not breathe.

"A marquise, perhaps. A lady of the court."

Colbert held the box out to Papa again, and this time Papa took it, though his hands shook as he did.

"Make it shine, Pitau! Make *me* shine!" the king said, his eyes already alight with the idea of it.

"Yes, Your Majesty," Papa said. He snapped the rosewood casket shut and, bowing deeply, backed to the door to take his leave.

"A title, Jean!" Maman was beaming as we made our way home in the carriage. "A title and an estate! And a fine marriage for Juliette. It is everything we ever wanted. This is the opportunity of a lifetime!"

It was exactly what I was thinking too, and yet Papa's manner confused me. He looked out the carriage window and said nothing, the melancholy that had come upon him in the king's chamber only deepening.

"And you, Juliette," Maman continued, as if unaware of Papa's despair, or perhaps trying to dispel it. "An auspicious night for you as well. Complimented by the king himself! And I daresay you had an admirer in Monsieur Relieur. What do we know of him? Who is his family?"

I smiled, savoring the night, despite Papa's gloom. "We did not speak of his family," I said. "His father sent him to work with Colbert three years ago."

Maman returned the warmth of my smile. "Perhaps the younger son of a country gentleman," she speculated. "That would be a worthy match for you, Juliette."

I glanced at Papa as Maman went on imagining bright things for our future. His lips tightened into a thin line and his hands gripped the wooden jewel box until his knuckles whitened. When our carriage arrived home at last, he stepped from it without a word. He locked the diamond away in his secure hiding place in the workshop, then trudged up the stairs to his bedchamber without so much as a *bonne nuit* to Maman and me.

I retired to my own bedchamber, but sleep would not come. When I closed my eyes, I heard again that tremor in Papa's voice. I could not understand—he'd never shrunk from a challenge before. This was the greatest commission he could hope for. At last, I rose from my bed and stole downstairs, wanting another look at the diamond, hoping to see what Papa feared.

I was startled to find Papa in the workshop, his head in his hands. Papers were strewn across the table, surrounding the Violet in its box.

"Papa?" I said, touching his sleeve with timid fingers.

He raised his head, but his eyes rose no further than the Violet.

I stepped closer and bent over the stone. In the light of a single candle, its dark heart was opaque. The thin light could not penetrate but slid, slick and oily, across its surface. I remembered the king's question and Papa's slump of despair.

"What *do* you see in it?" I asked him.

"Darkness to consume the soul," he said.

I shuddered as I leaned closer, searching for the dark omen but seeing only a stone. "But this is a great commission, isn't it?"

"It is impossible, Juliette. It cannot be done. And yet I must do it."

"But surely . . ." I let my words fade away, not knowing what else to say.

Papa sighed heavily. He gathered his papers and the gem itself and put them back into the compartment in the wall, locking them securely away. "Louis wants me to make it like the Mazarins, with fire in its heart. But when I look into the heart of this stone . . ."

He broke off, the tremor once again in his voice.

"What, Papa? What do you see?"

"Failure, Juliette," he said. "Failure and ruin and death."

FIVE

The tight pinch of René's lips has relaxed, replaced by a crinkle of pleasure at the corners of his eyes. For all his anger, my retelling of that feast conjured feelings of delight in him. And that gives me hope. But he stiffened again as I spoke of our return home and Papa's dismay, and this compels me to break from my story.

"Papa always feared that diamond," I say, reflecting back over all that's happened. "From the first time he saw it, he foresaw the truth of it."

"Do not expect my sympathy if your father's lust for glory overreached his skill," René says. I can hear the effort it takes to haul up this resentment after indulging in the pleasant recollections of that night, and I sigh with annoyance. How long can he keep this up?

"It was the diamond. The Tavernier was not a stone that could be shaped as the king demanded," I continue, though his words have stretched my patience as tight as a bowstring.

I did not understand at first, either. Surely, fashioning the Tavernier Violet for the king of France was the greatest commission in the world. I did not understand how Papa could shrink from this great work, but shrink he did. For a month he did nothing but sit in his workshop, despair hunched on his shoulders like the gargoyles of Notre-Dame.

At last, he created a mold of the diamond, and excitement coursed through me. This had to mean that work would begin. He would make a glass model on which he would cut a replica of his intended design for the king's approval. How it pained me to sit with my tutors (Maman had engaged several to prepare me for a noble marriage) when I longed to be in the workshop, watching the model take shape. Finally, one afternoon, a month after Papa created his mold, I escaped my Latin tutor, claiming the need for a privy, and slipped out of our apartment and down the narrow staircase that led to the workshop. I paused on the landing where the stairs turned and I could spy without being seen.

Papa was seated at his grinder with his back to the stairs. He was bent over the spinning grinding plate, driving the flywheel with his foot. Two glass models of the Tavernier lay on the workbench beyond him, both partially shaped but broken.

Attached to the grinder was an awkward arm of metal and wood, held in place with leather straps and a steadying hand from André. A clamp at the end of the arm held another one of the glass models of the Tavernier. As I watched, Papa gave instructions, and André lowered the model onto the grinder's spinning surface.

For a brief moment, the glass sparked against the steel plate, and I thought a facet would begin to form. But then the arm shifted with a screech, and the glass model popped free of the clamp. It tumbled twice across the spinning grinding plate before being propelled off at a wild angle. Papa made a grab for it but missed. It slammed into the stone chimney of the forge and shattered, sending a spray of sparkling shards around Papa and onto the floor.

"*Merde!*" Papa growled. "*Merde, merde, MERDE!*" He scooped up the other two models and hurled them after the first. Then he snatched the pages of calculations and threw them into the forge. André, in shocked silence, watched the parchment curl and blacken while the air around him sparkled with broken glass and rage.

"Go, André," Papa said, with a sweep of his hand toward the door. "Take the afternoon off. Enjoy yourself."

André hesitated, glancing nervously toward the forge. "I—I don't mind trying again, Master Pitau," he said.

"Go!" Papa bellowed, and this time André scurried out the door. When he was gone, Papa collapsed against the counter, his head in his hands. His shoulders heaved, and I realized he was crying.

I wanted to sneak away, back upstairs. I had never seen my father weep, and I didn't want to admit to my spying now, but I could not bear to leave him in such distress. So instead, I crept down the stairs to his side.

"Papa?" I laid my hand on his shoulder. He raised his head and squared his shoulders at my touch. "Papa, how can I help you?"

He gave me a weak smile and patted my hand where it rested on his shoulder. His fingertips were callused hard from years at the grinder.

"If only it were so simple that your soft hands might solve it," he said.

"I don't care about soft hands, Papa. I'll do anything to help." To prove my point, I retrieved the broom from the corner and swept up the shattered remains of the models.

He shook his head. "What the king asks—I haven't the means to do it."

"But, Papa, you've cut dozens of stones for the king. You're the most skilled jeweler in all of France! The king himself says so."

"You have seen the Mazarin diamonds, Juliette. They are like no other stones in the world. That is what the king wants for the Violet."

"It's not your fault if the king's diamond is different from those."

"Fetch me a glass of water, Juliette. A clear glass—one of your mother's crystal goblets. And bring a spoon too."

I scowled, thinking he was cutting off our conversation, but I did as I was told. When I returned, he set the glass on the counter before me and put the spoon in it, the handle resting against the edge of the delicate crystal, which would have raised a protest from Maman if she had known. He bent and rested his chin on the workbench so that his eyes were level with the water in the glass. I did the same beside him.

"Look at the spoon, Juliette. See how it seems to bend where it enters the water? But it's not bent—not really."

He lifted the spoon from the glass and I saw exactly what he meant. Where the spoon entered the water, it seemed to shift in space, but as he lifted it out, the handle was as straight as always. "*Oui*, Papa."

"You see? It is not the spoon that bends in the water; it is the light."

"The light?" My eyes wide, I bent closer to the glass.

"Light can be bent, just like gold or silver. But to bend light, you must shine it through something, like water."

"Or a diamond?" I said, feeling excitement as I began to understand.

Papa straightened and smiled at me. "That's my smart girl." He took a paper from his work cabinet and laid it on the workbench beside the crystal goblet. On the page was a drawing of the largest Mazarin diamond, but in addition to the lines that formed the outline of the facets, there were lighter pencil lines drawn through the surfaces.

Tracing the pencil lines with his finger, he explained how different gems bent light differently. It made sense, but there was still one thing I did not understand.

"If any diamond bends light, what makes the Mazarins different?" I asked.

Papa gave me a conspiratorial smile. "That is the secret that earned me my position. You see, when we cut a diamond as we always have, like this one"—he held up a small rose-cut stone he was resetting for the queen—"the light comes in here, bends, and goes out there." As he spoke, he touched the facets with the tip of a goose quill. "The Mazarin has been faceted on the bottom as well as the top, at very exact angles. So when the light tries to leave here, it is thrown back and hits here, where it bends again. The light is trapped inside the gem!"

"But it must come out eventually," I said, following the lines on the page with my eyes as he traced them. It was hard to imagine—bending and trapping light as if it were a tangible thing—but I looked again at the spoon in the glass and knew it was true. Why had I never noticed before?

"That is the genius of the Mazarin gem-cutter," Papa said. "He has manipulated the angles of the facets so as to turn the light completely. It finally comes back out the same surface it went in—right back at the person viewing it. That's why the stones sparkle and flash and seem so much brighter than other diamonds: the light is shining right back into your eyes. It takes great precision."

Papa laid a second page next to the first, and there he had traced the Tavernier Violet. Beside the drawing, a stream of calculations ran down the length of the page in Papa's tight, crowded handwriting.

"You see?" he said. "When we have the means to control the angles precisely, we can become gods, Juliette, molding light as easily as clay." His words had been growing more passionate, but then he sighed, and the gleam died in his eyes. "But how to achieve such precision eludes me."

"Surely you can find a way," I said, looking again at the strange contraption he'd attached to the grinder, now dangling limply from the leather straps that held it in place.

"I've tried dozens of such tools," Papa said, following my gaze. He gestured to a haphazard pile under the workbench. Arms, tongs, gears, and vises of various shapes and materials jutted out at odd, useless angles. The one on the grinder was only his most recent failure.

"How can I help?" I asked.

"Tell no one of this secret, Juliette," Papa said as he put the notes back in his cabinet and locked it. "If another gem-cutter— Paul Valin, for instance—were to learn the secret of the Maza-rins . . ." He left the thought hanging, the suggestion of threat more ominous for having been unspoken.

I snorted. "If you can't do it, Paul Valin wouldn't have a prayer. He's not half the artist you are."

He shook his head. "I have only one idea—one hope—left."

"Tell me what I can do," I begged.

"Help me convince your mother of my plan," he said, leaning close to me, drawing me in as a trusted conspirator.

I nodded, feeling important. "Of course, Papa. Just tell me how."

Papa glanced past me toward the stairs. "I think you had better attend to your own work just now and leave me to mine."

I turned and looked at the stairs. Maman and my Latin tutor were glaring down from the very spot where I'd spied on Papa.

I returned upstairs and contritely sat down to my lesson, but my mind was too filled with Papa's amazing discovery to concentrate on drab Latin conjugations. The problem ate at my mind as I stumbled like a simpleton through my lessons. I wanted to talk to Papa about it again that evening, but Papa had already moved to his last plan, and it quickly became apparent to me why Maman needed convincing.

"It's no use, Marie," he said to my mother once the fish was served and the servants had left the room. "It cannot be done. Not by me, at any rate."

"But surely—"

Papa shook his head. "I must go. There is no other way. If I go now, I can be home before winter."

"Go?" I said, looking back and forth between my parents. This was clearly something they had discussed before, but I knew nothing about it. It seemed I was not Papa's only, or even his first, conspirator. André, too, was staring at Papa in surprise.

Papa turned a sober look my way. "Only one man has cut diamonds in Mazarin's style, Juliette. I must find him. I need his help."

"But you are a master. The crown jeweler. Who could possibly teach you?" André said.

"I am not sure that what the king commands can be done, but if it can, there is only one man to do it. I must find him and learn his secrets," Papa replied.

I shuddered as I thought of what this might mean. From the earliest age I had been taught how important it was to protect a master's secrets.

"But, Jean, how will you even find him? It's a fool's errand!" Maman protested.

"Mazarin was born in Venice. It is the best place to start."

"You cannot take the king's diamond to Italy!" Maman protested.

"I will return the diamond to the king before I go," he said.

Papa turned his eyes to me, and I realized this was the help he had wanted—to convince Maman to let him go. To let him do this reviled thing: stealing another master's secret.

I swallowed the lump in my throat and put a hopeful brightness into my voice, though it sounded false even to me. "I am sure the guild in Venice will help a master of your standing," I said.

René's annoyed snort interrupts my story. His arms are folded and his quill lies useless on the table. I glance at the paper and see it remains nearly blank.

"Why aren't you recording this?" I ask.

"I haven't the paper to waste. This is not the confession you are meant to be making."

"I'm trying to explain the problem my father faced," I say. "The king must know the difficulty of the task and the extent of my father's desperation."

I wait for him to take up his quill, but he doesn't move, and I am left wondering if the man I once loved is still behind those amber eyes or not.

I tap the page in front of him with my finger to remind him of his duty. "There was no sacrifice that we did not make for the king's glory. That is why my father went to Italy—for the king's benefit, not his own. Write it down."

He raises his eyebrows. "You're saying he would not benefit from stealing another master's secrets?"

I purse my lips and look away, cringing at this portrayal of my father that no amount of loyalty can deny. "It was only so he could do what the king commanded."

"And be granted a title, and marry his daughter to a rich gentleman," René reminds me.

I throw up my hands and stalk away from the table, on the verge of snapping. This willful misunderstanding has grown unbearable. He knows how we suffered while Papa was away. He saw our misfortunes and was kind enough to ease my pain. That is the René I need with me here now, instead of this hard, embittered man who wishes me dead. I begin to despair that I can ever break through that bitterness to the wounded, tender soul beneath. The one that loved me. I close my eyes and cling to that ghost until I recover my composure, then turn back to René. My stomach clenches at the sight of the blank page before him. The king needs a confession, and the day is passing quickly.

"You must at least write down that Papa went to Italy to serve the king, and in doing so, he risked everything of ours, and nothing of the king's. He sent the diamond back to the treasury for safekeeping, despite what André wanted."

"And what did André want?" he says, his eyes narrowing and his voice taking on a jealousy that twists the conversation in an entirely different direction. I stand blinking, my mouth agape, a tangle of emotions keeping any answer from forming. André was never anything to me, and I'm sure I was never more to him than a means to an end, but René's fear of betrayal fills the room with palpable anguish. Perhaps I should feel saddened by his pain, but instead a small smile forms on my lips. One cannot feel jealous, after all, if affection is completely gone.

I proceed carefully.

"André wanted my father to pass him out of his apprenticeship before leaving," I reply. "To give him control of the workshop, and of the king's diamond, but Papa would not take such a risk."

At last, René writes this favorable information down.

"And what else did André want? Or more to the point, what did he get?" René asks, his tone accusatory.

I ignore his implication. "André got room and board and skills that could open doors at every court in Europe."

René slams his fist on the table and I jump.

"Don't toy with me, Juliette! I know you were alone with him all those months."

"Not by choice!"

"If nothing untoward happened in your father's absence, why did you refuse Paul Valin's help?" René asks.

A snort of laughter escapes me, as bitter as any grievance René has yet aired. "Can you believe for a moment that Paul Valin would have acted honorably in my father's workshop while Papa was away? You know how the Valins have treated us." Even mentioning it brings frustrated tears to my eyes, and I blink fiercely to hold them back.

There is a pause before René answers, and for the first time, his voice is soft. "I never condoned Valin's cruelty, Juliette," he said. "He has conducted himself dishonorably. But he was within his rights. If your father had not—"

"Don't you dare blame my father!" The force with which these words explode from my throat surprises even me. I turn to face him, tears streaked across my face. "Blame me if you must, blame the king and his vanity, but do not blame Papa. He sacrificed everything for the king. Everything!"

Again, there is a long silence between us, but this time I do not look away and I do not bother to dry my tears. My eyes stay locked on René, daring him to contradict me, hoping that he will apologize instead.

He does neither. He simply lowers his eyes to the page. I cannot tell if he regrets his words or if he simply wants to finish this task and get out of this stinking cell.

I inhale slowly to cool my anger and collect my thoughts. I cannot afford such outbursts, not when opportunities to gain René's understanding are so few, and so fragile. I must convince him to record something that will exonerate me with the king. Perhaps recounting the events of the next few months will soften both the king and René, as they once did.

All too soon, we were saying goodbye to my father, hugging and kissing him while his coach waited to carry him to the coast.

Tears were on Maman's cheeks. Papa brushed them away with trembling fingers.

"*Mon coeur,*" he said. Then he pulled her into a fierce embrace, as if she truly was his heart and to tear himself from her would be fatal.

"The sooner you go, the sooner you can return," Maman said, pulling away at last.

He nodded, but did not move toward the coach. He bent and swept up Georges, swinging him around before hugging him and kissing him on the neck. Then he shook André's hand. Yes, André was there, as if he was part of the family. Though he was an apprentice, he ate his meals with us and was always treated with affection by my parents.

Papa turned to me last. "Juliette. *Mon petit bijou*." He reached an arm toward me, and I rushed into his embrace. "Be a help to your maman," he whispered into my ear. "I'm counting on you to watch over the workshop. You know my most precious secret now; that makes you my partner in this great endeavor."

"*Oui*, Papa. I will, I promise," I said, squaring my shoulders, proud and determined to live up to the honor.

He let go of me, touched Maman's cheek one last time, then hurried to the carriage and climbed inside. With a clatter of hooves and a grinding of wheels, he was gone, in search of a stranger in a strange land. Leaving me bound by a promise far greater than I could have imagined.

Six

"So all that time, your father was in Italy looking for this mysterious master?" René asks. "Not looking for gold as you told Colbert?"

"If Louis had known the truth about why Papa left, we would have lost everything—our position, our home, Papa's reputation."

"Your chance of a noble marriage," he slips in, as if this transgression galls him more than all the rest. I don't understand. He had no objection to me or my status as a craftsman's daughter when we met that night at the king's banquet. It was he who sought me out, he who wooed me all those months after. Why does he despise me for my wish to marry a man of his status now?

I scrutinize his face. The lingering injury I can see in his eyes fills me with a tender longing to hold him and soothe away the hurt, whatever its cause.

"When I met you, I thought you were different," he continues, "but you're like all the others at court, saying anything that will get you ahead."

I shake my head. "I never lied to you, René."

"You lied about your father's absence."

I bite my lip. Surely he can see that that is not what I'm talking about now. I want to talk about us. About how I hoped to marry him because I *loved* him, not because I craved position. But first, it seems, I have to justify keeping a secret I'd promised my father I'd keep. This defense only makes him scoff.

"Your father never meant to bind you. It's merely what a father says to a child to comfort her upon his departure."

His suggestion—that I, at sixteen, was a simple child—makes me grind my teeth, but I say nothing. Soon enough he will see that what I have done is no mere child's play.

Papa was gone and the Violet was safely back in the king's coffer, but that didn't stop me from thinking about how it might be cut. With my promise fresh in my mind, I dedicated myself to better understanding what Papa had tried to teach me about angles and light.

My tutor was surprised by my newfound interest in math, a subject that until then had not held my interest, and that he did not consider ladylike. To quell my relentless questions about the symbols and calculations I had seen in Papa's notes, he grudgingly provided me with a hefty, dry tome by René Descartes and left me to try to decipher it while he turned his attention to teaching Georges his sums. My promise to Papa pushed me to glean what I could from the book. I had no clear plan or idea in mind, but I wanted to be ready to help when Papa returned from Venice with the skills to do the job. Meanwhile, André worked in the workshop, completing the settings on a few jewels the king would give as gifts. Papa considered him far enough advanced in his skills to be trusted alone on the king's lesser projects, and André took these to heart, always happiest when he had free rein over a project and could add something of his own vision to it. He did not much miss Papa, at least not at first. I would work alongside him whenever I could, but I kept my study of mathematics to myself. If Papa had chosen not to share his secrets with his apprentice, it was not my place to reveal them.

Though we were insulated from the gem-cutters guild by our position among the king's artisans, news had a way of getting quickly to the ears of the guild master. Papa had been gone from the city for scarcely more than a day before his wife, Madame Valin, came nosing around the workshop. Maman rolled her eyes at her arrival, but invited her to take tea in the parlor, knowing that any rudeness would only inspire more nosiness.

Madame Valin glanced covetously around the room before installing herself regally in Papa's chair by the fireplace. She noticed me by the window, a heavy book before me, and wrinkled her nose.

"To what do I owe the honor of your visit, madame?" Maman asked, before she could offer her opinion of my studies.

Madame Valin squared her shoulders and spoke. "I heard a rumor that Master Pitau is away."

Maman nodded.

Madame Valin waited with raised eyebrows.

Maman poured the tea.

"I understand he has gone looking for fine gold?"

"That's right," Maman replied, handing her a cup. I bit my lip to keep my expression from revealing anything. I was glad that Madame Valin's sources had gotten it wrong. I was glad, too, that Maman did nothing to enlighten her.

"Then he will have gone to Spain, I suppose?"

"He will go wherever he needs to," Maman said.

Madame Valin took a dainty sip from her cup before trying a different tack. "Of course. I am just surprised that he is working on the jewel's setting, when he has not yet cut the stone. That seems an odd priority, don't you think?"

She smiled as she waited for Maman's reply, but her eyes had the sharp look of a vulture. Maman gave away nothing, only smiled blandly back.

"My husband is a master craftsman, and crown jeweler to the greatest court in Europe, madame. He knows well enough what he is doing."

"But they say he has returned the Tavernier Violet to the king untouched. I hope he is not having any difficulty with the commission?"

"He would not leave the city without ensuring that the stone was in safe hands," Maman said.

"But he hasn't begun to cut it," Madame Valin persisted.

"Do you think such a stone could be cut in a mere two months?" Maman said. "Surely your husband makes plans and models before he begins work on a treasure such as that."

"Of course, of course," she said, with a wave of the hand. "I only came to offer my assistance to you while your husband is away."

"How very kind," Maman said in a voice that carried no gratitude.

When our guest was finally gone, Maman gave a growl of disgust. "Insufferable woman!" she said.

"I'm glad you got rid of her," I said.

"Oh, she'll be back. But tell her nothing, Juliette."

"Of course not!" I replied. I would never betray Papa's secrets, but especially not to a nosey old cow like Madame Valin, and I said so.

Maman gave me an understanding smile, and a warning. "Don't call her that, *ma cherie*. Always show her respect. She's a dangerous person to offend."

I wish now that I had heeded that warning, but even if I had, it might have done me no good.

Spring gave way to summer and Paris sank into swelter and fume. In the market stalls, the vegetables were limp, the cheeses sweated grease, and the meat and fish swarmed with flies. The reek of stagnant mud and sewage rose like a fog off the Seine.

Across the river on the Right Bank, the elegant homes of the nobility in the Marais district took on a still, cast-off air of abandonment. The Manufacture Royale saw no such quiet. Painters, sculptors, silversmiths, glassblowers, cabinetmakers, and weavers all worked on busily for the glory of the king, though our royal patron was at his leisure at Fontainebleau. The neighborhood sang from dawn until dusk with the pounding of hammers and chisels, the clatter of looms, and the creak and puff of bellows.

We kept working along with the rest. André had the projects Papa had left him, but had also begun a body of work of his own, to demonstrate the skills needed to advance out of his apprenticeship. The heat of summer was intensified by the forge in the workshop below our apartments. When it became unbearable, Maman would allow Georges and me to suspend our lessons. She and Georges would set out into the city on errands, but I seldom accompanied them. My promise to Papa bound me to the workshop. I wanted to keep an eye on André, who, when left to his own devices, was prone to overstep his bounds. I wanted to study Papa's notes too. Whenever I was alone, I took the key from Papa's hiding place and examined his papers. I copied calculations I didn't understand, and at night, I sat on my bed, deciphering Papa's greatest secret by the light of a single candle, and practicing equations until I understood them.

When I finally conquered the math, I began to read Papa's notes on every stone he'd cut for the king. For each one, he had worked out the angles, but he had only been able to approximate those angles as he held the stone on the grinder by hand.

On every page he'd kept final notes that documented his disappointment and growing frustration at his inability to achieve accuracy. If he couldn't cut precise angles on softer stones like topaz and amethyst, he would never succeed with a diamond.

That was why he had feared the Tavernier Violet, and why he'd flinched when the king forced it into his hands. I understood now, and I ached with worry. We had received word of Papa's safe arrival in Venice, but no word that he had found any answers.

I was studying Papa's notes about an especially complicated design one day in July when our maid rushed in from the street. She stood before me, wringing her hands and chewing her lip, until I looked up.

"What do you want?" I snapped impatiently.

"Mademoiselle, you must find the mistress and young master. They must come home!"

"Why? What is the matter?" I glanced toward the window, but saw nothing unusual, only the comings and goings of tradesmen, the same as always.

"Fever," she whispered, as if speaking of the thing too loudly would bring it down upon us. "I heard it from the butcher. There were heavy vapors off the river last night, and today there's fever in the city."

"I'm sure we have nothing to worry about here," I said.

"But the mistress," the maid said, twisting her apron in her hands. "She's gone to the river! We must fetch her back! The air is unsafe there."

I told the maid I would go, and sent her off to the kitchen, but I did not rush out right away. I had little enough time to look at Papa's plans, and I wanted to finish examining the angles. I did not think a few hours would matter. I shall never forgive myself for that. Because you know, René, what happened.

"Yes, I know," René says. He looks up from the page. His shield of anger is lowered, and my breath catches at the raw, exposed sorrow in his eyes. Such unexpected kindness weakens me in ways that all his railing could not, and before I can catch it, a sob escapes me, gouging across my battered ribs. I double over with the pain.

I feel the comfort of his presence beside me even before his hand touches my elbow, supporting me and gently guiding me to the cot. Gratefully, I sink onto it.

"I know how hard it is to lose someone," he says, his voice solemn.

I look up into his deep, compassionate eyes. Not a shallow sympathy, but the understanding of one who has also known loss. "You too?" I ask.

"Not in the plague. My elder brother was a soldier on the Spanish border. But what you suffered . . ." He pauses and shakes his head as if no words can express the unfairness of it. "To lose your mother and brother all at once. And while your father was away too. I don't know how you carried on."

"It was a great deal to bear. Georges, my father's pride and joy. He was so little, René. And the way he suffered . . ."

Seeing the tears that are streaming freely down my face by now, he unfurls a clean white handkerchief from his pocket and holds it out to me. I take it gratefully and wipe my eyes and nose. It comes away from my face ruinously brown with grime.

"Maman too. She didn't tell me she was sick, and I didn't see. She sat by Georges's bed, day after day. It wasn't until the morning he died that she succumbed. I found her beside him, delirious with fever, still holding his cold, dead hand. And when I put her to bed, I saw the blisters she had concealed beneath her sleeves."

"Shh," René soothes, his hand rubbing gently up and down my back, offering the only comfort I have had for days. I lean into him, into his aura of calm, and he offers it freely.

"You did what you could for them, Juliette," he says kindly.

"No, I didn't," I say, and though I have lived with this guilt for almost two years, I can scarcely choke out the words. "I didn't rush out to find them when the maid warned me. I let Maman sit by his bed when she, too, was ill. By the time I knew, it was too late. She died that very night."

"You mustn't blame yourself," René says, laying a reassuring hand on mine.

We sit like this until my tears subside. Then, to my disappointment, he pulls away. Perhaps I have presumed too much, leaning into him.

He goes to the door and bangs on it to raise the guard.

"It is time we had some sustenance, and not that prison gruel," he tells the guard. "Bring us bread and cheese from the guardhouse. And more wine. And another chair."

I continue to sit on the edge of the cot, twisting his ruined handkerchief in my hands and watching through wet eyelashes as he tidies his papers, averting his eyes so that I might regain my composure. His teeth are not clenched, as they have been for so much of the morning. His face has returned to the one that I love so much, unguarded and kind, and I find it hard to pull my gaze away. I could look at that face forever. Perhaps his gentleness is not a renewal of his love, but only the compassion he would have extended to anyone reliving the sorrow of death, but it gives me hope all the same.

I blow my nose and draw some calming breaths, and when he has his pages in order, I take up the thread again.

I remember little of the next few days. We were lucky, I suppose, that they were among the first to die in that horrible summer of fever, before bodies piled like cordwood in the streets and funerals and private graves became impossible. Papa had long been a patron of the Monastery of Saint-Éloi, and so the brothers agreed to bury Maman and Georges in its cemetery.

I do not know how word of our tragedy reached their ears, but a handful of artisans from the Manufacture Royale and guildsmen from the gem-cutters' guild arrived at the church for the funeral mass. Among them were Master and Madame Valin, who followed the coffin out to the grave. I shied from them, bumping into André, who took my hand and held it until the prayers were finished and the mourners streamed by me to offer their condolences. Don't glare, René—it was only as a friend that he comforted me then.

The Valins were the last to console me. Master Valin only

muttered a few words, then moved off to talk to André. His wife stayed behind, taking both my hands into hers.

"Oh, you poor, poor child, all alone. You should have sent for us. The guild helps its own, my dear."

I only stared at her, unsure if this was chastisement or sympathy.

"Come back to our home with us, or we can come and stay with you for a time. You will have to sort out your household affairs, after all, and we can help you. The guild has funds for widows and orphans."

"I am not an orphan!" I protested. "My father is in Venice."

Her eyebrows lifted. "Venice, is it?" she said. I pulled my hands from hers. How dare she use me in my grief to pry into Papa's secrets.

"He's due back any day now," I lied.

"Perhaps we can bring you some food, and I could stay for a day or two. You look pale, Juliette," Madame Valin said, prying at every crack to get into Papa's workshop.

I looked into her eyes and gave a sickly smile. "I feel pale, madame. I'm afraid the contagion still lingers in our home and will soon take me as well."

At that, she yanked her hands from mine and took a quick step backward. Covering her mouth with a handkerchief, she hurried to her husband, who had been speaking to André, and pulled him away.

André turned an appreciative smile to me and returned to my side.

"What did the guild master have to say?" I asked.

"Only what you would expect. He wants to supervise my work. I assured him I had completed all the tasks your father had left for me, and that we expected his return soon."

"You haven't completed all the work," I said.

"He doesn't know that," André replied, "and if we want to keep them out of your father's workshop, we need to keep him from finding out. He has the authority to take over in your father's absence, you know. It's as I said before: your father should have made me a journeyman before he left."

I sighed, feeling too heavy and lost to listen to that old gripe. Of course, I wanted to protect Papa's workshop, but I was thinking of the way Maman and Papa had parted. *Mon coeur,* he had called her. How was a man to survive without his heart? And Georges had been his only heir. I had promised to help Papa, but I had been negligent when it mattered most. Perhaps I was no better than Master Valin, trying to unravel Papa's secrets at the expense of all else.

"What are we going to do, Juliette?" André asked. "How are we going to keep the Valins from our door?"

"I will write to Papa to hurry his return," I said, though I knew the chance of a letter reaching him, when we didn't exactly know his whereabouts, was low at best. But I had to try.

I wrote the letter that very evening, and André found a merchant bound for Venice who could deliver it. Then all we could do was carry on, grieving, holding the world at bay and praying for Papa's prompt return.

Seven

The prison guard arrives carrying the food that René requested, as well as a small stool. I seat myself on the stool while René tears the loaf and hands me half. I bite into it ravenously, having had nothing to eat since the day before. René watches for a few minutes before handing me his half as well, along with a generous chunk of cheese. The loaf is a little stale, but René's kindness makes it a feast in my eyes.

René pours a cup of wine, and when I take it from him, our fingers brush, an accident that is not wholly accidental. A shiver of delight runs through me, as it did the very first time we touched in such a way. I raise my eyes to his with a smile of thanks, but the crease in his brow does not relax. Sorrow, perhaps, or pity for my lonely plight in that difficult summer of loss.

"You were the only bright thing for me in those hard months. I might have given up but for you," I tell him.

The crease only grows deeper. "Nonsense. When I arrived back in Paris, you and André were busy at work."

André again. How quick men can be with unwarranted jealousy, and how slow to be convinced it is unwarranted. It is true that André was my only confederate in those long days after the death of my family. Papa had treated him as a son, and though I'd never taken to him before Papa's departure, in those long, hard months, he became like a brother to me. Necessity and grief will do that. But to imagine my feelings could ever have gone beyond that to attraction—nothing could be further from the truth. Denying it yet again is tiresome, and no doubt futile, so I take a long gulp of my wine and ignore the insinuation of his words.

After their deaths, our only solace was in work, keeping our hands and minds busy enough to forget our sorrow. André worked on some small tasks that Papa had left him. I traced Papa's drawing of the Tavernier Violet, and in the evenings, I began to sketch designs for how the stone might be cut. Night after night, when I could not sleep, I would take up parchment and quill. I drew the diamond, depicting it in increasingly grand ornaments. By the time the court returned to Paris, I had dozens of sketches and calculations, meant only as a distraction from my loss and my fear that Papa might not return.

Then came the day when you arrived at our doorstep, René, in Monsieur Colbert's conveyance. You had come on business and spoke in an appropriately formal manner, but my heart swelled with joy at the sight of you. It was the first bright moment in months.

Of course, you were not there to see me. You entered with condolences, having heard rumor of our sorrows, but eager to talk to my father. Monsieur Colbert waited in the carriage for you to send Papa to attend him.

"I'm afraid my father is abroad, seeking out the very finest gold, worthy of the king's diamond," I said in response to your inquiry. "But if you and Monsieur Colbert would like to come upstairs to my salon, I can offer you some refreshment and share what I know of his progress."

Do you remember, René? You smiled so broadly at the invitation that it made me blush. At once, you carried the invitation to Colbert.

"Your father's progress?" André said from the corner, where he'd been watching the whole exchange. His eyes were wide and incredulous. "What do you mean to tell them, Juliette?"

I did not have time to answer. Colbert was already stepping down from his carriage. As I turned to lead him up the stairs, André threw one more suspicious glance my way.

In the salon, I invited Colbert to sit and rang for refreshments, praying that a servant would answer properly. Our servants had been reduced by the plague, and the few who remained had become lax and sloppy in the absence of a proper master.

At last, I had to address Colbert. "My father is making excellent progress in his plans for the Violet, Monsieur Colbert. I am sure the king will be most pleased," I said, trying to convey a confidence I did not feel.

"Why has he not presented his designs for my approval?" Colbert asked.

"Papa will not offer the king anything less than perfection, monsieur," I said.

The maid arrived, and I breathed with relief to see she wore a tidy apron and carried a well-arranged tray. Still, my nerves rang with tension while she served, and my cup jittered on the saucer when I took it from her. I quickly set it on the table beside me. Colbert's eyes followed it before returning to my face.

"Well, mademoiselle, I am not the king," he said. "And I would like to see his plans, and any models of his designs he may have created."

"My father keeps them locked away, monsieur," I said.

"I'm sure he left a key," Colbert said, stirring his tea with a silver spoon that could have used a polish. "Perhaps among your mother's household keys?"

I took a deep breath. If I was to satisfy Colbert, I had to produce a drawing, but Papa's only drawing of the Tavernier Violet had all his calculations on it. I did not know if Colbert had the knowledge to decipher the formulas, but I would not risk it. I had promised Papa.

"Sir," I said, "I am not sure which design he has settled on. He often makes several before perfecting the right one."

"Retrieve all the drawings," Colbert said.

I could make no further delays. I left the salon and retreated to my bedchamber. I sorted through my best drawings, looking for ones that might be mistaken for Papa's work. I selected four—a large starburst, a fleur-de-lis, and two sketches of the finished stone—and I returned to the salon. There I laid the drawings out across the table for Colbert's examination.

At once, Colbert bent over the drawings, taking in every detail, making small noises of admiration and approval as he moved from one to the next.

"You understand, these are his rough drawings," I said, nervous that Colbert would recognize the inferiority of my work. "He always does a much better one for the king's final approval."

Colbert picked up the two drawings of the settings. He compared them for a long moment before setting the starburst down and handing the fleur-de-lis to you, René, along with the better sketch of the cut stone. "Thank you, Juliette. I am sure the king will be satisfied when he sees this."

"But, sir! Papa has not authorized me to—"

"I am authorized, mademoiselle. By the king."

"But—"

"Good day to you, Juliette. Come, René," Colbert said, already striding toward the door.

"You mean, the design the king approved was yours?" René says, looking up from his papers with wide, incredulous eyes. I can't help smiling at the admiration I see there, but he does not smile back. In fact, his countenance quickly darkens into disapproval, and I realize my mistake. He has been softening toward me, remembering the tragedy of my family, but now he is no doubt reminded of the overreaching ambitions of which I stand accused. Counterfeiting my father's work is undoubtedly just one more proof of guilt in his eyes. But surely this time he can see that it was an accident. He saw for himself my hesitation.

He must realize I never intended for Colbert to take my drawings to the king.

I look him square in the eye and speak in the most reasonable voice I can muster. "What would you have done, René?"

"I wouldn't have lied to the king," he says. "But then, perhaps lying doesn't come as easily to me as it does to you."

"Easily?!" I round on him, all reason flown. "Do you think it was *easy* for me to bury my mother and brother? To go on, day after day, not knowing where Papa was or if he was coming back? To try to satisfy Colbert when he was demanding something I couldn't give?" René looks away, but I refuse to let him dismiss me. I step around and plant myself where he cannot avoid me. "Do you think it's easy to be here now, facing execution and heaped with scorn by the man I love, all because I tried to save my father and please the king? Is that what you think?!"

René does not answer. Nor will he look at me. He puts down his pen, rises from the table, and paces to the door, as if wishing to be free of his onerous duty. To be free of me.

I let my breath out slowly and force my voice back to a calmer register. "I am sorry, René. I am sorry for all of it: for deceiving Colbert and the king and, most of all, for hurting you. I wish you could believe that."

I wait for any sign that he accepts my apology, but there is only silence between us for a long, heavy moment. When at last he speaks, he has changed the subject, neatly avoiding any discussion of what we once had. "It was a beautiful design," René says, and despite my disappointment, I'm touched by his compliment. "You inherited your father's skill. It is a pity—" He breaks off and I am left wondering what he meant to say. A pity I am a girl who cannot be a jeweler? A pity I compromised Papa's reputation? A pity I've brought myself to this early end?

Suddenly too tired to argue, I cross to the cot and sit down on it, my head in my hands.

René sighs and rubs his neck, leaving a streak of black ink on his fine white collar. He turns back from the door and, avoiding my eyes, sits again at the table.

"I shouldn't have said that," he says, his tone contrite. He takes up his quill and waits for me to speak, but I do not. How can I? He would have me be silent on what happened next, and the joy it gave me in those long, lonely weeks of my father's absence. He wants to obliterate all record, all memory of what happened between us, but I need something to hold on to.

"Come," he prompts. "What happened next?"

I will speak of it, though he will not write it. How he returned to me with news of the king's approval. That he took my hand gently in his and asked, shyly, if he might court me, assuring me of his gentlemanly behavior in my father's absence. He frowns, and writes nothing down, but he does not stop me as I recount our autumn walks and the cups of *chocolat* we shared in sunlit cafés. The moments at his side that brought me back to life after so much grief and fear.

Of course, André thought I was only stepping out with you to gain Colbert's favor, but André has always been inclined to see conspiracy everywhere. You may remember, he was there in the

workshop that morning you returned with the approved drawing, the king's seal pressed in crimson wax on the bottom of the
page, and he demanded to know what had happened as soon as
you left. Reluctantly, I showed him the drawing and admitted
the truth: that the drawing was not my father's. I explained my
insomnia, and how I had spent it in creating designs for the Violet. I did not tell him that I had been practicing or applying
equations to understand my father's secret. I had grown closer
to André in the months we had to rely on each other, but not so
close as to trust him with that.

As I explained to him about Colbert demanding a drawing,
André examined it closely. "This is good, Juliette," he said when
I had finished.

The words drew me up short. "Is it?" I looked again at the
image. It was a large, golden fleur-de-lis, the Tavernier at its center, cut like the largest Mazarin diamond. Along the sweeping
petals of the lily, among curls of gold, I had drawn emeralds and
citrines and tiny white diamonds. I had done my best to copy
Papa's style, and I felt a surge of pride that my design had been
mistaken for my father's by the king himself.

André looked up from the sketch. His eyes scrutinized my
face. "You know, don't you? He's told you the secret of the Mazarin cut."

I took the paper from his hand and turned away, but not before André saw the confirmation of his suspicion in my face.

"Don't you see what this means, Juliette?" André said, following me up the stairs to the apartments. "We have an approved design, and you know the secret of how it's done. We

don't have to wait for your father's return. We can start now!"

"Don't be ridiculous, André. It's not even his design!"

"But it could be. You have mimicked his style perfectly. He will approve this design when he sees it—I'm sure of it," André said.

"We cannot start anything without Papa here," I insisted. I was flattered by the compliment, but appalled that he thought we could do such important work for the king—he only an apprentice and me not even that. "We don't have the diamond, and even if we did, we don't know how to cut it."

André frowned at me for a long moment before speaking again, carefully advancing into dangerous territory.

"Master Pitau should have been home weeks ago, and yet we have heard nothing from him," he said.

"He will be here soon." I had said this a dozen times, to Valin and Colbert and everyone who asked in the market or at church, but saying it now, my conviction sounded limp and worn-out.

"You should be planning, Juliette," André said, his expression serious, and a little calculating. "We should be prepared for the possibility that he isn't coming back."

EIGHT

I hated André for saying what we'd both been thinking. Now that it had been said out loud, it could no longer be denied, but I could not bear to move on. So I waited, paralyzed, while six more weeks passed, and still no word came from Papa. Master Valin continued to nose around us, trying to learn the truth about Papa's extended absence. Colbert, too, inquired frequently. And all the while, the nameless fear I had kept at the edge of my mind was eating at me, silent but persistent as moths in wool. André's words repeated endlessly in my mind. *What if he isn't coming back?*

André continued to press me to begin work on the ornament, if not the diamond itself. With each passing day I resented his pestering more. He didn't voice our worst fear again, or his own thoughts about it, though they were plain on his face. If Papa didn't return, André's own work would be seen by the king, just as my design had been.

I did not want him to craft anything for the king, but as the weeks passed, I conceded. I agreed to let him sculpt the setting in wax, the first step for creating the mold. I could not bear to be with him as he worked. It felt too much like a betrayal of my father—a loss of faith, a broken promise. So I left André to do as he pleased while I took my respite in your attentions, René: in walking home from church with you, or strolling the broad avenues of the Right Bank, enjoying the golden evenings of autumn, and, when they darkened into winter, retreating to the cozy comfort of shared books beside the fire, André and my lady's maid on hand to keep us proper. I regret nothing of those days, when I forgot my grief and fear and worry as we read poetry together in the raw evenings of winter.

As I had paid André's work no attention, I shouldn't have been surprised in early December when he announced he had completed the wax model and was ready to make a mold and cast the gold. I shouldn't have been, but I was.

"In your father's absence, your mother had the authority to oversee my work. She could have given her approval. As she is not here, I believe you could act on his behalf," he said. The wax model lay on the table before me for my inspection, not that he would have listened if I had suggested changes. "We need six ounces of gold from the royal treasury."

I stared, openmouthed. How could he possibly expect me to ask the king's treasury for gold? "It's a fine model, André, but it isn't even Papa's design. I don't think we should put the king's gold into it without Papa's approval."

"We have Colbert's approval," André said. He was not going to take no for an answer.

"Two more weeks," I said, hoping I could come up with a better argument by then. "Give Papa two more weeks, and if he has not returned, we will take your model to Colbert for his approval."

A week and a half later, when Papa still had not returned, I reluctantly gave André my blessing. A few days later, I was in the workshop comparing his wax model to my drawing when a heavy coach drew up outside. The footman opened the carriage door and Papa stepped to the pavement.

I blinked, unable to believe my eyes, but it was truly Papa, weary to the bone and home at last. A month at sea had left him thin and pale from poor food and seasickness, and his beard had grown into a gray-streaked shroud that hid his usually clean-shaven face. From the sag of his shoulders, I knew at once that he had been unsuccessful, but I did not care; I was so glad to have him back. At least until I remembered the empty house upstairs, without Maman and Georges. How could he bear up under the weight of their loss?

André rushed to him, shook his hand with vigorous enthusiasm, and hurried to gather the trunks and baggage. I remained frozen inside. He didn't see me until he was through the door, André close on his heels, talking excitedly about the golden fleur-de-lis he was ready to cast. Papa wasn't listening. When he saw me, his tired eyes brightened and his lips stretched into a smile. My heart split open.

"Papa!" I flew into his outspread arms, then burst into tears.

"Juliette! *Mon petit bijou!* Hush now, I'm home. Safe and sound," he said, stroking my hair as I wailed like a lost child. He held me while my tears awakened the salty, sweaty smell of the sea in his woolen cloak. At last, when I had calmed, he stepped back from me.

"Where is your mother?" he said, and before I could answer, he started up the stairs. I stared after him, shocked by the question. It wasn't until we were in the apartments and he was moving through the empty rooms that I could speak again.

"Didn't you get my letter?" I asked as he stood in Maman's doorway. His blank confusion told me he had not.

I swallowed the rising bile in my throat. "There was fever in the city," I began, my voice trembling.

I watched as my meaning broke over him and dashed the color from his face. "Fever," he repeated. "When?"

Tears were streaming down my face now, as his pain doubled my own. "In the summer," I choked out. "July. It was hot . . . They went to the river . . ."

"They," he repeated. He staggered and clutched the back of a chair for support. "Georges too? Marie and Georges? Oh, Juliette."

I could not speak, but he could read the answer in my face. I reached a hand toward him—whether I was offering comfort or asking for it I cannot say. He pulled me again into an embrace, but this time he, too, was crying. He, too, was breaking apart.

"I wrote to you, Papa, but I didn't know where . . . I didn't . . ." The words were streaming out with the tears now, senseless and out of order. "We buried them at the Monastery of Saint-Éloi. The Valins have checked on us, and André has kept the work going in the workshop, and Colbert has been here, and . . . oh, Papa, I've missed you!"

Unexpectedly, Papa's arms fell from me, and he stepped unsteadily back, his expression dazed. Without a word, he stumbled from the room, down the stairs, across the workshop, and out the front door. Once again, everything was as still and empty as before. We waited for his return until dusk settled over the city.

"Where can he be? Do you think he's gone to the king already?" André said as we sat together, sharing a meager evening meal. Hardly the fine feast I'd hoped might celebrate Papa's return.

I shook my head. "He is grieving."

"But where?"

I retraced the words I had spoken before he left. "I told him we buried them at Saint-Éloi. That is where he will be."

André pushed away his plate and stood. "It's growing dark and cold. We must fetch him home."

We set out together, through an evening gloom deepened by winter drizzle. Though André urged me to haste, my feet were slow and heavy. I did not want to visit Maman's grave. I did not want to intrude on my father's deepest grief.

He was not in the great church, nor was he praying in any of its alcoves, so we ventured into the graveyard. The summer fevers had left the once-placid space churned and mounded with new graves. A vague stench of decay lingered on the air. I did not see Papa until we were nearly upon Maman's grave. He was sprawled upon the ground, his cheek to the earth and his face streaked with muddy tears.

"Papa!" I cried, putting my arms around his shoulders, trying to lift him up. He did not respond, but only continued a low keening. I pressed myself to him, my own grief freshly torn open as I realized his keening had words. A steady stream: "Marie, *mon coeur*. Georges! My son, my precious boy. Marie!" And on and on, calling to two who would never answer again.

"Come away, Papa," I begged. "Come home. Please." He resisted, clinging to the earth until his strength gave out. Then he let himself be lifted, his limbs limp as old rags. He was soaked through from lying on the wet ground in the drizzle.

André and I on either elbow, we walked him back through the dark streets to our home. He was shivering with chill, so we took him to the kitchen. I stoked the fire and André found a bottle of brandy and filled a cup, to warm him from within. I hurried to his room for dry clothes, but when I returned to the kitchen, he was no longer at the table. André pointed helplessly toward the stairs that led up to our bedchambers. I followed the trail of wet footprints to the closed door of Maman's bedchamber.

I knocked, but Papa did not answer, so I cautiously peeked inside. He lay curled on the bed like a small, abandoned child, one hand pressing Maman's linen nightdress to his cheek, while the other gripped the brandy bottle. Without a word, I closed the door and retreated to the kitchen.

"I cannot tell that he had any success, can you?" André said gloomily as I warmed myself by the fire.

"How can you think of that now? He is grieving!" I said.

He sighed. "Forgive me. I know his loss is great, and yours too, Juliette. But we have a commission from the king to think about. We need his attention here—on our work."

I softened a little. Papa's long absence had been hard for André too. But I could not deny Papa at least one night to grieve. "Tomorrow, André," I said. "We will talk to him of business tomorrow."

The next morning, while Papa slept late, I sent the maid to the market for a joint of beef, fine cheese, delicate pastries, and other tempting delights. I hoped a proper French supper to celebrate Papa's return would revive him, and give André and me a chance to tell him of the design for the king.

Our maid had just left when a carriage pulled up in front of our door and Madame Valin stepped from it. Cursing under my breath, I hurried down into the workshop, determined to keep her from the apartments. I did not want her disturbing Papa— or, worse yet, reporting back to the guild should he emerge unwashed or drunk.

She was already in the workshop when I descended the stairs. André had greeted her, and she was bending across the counter, trying to steal a glance at the design stretched before him.

"Madame Valin," I called loudly in greeting from the stairs, forcing her to turn her eyes toward me. André, with a grateful glance at me, turned the design facedown as soon as her eyes shifted from him.

"Ah, Juliette. I hear your father has returned at last," she said, a hungry smile making her sharp face ugly.

"News travels fast," I replied.

"It is true, then?"

"He arrived last night, after an arduous voyage," I said, wanting to give her as little information as possible.

"I thought I would find him at work this morning. After all, he does have a great project to complete for the king." She glanced around the workshop, as if she thought he might be hiding under the workbench. Not seeing him, she took a step toward the stairs, but I remained firmly planted in front of her.

"He is resting. If you have a message for him, I will be glad to convey it."

She glared at me, as if she might force me out of her way with her look. I held my ground.

"I only came to welcome him home and see what help the guild might offer him," she said. Still, I did not move.

She hesitated a moment longer, glancing between me and André and the now-hidden design for the king's jewel.

"Give Master Valin our kindest regards," I said.

Her nostrils flared at the dismissal, her lips squeezing together so tightly that her chin puckered. When she turned and left the workshop at last, it was on brisk steps of protest.

André let out a long breath. "If she knows, the king knows, or will very soon. You've got to rouse him, Juliette."

I returned upstairs with rising desperation, straight to the door of Maman's bedchamber, and knocked hard.

There was no answer.

I pushed the door open anyway. Papa was still huddled in a rumpled heap on the bed, clutching Maman's shift. He had dropped the brandy bottle, which lay empty on the floor. Only a drop of brandy had spilled, confirming my fear that he had drunk the whole thing.

I shook his shoulder and called to him. "Papa, you must get up and eat something."

He stirred, opened his eyes, and looked up at me. "Marie?" he muttered.

"No, Papa. Juliette. Come now." I coaxed him up, realizing as I did that the bed and his clothes beneath him were still damp. My stomach knotted. I had let him sleep all night in wet clothes. What if he, too, took ill?

"Juliette," he said slowly, trying to decide if he could settle for me.

He let me help him to his own room, where he sat, despondent, on the bed while I pulled a fresh shirt, breeches, and hose from his wardrobe and laid them out beside him on the bed. He was still sitting, staring dully into space, when I brought him a basin of water and a bar of soap. When he emerged later, he had neither washed nor changed his clothes.

"Come. Eat something. A fine meal is prepared," I said, coaxing him to the table.

The maid served the soup and poured the wine. André and I picked up our spoons and began to eat, but Papa only pushed a chestnut around his bowl with his spoon.

"Papa, you must eat," I said. "You look so thin."

He sighed.

"Tell us of your adventures, sir," André said, a bit too brightly. "What did you learn in Venice? Did you find the workshop that cut the Mazarins?"

Papa looked at André with dull eyes, as if dredging up the memory was too great an effort. "Venice is a decadent city," he said at last.

"I've heard it's very grand!" I said, following André's lead with all the cheer I could.

"Masked balls, night and day. Boats full of lovers crowding the canals," Papa said, and drained his glass. "It's frivolous, and immoral."

"But what of the workshops there, Papa?" I persisted, nodding to the servant to refill his wine, hoping to relax him.

He shook his head. "If Mazarin's gem-cutter ever lived in Venice, he did not pass on his knowledge. I saw nothing as fine as what our guild here produces. The doges have lost their power. Venice is in decline."

"Are there no craftsmen at all in the city, then?" I asked.

"There are great glassworks. You should see the ceiling of the basilica, how it shines with mosaics of glass that mimic pure gold or precious gems. But as for real gems, and gem-cutters . . ." His words trailed off and he shrugged.

"Perhaps Mazarin's master moved elsewhere?" André suggested.

Papa swirled the wine in his cup before lifting it again to his lips for a long drink. He hadn't touched his food. "The stone did not come from Italy," he said. "Not from Tuscany, or Rome, or the Kingdom of Napoli, or Amalfi. I begin to think the Mazarins do not exist at all. That I am searching for a specter of my own imagining." Again, he gulped his wine. Then he waved the maid to him and took the bottle from her hands. Gripping it tightly, he filled his cup until it was almost overflowing.

"Imagine! You may be the only man in all of Europe who knows the secrets of those stones. When you cut the Violet, you will be famous. The greatest jeweler in the world!" André said.

Papa shook his head. "What do I care for fame? I should be remembered as the man who abandoned his wife and son to die!"

"Papa, it's not your fault," I said, reaching across the table to place my hand reassuringly on his. "It's not anyone's fault!" The bitter tang of the lie burned my tongue, knowing there was more I should have done.

"The king is expecting to hear from you, Master Pitau," André said. "He will want to see you as soon as he knows you have returned."

Papa took another big swallow of his wine. He wiped his mouth on the back of his sleeve, adding a bright red streak to the filth of his shirt. By now he had drained the full cup, and was nearly through the bottle. I eyed it, wondering if I could get it away from him unnoticed, but his hand curled protectively around it. "I will go to the king tomorrow and resign my post," he said.

"But you can't!" I cried. No one would commission work from a gem-cutter who had failed the king. We would have to leave Paris, and that meant I would lose you, René, and that thought was unbearable.

"Don't worry, André," Papa said, ignoring my protest. "I will see to it you are housed in a new workshop with a great master. One who can teach you great things."

"I want to work with you, Master Pitau," André said.

Papa only shook his head. "Save yourself from this sinking ship, my boy. You will be better off elsewhere."

Papa reached a hand to me. "I had hoped in a few years to find you a husband at court," he said.

"Papa, there is someone," I began, but stopped, my heart sinking as his face clouded with a scowl.

"No one at court will want the daughter of a disgraced craftsman. And look at you—worn-out with cares before your seventeenth birthday. *Mon Dieu*, Juliette. How will you ever forgive me? How will God ever forgive me?"

I bit back all that I had intended to say. If my father fell into disgrace, what hope would I have of ever seeing you again, René? A gentleman's son could not afford such a low connection. I do not know much about your family, but I doubted that a father who had sent his son to work with the minister of finance at the age of fifteen intended him to marry a ruined craftsman's daughter.

The maid came in then, carrying a perfectly roasted joint of beef. It had been my plan for a celebration of Papa's return, but none of us had much appetite anymore. She set it before Papa to be carved.

Papa stared at the steaming meat in silence while we waited. Then he stood, picked up the bottle of wine, and shuffled upstairs to his bedroom. We heard the door shut behind him, leaving all my relief and hope in his return crushed by a swell of frustration. For many months we had struggled on without him, assuring ourselves that he would come back bearing salvation. Now he was back, but we were as desolate as before, with no solution to our dilemma in sight.

NINE

"Of course, you know what happened next," I say, glancing at René and feeling again my embarrassment of that morning more than a year earlier. "You arrived with Colbert while my father was still abed. I never did understand how news of his return traveled so fast."

René's mouth turns down as if tasting something vile. "Master Valin, of course. He was watching. He suspected that your father had died or abandoned your family and that you were covering it up."

"Papa would never have abandoned us," I say, indignant at the accusation, but as I say it, René's mouth tightens and I can see what he is thinking. Papa *did* abandon me, when he turned to drink. He's right, of course, but to say so would feel like betrayal. I hold my tongue, but I feel my cheeks flush, as I think of how Papa looked when I rushed into his bedroom and roused him, pushed his arms into a dressing gown, and pulled a comb through his hair. Even then, even as I helped him stagger out into the salon, he was barely presentable. I tried to convince Colbert that his rough appearance had resulted from long days of travel and seasickness, but looking back, he must have reeked of wine.

"If only Colbert had not shown up that very next morning," René says, "your father might have come to the king and resigned his post. Then none of this would have happened."

"I didn't want him to resign," I say quietly.

"That much was obvious, the way you spoke for him and talked Colbert into delaying his meeting with the king. But now I see it was more than that. You were hiding the truth from your father as well as us."

"Only until I had a chance to explain properly and to let him decide what to do. You didn't give me that chance, barging in on the heels of his return." I know it's not fair to blame René—he has no control over Colbert's decisions—but it feels good to have an accusation I can finally lay at his feet instead of the other way around.

René rubs his neck again, his brows drawn down hard over his eyes in a new expression. When he speaks, his words have lost their sting and taken on the tired tone of one who must correct a child's error for the hundredth time. "Your father was ready to resign, Juliette. You should have let him. But still you dreamed of glory. Tell yourself what you will, but you weren't protecting him. You were forcing him."

I open my mouth to protest, but close it again as his words sink in. *Was* what I wanted for Papa really what was best for him? Surely staying at court was better than being cast out. And yet . . . I clamp my lips between my teeth and squeeze my eyes shut. Was my father's collapse *despite* my effort, as I have told myself, or *because* of it?

René busies himself sharpening quills, pretending ignorance while I wrestle with this new revelation. I am grateful that he is too kind to revel in having scored this point against me. When I speak again, it is with new humility, no longer wanting to prove myself right so much as to prove myself worthy of him.

I did tell Papa the truth. As soon as you and Colbert left, he questioned me and I told him everything—of the design and how it had gotten the king's approval. He listened with anger rising to a boil in his eyes.

"Do you have any idea how many guild rules you have broken?" he shouted when I had finished. His face was purple with rage. "They could bar me for such transgressions. And what of the king? How will I face him after a novice drawing has been passed off as my work?"

"I didn't mean for it to go to the king," I whispered, my eyes on my feet.

"But it did."

I bit my lip and nodded.

"Bring it to me," he demanded.

I raced down the stairs, my feet pounding a rhythm of fear and hope. Papa was angry, but at least he was thinking again about his craft.

When André saw me retrieve the design, he grabbed the wax

model he'd made and followed me. I handed Papa the drawing with the king's seal of approval attached. Without a word, but with distinct pride, André set the matching wax model on the table before Papa.

Papa stared at the design for a long time. I waited, chewing at my lip, praying he would see something of value in it. Instead, he only dropped the design to the floor. Then, catching sight of André's wax model, his face went red again. He snatched it off the table and crushed it in his fist before throwing it to the floor. André winced, as if he himself was being crushed.

"Monsieur Colbert has arranged an audience for you in two days, Papa. You can tell him then that you have a new design. A better one," I hurried to say.

"You should not have done this, Juliette. You had no right!"

"Colbert was here, and he was asking—"

"You had no right!" he said again, coming to his feet on a sudden surge of anger, stepping on the design where it lay on the floor. "I cannot do this! I will not! Marie would never have let this happen!"

"I'm sorry, Papa," I said, my voice shrinking to a whisper.

"If only she had lived, instead—" He bit down hard on the thought and a black silence filled the room. Then he strode from it, back to his bedchamber, where he slammed the door behind him.

I stood still, letting his hard, unspoken words saturate my heart. Instead of what? Instead of me? Is that what he had been about to say?

"Juliette. He didn't mean—" André couldn't find a comforting word to finish the thought.

That's when I knew I wasn't mistaken. In my father's eyes, I was the one who should have died. I was not his little jewel; I was the millstone around his neck. I wiped my eyes on my sleeve and picked up the drawing off the floor.

"Does he really have an audience with the king in two days?" André asked.

I nodded. "Colbert's arranging it."

"Then we will get him ready. We must convince him to keep his post. We've got a good start on a design, if he will just apply himself," André said.

I straightened my shoulders. I wasn't blinded by ambition the way André was, but I knew Papa could do this, if he would just try. If he would get back to work, we could begin to put our lives back together. It was all that was left to us, after losing Maman and Georges, but surely if we clung to each other, comforted each other, worked together as the partners Papa had said we were, we could come through this.

For the next two days I held that belief in my heart as I brought Papa meals of the finest food. I hid the wine, and I called a barber to shave him and trim his wild hair. I set servants to airing and pressing his finest coat, polishing his best shoes, and starching his best shirt.

André, meanwhile, coaxed him into the workshop, to show him all we had done in his absence, and to try to get him to consider the merits of the design. He would not. He only shook his head whenever he looked at it, pushing it away from him. It vexed André—who thought the design was suitable and was eager to start—but it worried me. If Papa still planned to resign his post, there was nothing more I could do to prevent it.

I kept up a cheerful banter over breakfast and in the carriage the next morning, speaking of the great opportunity that lay before us. André accompanied us with the excuse that Papa might need the assistance of his apprentice. I had little excuse, but hoped I might bolster him, or, if the worst happened, confess what I had done and take my punishment. Perhaps then Papa would be given a second chance.

The king was alone in his private office when one of Colbert's assistants escorted us to him. He sat behind a finely inlaid desk, papers and quills set out before him. There were no other chairs in the room, so we struck a meek pose as his gaze ran over us: father, daughter, and apprentice.

"Monsieur Pitau," he said, in his languid, mocking tone, "at last you find yourself at leisure to spare a moment for me." I bit the inside of my cheek and lowered my eyes to the floor.

Papa only nodded with a bland, empty expression.

Louis's voice and eyes hardened. "It has been nine months since I set you the task of cutting it, and yet nothing. I had hope when I saw your design. I thought, now at last, he will begin his work. And yet time slips steadily on, and Monsieur Colbert tells me you have not even taken the Tavernier from the treasury."

"Thought and planning must come before shaping such a grand stone," Papa said.

"You have had ample time to think!" the king bellowed so that I took an involuntary step back. "I've approved a design. I've given my instructions. I command you to cut the Violet, Jean Pitau!" Louis was banging his fist on his desk now like a petulant child. A very powerful one at that.

"The sun is not blue, Your Majesty," Papa said quietly.

Beside me, André drew in a sharp breath. I did too.

To my surprise, however, Louis seemed to take Papa's blunt words into consideration, for when he spoke again, his tone was reasonable. "Tell me, then, Master Pitau, what would you recommend?"

"Rubies and citrines in the fleur-de-lis, Your Majesty. The sun and the symbol of the king united," Papa said.

Louis slammed his fist against the desk again, rattling the inkwells. "I did not acquire the hoard of Tavernier so that I might wear citrines before the courts of Europe!"

"Of course not, Your Majesty," Papa said with a sigh.

"Perhaps you have not heard, Master Pitau, in your self-imposed solitude, but my esteemed cousin and ally, His Majesty King Charles of England, will be here for the grand fete at Twelfth Night. Would you have him return to England saying the Bourbon court cannot be distinguished from beggars?"

"I would have them say, Your Majesty, that the great Louis XIV outshines them all, with the greatest diamonds in all the world at his breast," Papa replied obediently.

"I *will* wear the greatest diamond in the world! I will not be outdone by an English upstart who can barely hold his own throne!" Louis proclaimed.

My heart dropped to the palace foundations. Wear the Tavernier for Twelfth Night? It was already December—Twelfth

Night was scarcely a month away! Even in the best of conditions, a diamond the size of the Violet could not be cut in a month.

But Papa only gave a small bow, and said, "Of course, Your Majesty."

André made a small, strangled noise.

"Shall I take the stone now, or will you send it with your guard?" Papa asked.

The king's eye turned to Colbert's man. "See to it Pitau receives all that he needs."

Our escort bowed and backed from the room, and we followed. We walked in silence through the corridors of the Louvre and into a plainer wing of the vast building. Here various ministers and their clerks scurried in and out of offices carrying ledgers and scrolls, the king's business hurrying their steps.

Colbert's offices filled a suite of rooms along the second-floor corridor. A number of men milled around the hallway outside the entrance to the suite. I recognized some of them from the Manufacture Royale—cabinetmakers, painters, architects. Others were distinguished by their clothes as men of the church or of noble lineage. All were waiting their turn to speak with the king's top minister. We passed through them like water, leaving behind us a wake of mumbled complaints and annoyed glances, and entered directly into Colbert's offices.

Though the corridor was plain, the offices were richly appointed, as one might expect for a man of Colbert's importance. We stepped from the hallway into a spacious room, the walls covered in red silk. A huge painting hung on the wall opposite the door, depicting the king riding into battle amid roiling masses of people and horses, his victory certain in his expression. A single desk was positioned in the room so as to block access to the door behind it. Neat stacks of papers stood in rows on the desk. My heart quickened when I saw you seated there, René, even before you looked up and saw us. When you did, you leapt to your feet.

"Master Pitau." Your eyes darted to me and back to Papa, and I could see how nervous you were. I was nervous too, being there with you in the presence of my father. You bowed, more deeply than my father's rank required.

"His Majesty sends Master Pitau to receive the Tavernier Violet diamond," our escort said.

"Of course," you said. "We have been expecting you." You led us through the door behind the desk and through several more offices, each more elaborate than the last, until we came to Colbert's personal office, where the minister sat surrounded by nearly as much wealth and splendor as the king himself. Gold sconces on the walls dripped with crystals and held solid beeswax candles. Between them, the walls were covered with tapestries so intricately crafted that the figures might have stepped from them to sweep us into their woodland dance.

The whimsical impression lasted only until Colbert rose from his desk and addressed us in the most businesslike tone. "Ah, Master Pitau. You will begin at last, *n'est-ce pas*?"

Papa said nothing, only gave a single nod of his head. Colbert took a large ring of keys from his desk and unlocked a door on the far wall. Behind it was a bare-walled flight of stone stairs. We descended the narrow staircase single file, Colbert leading the way, leaving you, to close the doors behind us.

Several flights down, we found ourselves in a small room, where the rosewood box awaited Papa on a table. We watched as Papa opened the box and inspected the stone.

Do you remember, René, how in the stillness, your hand grazed mine? I was delighted, and my cheeks warmed with what I hoped was a pretty blush.

"It is magnificent," Colbert said, looking at the diamond over Papa's shoulder.

It is indeed, I thought, as I shifted my hand in response to your touch, so that our little fingers momentary curled around each other. I stole a glance at your face and saw the smile you were trying to hold in check.

"And you will make it more so," Colbert continued. "You will make Louis the envy of the world."

"Louis's place in the world is ordained by God," Papa said, "not me." Snapping shut the wooden box and lifting it from the table, he turned abruptly to leave, and for a moment, my heart froze, thinking he had caught us in our flirtation. But he was blind to us, his face set in grim lines as he accepted the task he did not want. I pulled my hand back and forced my lips flat, trying to erase any sign of my pleasure. I climbed the stairs behind Papa, returning my thoughts to Papa's predicament and my role in creating it.

Back in Colbert's chambers, Papa signed receipts for the diamond while an escort was summoned to ensure the safety of the Violet until it reached our workshop. When the escort arrived, Papa and André followed him at once. I cast a parting smile at you.

You caught me gently by the hand. "I am glad your father is home, Mademoiselle Juliette," you said. "I should like to do things properly now. May I come by your house next Thursday and talk to your father? I would like to have the opportunity to declare my intentions."

My heart swelled until I could not speak and had to answer with a giddy smile and a nod. You must believe me, there was nothing I wanted more than a life at your side. And surely, Papa would approve. With a smile I could not suppress, I hurried after Papa, my feet barely touching the marble floors as my happiness flew me from the Louvre.

TEN

René throws down his quill and comes to his feet so suddenly his chair topples backward. "It is just as well I was unable to declare those intensions. I could never have made you happy."

I am all at once startled and stung. I'd thought he was forgetting his grievances and remembering the love he once had for me. His walls had been crumbling, but now, for no reason I can explain, he is raging again like when we started. I extend a reassuring hand toward his arm, but before I can touch him, he swivels and paces, propelled by his seething temper.

"I was never happier than when I was with you." It's all I can think to say.

He peels off his fine court jacket and waves it in my face. "It was my silk waistcoats and embroidered jackets that made you happy. It was my life in the palace and the hope of marrying high. Don't deny it."

"It was no such thing!" But my heart sinks. I've already spoken fondly of my mother's desire to make a good marriage for me. Still, I never gave him cause to think I *only* loved his status.

"No?" He throws the jacket onto the prison floor with a challenging glare. I twitch, barely resisting the urge to rescue it from the filth. René's lips curl into a victorious sneer.

"What is wrong with wanting a good marriage?" I demand, trying to ignore the fine wool at my feet that by now must be soaking up bile and piss and God knows what else.

"What would you have done when you learned that I am not, as you have imagined, the son of some country gentleman? That my father is a mere bookbinder?"

I stare, dumbfounded. A bookbinder? Why hadn't he told me during the months we had spent together?

"But how . . . ? When . . . ?" I have so many questions, I am not sure where to start.

"I excelled at penmanship, dictation, and accounting, so my father saw his chance when he was working at the Manufacture Royale, and thrust me before Le Brun, who took me on as a secretary. Through my own hard work, I climbed from Le Brun's to Colbert's service, thanks to my skill at accounts and taking dictation." He glances down at the pages on the table, and my eyes follow, to the neat rows of elegant, flowing hand, the graceful letters so at odds with the confession they now record.

"You did not wish to follow in your father's profession?" I ask, thinking of my own father. It had been his dearest wish to have a son to take over his business.

"I would be very happy as a bookbinder, but my father had an abundance of sons. Only one was needed to carry on his trade," he says. He shrugs, pretending it is all matter-of-fact, but I can see it is an old wound for him. "I fared better than the two he sent as soldiers. We were all used to fulfill Papa's aspirations of power, much like you and your mother."

There it is again—his tiresome grudge against my marriage aspirations, only now I begin to understand. "Maman would have been content to see me wed to a craftsman's son if he was a man I could love and who could put food on the table," I say.

René pinches the bridge of his nose, as if speaking of this has given him a headache. I am aching too. At last, we are talking about us, and the misunderstanding that has hardened him against me, but my heart feels like it's caught between millstones. I thought I had already lost everything, but to learn now how well suited René is for me, in ways I hadn't even known, is almost more than I can bear. I think what it would have been like, working side by side with him in a bindery, and my heart swells.

"I embraced the dream of marrying a gentleman for a time, before I knew what such a life was like," I say, praying he will believe me. "But I have found so much satisfaction working beside Papa on the diamond. A craftsman is a much better husband, I think." The sick knot in my stomach tightens, because there will be no husband at all for me if I do not survive past the morning. Yet this makes me all the more hungry for him to understand. I go to his side and lay my hand on his arm, hoping he can feel the sincerity in my touch.

"After Maman died, you brought me back from despair. You helped me see the good in living again. That's when I knew—" I have to pause to swallow the lump rising in my throat. "That's when I knew there was no one in this world for me but you."

His shoulders tense at my declaration, but I do not take it back.

"It wasn't the feasting or the dancing, or the fine clothes, René. It was you. The man who made me laugh again. The man who, even now, despite his anger, still finds it in his heart to comfort me." I run my hand down his arm until our fingers twine. "How could I not want you?"

He stares at my hand for a long moment before, at last, raising his eyes to meet mine. Beneath his troubled brow, I see the struggle of anguish and doubt in his eyes. They search my face, and I gaze back, willing all the reassurance I can into my expression.

He draws a deep breath and lowers his gaze to the floor again. "I wanted to marry you, Juliette," he says, his voice wavering under the force of his grief. "I admired your loyalty to your family. I thought that you could be happy with a man who earned a living with his own hands."

I press my hand harder into his, so that he feels the rough skin, the calluses, the chipped nails that have come from long hours in Papa's workshop: the proof of the life I've lived, and wish to live with him.

He turns my hand over in his, running his own soft fingers over the evidence of my months of hard work. At last he sighs, revealing nothing. He drops my hand and returns to the table to start a fresh page of my account.

ELEVEN

Papa did not notice me falling behind when he left Colbert's offices, but André did. He gave me a meaningful glance, his eyebrows raised. I gave no answer, but I couldn't keep the smile from my face. At least, not until I took my seat in the carriage opposite Papa and saw the defeat weighing him down. Then my euphoria gave way to guilt. I was selfish to be thinking of romance when Papa was bearing such a burden—especially when the burden had been of my making.

We rode in silence, Papa's heavy gloom muffling any conversation among us. When we were once again in the workshop, André broke the silence.

"Master Pitau, what is your plan? Twelfth Night is scarcely more than a month away. What do you need me to do?"

Papa dropped the jewel on the worktable and shrugged. "We will use Juliette's design. It doesn't matter," he said, crossing the workshop toward the stairs to the apartments.

"Where are you going?" I called after him. I was hopeful at

his words, but confused by his despondent trudge to the stairs. "We must get to work at once if we are going to satisfy the king."

Papa gave a dry cough of laughter as he turned back. "We are not going to satisfy the king, Juliette. You can be certain of that."

"Then why did you promise?"

"Louis will not take no for an answer. Even when he asks the impossible."

"It's not impossible!" I insisted, trying to keep the annoyance from my voice. "Someone cut the Mazarins. And he has approved a design already."

"Oh, yes, your design." He crossed back to his workbench where André had left the crumpled drawing. "Did you learn nothing of what I told you?"

His words stung after my long hours of study. "I did, Papa. That the angles had to be precise."

"And yet you draw this ridiculous fantasy?"

"But"—I looked down at the drawing, my face growing hot— "I used your calculations."

"Well, you used them wrong. You've only accounted for the Violet's length and width. You didn't figure its actual depth."

I bit my lip. I had only had Papa's sketch to work from, and it had only shown two dimensions. "Does that matter?" I asked, but I knew the answer. It was sinking like a stone into the pit of my stomach.

Papa opened the rosewood box where it lay on the workbench. The Violet looked like a great bruise nestled against the red velvet. He picked it up and held it out flat on his palm.

"Look at it, Juliette, and tell me whether it matters."

I saw at once what he meant. The stone was long and flat, like a thick slice of cheese. Far too thin for the proportions I had drawn.

"This diamond is one hundred fifteen carats," Papa said. "The largest of its kind. The size of the cut stone, though, is limited by its smallest dimension. If I could cut this in the Mazarin style—which I cannot, but if I could—how big would it be then?"

I swallowed, my mouth too dry to speak.

"Go on, Juliette," Papa said, sliding the paper toward me. "You deem yourself worthy of designing for the king. Do the calculation for a stone this flat and tell me what we would have left."

I took the paper and a stub of pencil, and with a trembling hand, I began the calculation I had practiced so many times in my room. This time, though, André and Papa were watching. It took me several tries to get it right. At last, I had a new set of dimensions, based on the actual depth of the stone. I stared at them, blinking in horror, hoping I was wrong.

"Well?" Papa said.

I swallowed. "It would be no bigger than the tip of my thumb," I said.

"Twenty-two carats," Papa confirmed. "So, you see, even if I had brought back the means to cut the stone, I would not be pleasing Louis. Not by Twelfth Night. Not ever. Because we have only two choices, Juliette. Reduce the king's great diamond to almost nothing, or leave it in the dark. Tell me, which do you think will satisfy Louis?"

He turned again toward the stairs. I glanced at André, hoping for his support, but he was absorbed, studying my calculations, trying to decipher for himself the secret of the Mazarins.

I snatched the paper out from under him and lunged around Papa, blocking his path to the stairs.

"You promised the king a jewel, this jewel—for Twelfth Night!" I thrust the design at him. He looked down at it but did not take it from me.

"We all know the Violet can't be cut by then, but you *can* make this brooch, Papa. You must! You've promised the king!"

Papa shook his head again.

His refusal sent the blood pounding at my temples. André and I had struggled too long and hard without him to let him just crawl back into his bed while humiliations were heaped onto our heads.

"You are the crown jeweler, Papa. You are the one who created a scepter so glorious it defeated the English!"

A ghost of a smile crossed his face at my exaggeration, so I plowed ahead. "Make the fleur-de-lis. I know my design isn't good enough, but it's a start, *n'est-ce pas*? I know you can fix it."

"Perhaps we could set the uncut Violet in it," André said, "and use already-cut stones to add sparkle."

Papa's expression softened as we spoke. He glanced from me to André and back. Perhaps he was inspired by our zeal. More likely, he was moved by the desperate hope on our faces. Slowly, he took the design from my hand and examined it.

"Perhaps some other embellishment around the Tavernier . . ."

He returned to the workbench and, taking up the stub of pencil, began marking and remarking the pattern, adding a flourish here, removing a gem there, changing the shape of the ornament a little with each expert stroke.

André and I smiled at each other. At last, the Papa I knew and loved had returned.

TWELVE

"Truly?" René says. I cock my head and look at him in confusion, unsure of what he is talking about.

He gives me a sheepish grin. "You would have married me, even knowing I was a craftsman's son?"

A little wave of happiness washes through me—all this time while I've been talking on, he has been thinking about marrying me. I place my good hand atop the one he has resting on his knee. He should see the truth by now, but I will say it a hundred more times if it will make him believe. "I would have married you if you had been the son of a ragpicker and aspired to nothing greater."

He stares at me for a few long seconds. Then, as if by the grace of God, he lifts his hand and, with a single finger, pushes back a stray lock of hair from my forehead. I close my eyes, tingling from his touch.

"Pardon my interruption. Pray, continue," he says, pulling his hand away. He is trying to sound formal and official once again, but when I open my eyes his face is shining with a dreamy smile, and I feel as if the sun has broken free from a long, dreary winter at last.

By the next morning, Papa had a design that satisfied him. It was wider and taller than mine had been, to accommodate the uncut violet. He replaced my emeralds and amethysts with rubies and citrines, their red and gold evoking the sun, and hopefully compensating for the dark Violet. Around the uncut diamond, he added an encircling band of small pearls, their pale, lustrous surfaces offsetting its darkness, like moonlight on black water. He added flourishes to the goldwork that alone would take most of the month. We had long hours ahead of us, but I wasn't afraid of hard work. Especially if it meant making up for my error.

Although the changes to the design required the king's approval, we set to work on it at once, trusting that the approval would come. We needed every minute to complete the work in the scant month we had. In that rush, I forgot about your visit, René, until you arrived that Thursday, intending to ask my father's permission to court me. Though there was nothing I wanted more, Papa's frequent sighs and trudging pace told me his renewed interest in his work remained fragile, and his mood volatile.

I was afraid he might turn you away, so I snatched my cloak and hurried out to meet you on the street before Papa noticed. A damp chill hung in the air, threatening drizzle at any moment. I wrapped the cloak tight around me as I spoke.

"I'm sorry, René," I said, "but we have so little time before Twelfth Night. It will take a small miracle to finish in time. It would be better if you waited to speak to him after the fete."

Your disappointment was plain, but you nodded and smiled graciously. "Of course. You must be very busy."

"There is something you could do for me, though," I said. I explained about the changes to the design. "The king must be forewarned that the Violet cannot be cut by Twelfth Night. He must be assured that the brooch will be magnificent all the same."

"You want me to present your new drawing to Colbert? I can take it now."

I hesitated, glancing back into the shop. "Papa is starting to craft the wax model to cast the gold," I said. "He needs the drawing for reference. Could you make an appointment for me, and I can bring the drawing, so that Papa is not without it for days? We don't have time to spare."

"Colbert confers with the king's artisans on Wednesdays," you said. "Come in the early afternoon, and I'll make sure you can see him then."

You kissed my hand before parting, and though I knew Papa needed me inside, I stood on the stoop watching you go and basking in the pleasure that flowed from where your lips had touched me. I was roused at last from my daydreams by a soft tapping. Turning, I saw André at the window, beckoning me back in.

"You don't need to keep buttering him up, Juliette," André

said when I returned inside. "Now that your father is back at work, we don't need his favor anymore."

I ignored André's comment and told Papa that I had an appointment to present the new drawing to Colbert on the coming Wednesday.

The day of my appointment, I instructed my maid to take extra care in arranging my hair and rouging my cheeks before I went to the palace. As I selected my prettiest gown, I told my maid it was to look my best before Colbert, but she smiled knowingly. She had seen you and me together too many times to believe my excuse.

At the Louvre, I went directly to Colbert's offices. As before, a small crowd of men milled around outside the door. I sat on a stiff bench and waited, holding Papa's new drawing, rolled and tied with a ribbon to keep it safe. After only a few minutes, you summoned me inside, smiling but remaining businesslike as you escorted me to Colbert.

I curtsied before the minister and explained the necessity of the changes before handing him the paper. He gave it only a cursory glance.

"I cannot approve such a large change without the king's consent," he said. He handed the paper back to you and dismissed us with a nod.

"Can't I even plead my case?" I asked as you led me back out of the office and into the corridors of the Louvre. I had planned all the things I might point out on the design—all the improvements and refinements Papa had added. I had been dismissed too quickly to say a thing.

"You can, but before the king," you said. I still remember how calm you were, leading me not out of the Louvre, but rather inward, toward the offices of the king.

I stopped in my tracks. "The king! But . . ."

"Colbert reported to His Majesty that there would be changes," you explained. "The king insisted they be sent to him at once."

"But I've never spoken directly to the king!"

"The design is beautiful, Juliette. All you have to do is present it and explain as you would have to Colbert."

"But how do I address His Majesty?"

"With humility and deference. Don't worry. He is a great lover of beauty." You gave me a flirtatious smile. There was reassurance in it, but my knees grew wobbly all the same.

"Be polite and flattering. Make sure he knows he will be greatly admired in this design, even with the Violet uncut," you said. By then we stood before a grand door, two of the *garde du corps* standing sentinel. You showed them Colbert's seal and the door was opened before us. On quaking legs, I stepped through, into the presence of Louis XIV.

He was seated behind an ornate desk, leaning back in his chair, listening with a bored expression as a gentleman detailed the concerns of some northern dukes. When the door closed behind us, Louis turned his eyes to us.

"Ah, Mademoiselle Pitau," he said, interrupting the petitioner mid-sentence. The man closed his mouth and turned to glare.

I dropped into a low curtsy. "Your Majesty."

"I understand you are asking to change the design of my diamond for Twelfth Night. Is this true?"

"To improve it, Your Majesty." My voice was thin and reedy with nerves. I swallowed and forced my next words out on a stronger breath. "The Violet is a treasure beyond all measure, and there is nothing that will do you greater honor than to perfect it, so that it may shine your glorious light for all the world."

The corner of his lips turned up in a tiny smile that only sharpened his piercing gaze. For a man so enraptured with flattery, he was not easily taken in by it.

"Indeed," he said. "And yet you propose to leave it uncut." He snapped his fingers and a boy stepped forward to take the design from me and hand it to the king. I wondered how, when I had only just left Colbert, the king already knew the content of my request. Perhaps there was nothing in the Louvre that Louis did not know. Perhaps nothing in all of Paris.

"What my father proposes, Your Majesty," I said while he examined the design, "is a finer ornament for Twelfth Night. As you can see, he has embellished the goldwork, and added more brilliance to it through the use of citrines and rubies in the petals of the flower."

"Really, sire," interjected the young nobleman who had been speaking when I entered. "I think the concerns of my duchy are of greater urgency than some girl's trinket for a ball."

Again, the king's lips twitched. He was enjoying the insult he was dealing the duke. "The goldwork is magnificent, I grant you. But I believe I voiced my opinion of citrines and rubies once before."

"You will see that the Violet is still at the heart of the design, surrounded by pearls. With the red and yellow stones, it will create the impression of sun, while the Violet reminds one of moonlight."

"Am I to be called the Moon King, then?" He looked up at me, raising an eyebrow. I pressed my knees together to keep my skirt still.

"To cut the Tavernier Violet by Twelfth Night would be foolish, Your Majesty."

His eyebrows rose higher, waiting for my reasoning, or perhaps wondering if I had just called him a fool. I hurried on.

"Perfection cannot be rushed. To cut a diamond takes not only great skill, but precise calculation. Give my father time, and he will harness the sun for you. He will mold light itself, to your eternal glory. But rush the cutting, and the chance will be lost forever."

The duke opened his mouth and uttered a word of protest, but I charged on. "Once cut, the stone cannot be returned to its former shape. My father could cut the stone for Twelfth Night, and all the English court would admire it. It would shine with the light of a hundred candles. But you are not the Candle King, either, Your Majesty. You are the Sun King. Give him time, and he will put the sun in the heart of the Tavernier."

The young noble gave a snort of derision and tried to speak again, but I rushed on, raising my voice to speak over him, bold as any man.

"This design will shine, Your Majesty. No one will doubt your praise of the sun. The Tavernier Violet, by contrast, will be a dark mystery at the heart of the bright jewel. Let them wonder at the mystery for now. There is power in mystery too, *n'est-ce pas?*"

"You speak well for such a pretty child, mademoiselle. But I do not think I need a lesson from you in power," the king said. Perhaps he meant to quell my boldness, but there was no anger in his eyes. In fact, he looked amused. So I continued.

"Of course not, Your Majesty. Which is why I don't need to tell you how much greater the effect will be on those who have seen the dark mystery of the uncut stone when, in a year's time, you are wearing the captured sun upon your breast."

Now the king's smile widened, lighting even his eyes. He sat a moment considering. Remembering the advice about humility, perhaps later than I should have, I lowered my eyes to the floor and tried not to fidget while I waited for his decision.

At last, the king took up a quill and signed the drawing. He handed the paper back to his servant. "Tell Colbert to deliver the pearls, rubies, and citrines to Master Pitau's workshop. I look forward to the great mystery, Mademoiselle Pitau, and, of course, to the captured sun. *Au revoir.*"

I curtsied again, a shallow bob for fear my legs might not support more, and hurried from the room. Once outside, I let out a long breath.

"I remember that audience," René says. Though his tone still carries a shadow of censure, there is a crinkle of amusement at the corners of his eyes. "How you professed your fear of the king, like a timid mouse, but when you stood before him, you were fierce. Defiant even."

In keeping with his tone, I lower my eyes like a contrite maiden, but allow a little fierceness into my words. "You told me to be humble, and I had intended to be. But I had to get the king's approval to save my father."

René rolls his eyes. "After all this, you still can't admit it was your ambition that made you so bold."

I incline my head in a tentative acknowledgment of his point. "Perhaps I was prideful," I admit slowly, "but there was more than that. I was afraid that if Papa resigned his post you would not want me in my disgrace."

His brow wrinkles at this. "Do you think me so superficial that I would see your father's failure as a mark on your honor? You do me a grave injustice."

"I should have put more faith in you," I agree mildly.

His scowl softens a little at my apology, but he says nothing. With a pang, I realize that he sees me now as I have always seen André: too ambitious to form true attachments. Maybe my ambition is a fault, but my love for him is real. If he can just remember, as I do, our pleasure in our next meeting, perhaps that will persuade him.

"Do you remember what happened next?" I say. "You asked me if I would be at the king's fete on Twelfth Night."

"I asked you for the first two dances," René says, a warm glow in his eyes as he remembers.

"And you kissed my hand before we parted that day," I say, looking down at my wounded hand. Even now I can feel a tingle, remembering the thrill that came through me at the touch of his lips. "Perhaps you felt my pulse racing? That was not ambition, *mon chéri*. Nor was it thoughts of political advantage that had me dancing on air, giddy with anticipation until Twelfth Night."

Even now, I feel a little giddy remembering. I look up at René again, and only when his eyes widen in surprise do I realize I must be grinning like a silly schoolgirl.

He turns quickly back to the safety of his papers and ink, and I imagine, just for a moment, I see him color at the temples.

"This is not the story of us," he reminds me once again. "We should be speaking of the diamond and the plot."

"Of course," I say, content to continue and not disrupt the truce we seem to have reached. "All seemed right, until I remembered the promises I had made the king. The captured sun, I had said, though Papa had shown me why it was impossible. I had said too much in my desperation to have the design approved.

"But in my heart, I hadn't given up on the commission, or on Papa's skill. He would yet find a way. We can mold light itself, he had told me. We can be like gods."

I pause, and when I hear those words as René must hear them, the room seems to tilt. Pride, I realize, now that I face execution, is a mortal sin. René must know what I am thinking, but he mercifully remains silent.

I put a steadying hand on the table and try to frame it differently. "I wanted to see Papa honored. I wanted to find a way to make the king happy—to make the Violet shine without reducing it to nothing. We had to. After my careless words to the king, it was more than Papa's promise to Louis now. It was mine as well."

Thirteen

Over the next month, Papa threw himself into his work with a fever, much as André and I had done after Maman and Georges died. Fires burned constantly in the forge, and hammers and grinders could be heard all day and into the night as the jewel took form.

Papa widened the central petal of the fleur-de-lis to hold the great Tavernier Violet in its uncut form. He switched the small pearls for larger ones to make the darkness even more dramatic. For more fire, he added Mazarin's large pale-yellow diamond, beneath the Tavernier. Around them all, the gold swooped and danced in intricate patterns.

It was a fine brooch for the king to wear upon his breast, a true masterwork. Papa never made anything less. But when he set the final stone, only one day before Twelfth Night, and stepped back to admire the final piece, it was with disappointment. The Violet was not the mystery I had promised. Enthroned at the center of the great lily, it looked more like a murky swamp than a moonlit pool.

"I still have to polish it," I offered, but we all knew that would not be enough to save it.

"There is one more thing we can do," André volunteered, with a hesitant glance at Papa.

"And what is that?" Papa asked.

"We could foil the Violet," André said.

Papa's face turned red with indignation. "Never!"

I was shocked that André would even suggest such a thing. Foiling was the trickery of inferior craftsmen who defrauded their clientele by adhering a thin layer of gold to the backs of worthless stones to temporarily brighten them.

"Louis has commanded us to make it sparkle," André said.

Papa shook his head. "We are the king's jewelers. It is not for us to resort to petty tricks."

André glanced at me for support, but seeing none, he dropped his gaze to his shoes and clamped his mouth into a tight, thin line.

I looked at the band of soft, lustrous pearls surrounding the Violet. If sparkle and fire came into a stone with the light reflecting back and forth across its interior, it stood to reason that light might be bent and projected into the Violet to brighten it from faceted gems around it.

"What if we replaced the pearls with small diamonds—ones that are already cut? That might add some light to the Violet, mightn't it?" I said, and I explained my thinking.

Papa cocked his head, considering. "That might have worked. But the only diamonds I might have used are currently set in the queen's necklace. I would not wish to insult that great lady. She, too, must shine for Twelfth Night." He ran his fingers over the surface of the Violet and shook his head with a sigh.

"This will have to do. Polish it, Juliette," he said. Then he turned and, with sagging shoulders, climbed the stairs to our apartments.

André glared after him. "He won't even try."

"He's done his best," I snapped. André had no place criticizing, and anyway, what use was grumbling?

I polished every stone and pearl and fleck of gold that evening, but even as they grew brighter, I sank into gloom. So much work, so much skill, and still the Violet had defeated Papa. All I could think, as I locked it away in its secret cabinet for the night, was how the whole court would see the king's disappointment. Louis was not one to restrain his contempt when he was displeased. I only hoped he didn't throw my foolish promises back at Papa, when it was my fault.

If only we had bright, faceted diamonds to throw light onto the Violet, it might be the fascinating secret I had promised the king. Through the evening, the idea grew, until it burned like a sun, blinding my reason. After André and Papa retired for the night, I returned to the workshop to look again at the jewel.

To my surprise, André was there already, seated at a workbench. At his elbow, the jewel's box was open, and the Violet, removed from its setting, lay facedown before him. Using a soft brush, he was painting egg white onto the back of the stone to glue down a thin layer of gold leaf.

"André! What are you doing?" I said.

Startled, he dropped the paintbrush. When he saw it was only me, he quickly regained his composure. "Someone has to do something if your father won't," he answered simply.

"Papa strictly forbade foil!"

"Shh!" he hissed. "At least see how it looks, Juliette. You don't want your father disgraced in front of the whole court, do you?"

His words probed my deepest fear. I knew foil had been banned by the gem-cutters' guild, and the penalty was severe. But my fear of Papa's disgrace was stronger than my fear of the guild, so I did nothing to stop him.

When he finished applying the gold leaf and turned the stone over to examine its face, I had to admit, it was a little brighter. My resolve to do what was right weakened even more.

"We should show Papa," I said, though I did not move to get him.

"He will be in bed by now," André said.

"But—"

"I wish we could do more," André said, ignoring my pleas. "What was that idea you had? Diamonds instead of pearls?" He ran his fingers along the pearls, fourteen in all, surrounding the Violet. "If only you had thought of it sooner."

I hesitated. I had come down to the workshop because another solution had come to me.

"Do you remember when Papa came back from Venice? He

said they make glass seem like gold and gems."

"Glass?" André repeated, his eyes sparking as the idea caught him.

"We don't have diamonds, but we might have time to make and facet glass beads that would reflect light into the Violet."

André nodded eagerly. "That just might work! Glass is easy to cut. But it would have to be high-quality glass to get much sparkle."

I hesitated then, because there was only one source of such high-quality glass in our house. The queen had made my father a gift of fine crystal goblets, two years previous, in appreciation of a fine necklace. Maman had prized the goblets above all things, not just for their beauty but because they were in praise of Papa and his work.

It was a terrible sacrifice, and a risk. The workshop had cut plenty of glass models of stones to test designs, but they were never as beautiful as the stones themselves. I just hoped that the fine crystal would make a difference and we could give the king the glory he wanted.

And so, with every hope and good intention in my heart, thinking only of pleasing His Majesty the King, I tiptoed into the dining room and took the most beautiful possession my family owned. My first theft that I must confess.

I set the goblets on the workbench and retrieved a hammer. André fed the forge and pumped the bellows until the heart of the fire glowed blue. The goblets caught the glow of the fire and sparked like miniature suns. Swallowing my regret, I raised the hammer and smashed the treasured gifts into a thousand splinters of glass.

I swept the fragments into a mortar and ground them into a fine grit, then poured them into a crucible. We worked through the night, transforming the grit into small droplets of glass, then into faceted beads resembling colorless diamonds.

It was nearly dawn when we removed the pearls from their settings and replaced them with the bright crystals. We gave them a hasty polish even as the floorboards creaked overhead, announcing that Papa was preparing for the day. Papa would be presenting the fleur-de-lis to the king in just a few hours' time. My heart quickened. How would we explain to Papa what we had done?

"You must be the one to tell him," André said.

I must have paled at the idea, because André went on forcefully.

"It has to be you—this was your idea. And anyway, you are his *petit bijou*. If he is angry, he won't punish you as he would me."

This argument did little to ease my sudden terror, but before I could give any further objection, he slipped away into the apprentice's quarters.

Panic washed over me as Papa's tread echoed on the stairs. He was sure to be angry. My courage failed. I slipped the jewel into its box and replaced it in the wall panel where I had put it after Papa's final inspection. Then I snatched up the broom and began hastily sweeping up the sparkling bits of glass around the grinder.

Papa looked at me quizzically when he saw me at work so early.

I opened my mouth to tell him the truth, but again fell into cowardice. "I want the workshop to look its best when the king's couriers arrive," I lied.

"Never mind that. Go make yourself presentable. You look like you only just crawled out of bed, without a thought to your toilette."

I nodded and hurried away. A pang of guilt stopped me on the stairs. I gulped a few deep breaths, hoping for the courage to go back and confess the truth.

But it was too late. I heard the clatter of a carriage in the street. I could do nothing more than watch as Papa, carrying the wooden casket carefully before him, climbed into the carriage.

In my room, I tried to rest, but sleep eluded me. What would Papa think when he opened the box and saw the changes André and I had made? And what would the king think of the ornament?

At last, I heard the carriage returning. I settled myself in the salon to await Papa, calling for refreshments for him: bread and cheese and wine, since it was early afternoon. When Papa entered, he crossed straight to the wine, filling a glass to the brim. He did not speak until he'd drained his glass in silence. When he had filled it a second time, I could no longer bear the silence.

"Papa?" I said, cautiously.

He lifted his glass and contemplated the bright liquid. "So this is what we've come to, Juliette? Charlatans and tricksters."

"We had to do something to make the stone brighter, Papa. We would have told you—"

"Well, there's no point in telling me now, is there? It is out of our hands now. The king has his bauble, and we will have our share of whatever glory it brings him."

I was confused then, for his manner had not made me think he anticipated glory. "Then the king was pleased?" I asked.

Papa sighed. "Has it never occurred to you that I am a master for a reason? That it means something to be a master in a guild?"

"Of course, Papa!"

"You got lucky, Juliette, when they didn't see your deceit on the design. But you are a fool if you think your trickery will be indistinguishable from the true art of a man such as myself."

"I didn't mean—"

"What is done is done. It cannot be undone. We can only wait and see."

"But the king?" I asked again.

"Louis is a child!" Papa said. "He is eager to sparkle. But trickery cannot substitute for quality, Juliette. Not where kings are concerned. Sooner or later we will be found out as liars. And what then, *ma chérie*? What will become of us then?"

He drank down the wine from his glass in heavy gulps before striding away to his bedroom and closing the door behind him.

FOURTEEN

I have always adored Twelfth Night. What child doesn't love the eve of Epiphany, with its revels and feasts, its gifts and treats that mimic the gifts of the Magi? That year, I was no longer a child, but the delights of the holiday were no less promising. I would be at the king's fete, albeit apart from the nobility in the king's ballroom. Even so, there would be ample food and drink, entertainment and dancing—and the first two dances belonged to my beloved René. I had never had any doubt of my regard for you, René, which had grown steadily since we first dined at the king's table nearly a year before. This would be a chance for a public show of our feelings.

Still, as my maid curled the ringlets along my neck, I couldn't shake a deep unease. I had meddled in the affairs of kings. I had looked Louis in the eye and made promises, and I had engaged in a forgery to try to keep them. Fear hummed through my veins like a swarm of bees, and I jumped at every sound in the street.

Papa's words kept repeating through my mind: *Sooner or later we will be found out as liars. What will become of us then?*

That evening, Papa awaited me in the salon, dressed in his own finery, his jaw clenched too tight to speak. He offered no compliments on my appearance, though I wore my finest gown. When he extended his arm to escort me out, it was with none of the tenderness or pleasure that he'd offered to my mother on such occasions in the past. We descended to the street and the waiting carriage in grim silence.

With Louis entertaining the king of England, the Twelfth Night fete was the grandest I had ever experienced. The glittering galleries and spacious salons of the Louvre were crowded with revelers, all dancing and drinking and joining in the madrigals and farces of the night. Papa was drawn off with a crowd of craftsmen to enjoy conversation and cigars moments after our arrival. I wandered the grand gallery for a time, watching a juggler, listening to strolling musicians, searching the crowd for the one person I wanted to see.

The grand ballroom, with its crystal chandeliers, gilded walls, and marble floor, where the king watched over the courtly dances from his high seat at the head of the room, was beyond my reach, but there was still plenty of dancing to be had. The courtyard was filled with thousands of couples, some who knew the courtly steps, others dancing the simpler, lighthearted country dances. Torches and bonfires had been lit against the winter chill, but the crush of people and the flow of wine made them unnecessary. Here, the strict protocol of rank and etiquette were eased, and the crowd of wealthy merchants, craftsmen, artisans, and officers bubbled with mirth.

"Despite the churning mass of people, you found me almost as soon as I stepped out of the gallery into the night," I say to René, leaning across the table toward him as far as my broken ribs will allow. My side throbs, but it is worth the pain to be close to him as I remember that glorious dance.

"Of course, I saw you at once," René says, his voice a little dreamy. "You were the most beautiful thing in the palace."

I laugh at the audacity of this claim, but he does not take it back.

"I still remember every detail: the tiny white flowers woven into your hair, the graceful curve of your neck above the lace at your throat. The soft folds of dark-red velvet hugging your waist and flowing to the floor." He turns his eyes to me, and though the face before him is tear-streaked and bruised, for one unguarded moment his eyes caress me, as if seeing the girl he saw that night. It awakens a glow in my core that quickly radiates through my whole being. The corner of his mouth rises mischievously.

"And when you saw me, your cheeks grew quite rosy, just as they are doing now," he adds.

I cast my eyes downward in a confusion of pleasure and em-barrassment. "You treated me as if I were the only girl in the world that night. Like I would always be safe and want for noth-ing, as long as I had your arms around me."

He nods, though he does not take the hint about his arms. "I've never been happier than when we were dancing together that night, innocent of all that was to come."

The change in the tenor of his voice jolts me painfully, as if we were mid-dance and I'd just jammed my toe on a stone. Hastily, I try to regain the mood we had only a moment before.

"When you found me in that crowd, you bowed and kissed my hand as if I were the queen herself. You reminded me of my promise, but I hadn't forgotten, and I was more than happy to let the two promised dances merge into four."

It is no good. A morose expression has settled onto his features and will not be dislodged.

"That night went to ruin soon enough, so there is no point in remembering it," he says.

"Perhaps not for you," I say. "You can choose what to write, René, but not what I remember. I will not be denied the solace of remembering those hours that were the happiest of my life."

Even so, I must continue with my account, no matter how much I wish I could linger in those fleeting pleasures.

By ten o'clock, when a chime called us to the dining room for the feast, the crowd was rosy with dancing and wine. In the grand dining room, a long table was laid for the nobility. Louis and Charles sat side by side at its head, like old friends despite the opinion Louis had voiced a only a few weeks earlier. Around them the French and English dukes crowded the table, jockey-

ing for the best position. I was happy enough to sit at the opposite end of the room among the commoners—the guild masters,
wealthy merchants, and honored artisans of the Manufacture
Royale. Colbert's clerks were expected at his elbow, should the
king require anything, so you bid me *au revoir* with a regretful
smile.

I took a seat between Papa and Master Valin and his wife. I
was as polite as possible to the guild master, knowing that of all
people there, he was most likely to unmask the secret trickery of
the jewel, and wanting to give him no reason to do so.

The feast went on for hours, each course richer and more elaborate than the last: thick winter soups, shellfish in cream and fish
in butter, braised duck, stuffed peahen, weanling pork, breads
and puddings, Spanish oranges, wheels of well-aged cheese, and
concoctions of candied fruits and honey. Finally, the largest
galette des rois I had ever seen emerged from the kitchen on a
platter held aloft by four men. The huge golden mound of cake,
dotted with nuts and brandied cherries, was set before the Grand
Dauphin. As the youngest member of the household, the prince
was called upon by tradition to cut it and pass the slices around
to everyone at the table. Two real kings watched, smiling, to see
who would get the slice with the bean and become King of the
Feast and the third king at the table. Three kings that night on
the eve of Epiphany—perhaps that was a coincidence. Perhaps it
was God's little joke.

I glanced up and down the table, as eager as anyone for the
announcement.

"Who do you think will get the bean?" Master Valin said into my ear.

Before I could answer, a cheer went up among the entourage of the English court. One man in their midst rose to his feet, holding aloft an object too small for me to see, but of course, we all knew what it was.

"Ah," Master Valin said with a smile, "Sir Robert Vyner will be crowned."

"You know him?" I asked.

"He crafted the coronation crown for Charles after the original was melted down by that dog Cromwell. No doubt he's come along to see what makes our Sun King shine so brightly," Valin said, with a smile toward Papa that sent a shiver of misgiving through me.

I looked back and watched the plump Englishman being pushed forward by the laughing crowd, to take the empty seat between Louis and Charles. He was sneering, a crooked, smug expression, as a crown of paper and flowers was set upon his head. Such smugness—looking back, I wonder if it was a cruel trick of fate that thrust the English goldsmith forward that day, or a bit of counterfeit trickery when he saw the opportunity to humiliate his betters at the French court? He now had the authority to speak freely, and when I turned to Papa and saw him go white, I knew why the man's smile was so wicked.

In the good-natured spirit of Twelfth Night, the two great monarchs, Louis and Charles, bowed with flourish before the baronet, who smirked and raised a palm in blessing over the assembled crowd of his betters.

"Speak. What do you command?" Louis said, and the whole crowd leaned in to hear what revels the King of the Feast would call for. Instead of revels, however, he preferred to share his own epiphany.

"Where is my brother goldsmith?" he cried in heavily accented French, well soaked in wine. "Bring me the great glassblower of Paris, that he will adorn me in the true style of the French kings!"

Louis laughed at the fool's pronouncement, but with discomfort. What did the fellow mean, *glassblower*?

Papa glanced toward me as he got slowly to his feet. Enthusiastic hands pushed him forward to the new king. I saw you, René, laughing with the rest, unaware of the calamity to come.

When Papa stood before the King of the Feast, the man smiled with sharp malice. I tried to rise, to rush forward and take the blame as I should, but Valin gripped my arm and pushed me back into my seat.

"Be still, mademoiselle. Nothing will happen to your father that he doesn't deserve." I looked at him and saw the Englishman's malice mirrored in his gaze. Paul Valin and his wife were watching with the hungry, eager lust of vultures. Helplessly, I turned my eyes back to where Papa stood before Sir Robert.

"I say, Master Pitau," he said, his cheeks and nose rosy with drink as he wobbled on the dais.

"*Bonsoir,* Sieur Robert," Papa replied cautiously.

Vyner's smile widened. "Tell me, good sir, the secret of making your king so glorious. Did you yourself cut these trinkets of glass your king wears on his breast, or did they fall from the chandelier?"

Papa said nothing, but Louis reddened and looked down at the gleaming fleur-de-lis. His eyes narrowed as he saw what he should have seen before—the clear crystals where pearls should have been—and he understood the baronet's meaning. No doubt he saw, too, the spiteful pleasure flooding the faces of the English court. Even his own wife could not keep a small smile from her lips.

Sir Robert Vyner laughed and adjusted his paper crown. "I had heard that the sun ruled in France. Now I see he is only an elaborate candelabra."

There was a scandalized tittering of laughter from a few of the English ladies, and a gasp of horror from the French. Faces paled and mouths fell open across the room.

Papa shifted his attention from the insolent Englishman and bowed deeply before the French king.

"My liege. May your reign be long and triumphant," he said. Then he turned on his heel and strode from the room.

The silent horror of the French broke out into gossip and protest. Valin let go of my arm and leaned back, smiling, in his chair.

Freed at last, I ran after Papa. Near the door of the dining room, you blocked my way, René. Through the blur of tears, I saw the horror and shock on your face, and I could not bear it. I ran—from the hall, from you, from the very palace.

Papa's carriage was rolling away when I burst into the courtyard, leaving me to struggle home through streets crowded with revelers. By the time I reached the apartments, Papa had already locked himself in his bedchamber. I retreated to my own and cried bitter tears until the first light of Epiphany.

FIFTEEN

"I wanted to help you, Juliette," René says, his voice breaking. His hand is shaking, and a glob of ink escapes the quill to splatter on the page. "I was trying to help . . . but when you ran from me . . . I didn't know what to think."

My chest aches, the mortification as fresh and sharp as it was that night. I cross the room and sink down on the filthy cot, unable to look René in the eye.

"How could I talk to you? How could I talk to anyone after what my rash, vain actions had just done to my father?"

"You couldn't have known that would happen." René's voice is kind now, but still I cannot look at him. I fear it is not love but pity that makes him gentle, and to see his pity would undo me.

I pick at a loose thread on the thin blanket. "I knew it was not my place to tamper with the jewel! I never meant any harm, but my father was right. I presumed too much. Please write that, René," I say, trying to be a person worthy of his love, willing to take responsibility, though the consequences terrify me.

René does not pick up his quill. "Your desperation, though—that was your father's fault, leaving for so long and falling into drink at his return," René says. For a brief moment his understanding is reassuring, until he continues.

"I can only reflect with sorrow on the next day."

Yes. The next day. Even the thought of it knots my stomach.

Though it was midday on Epiphany, a holy day of obligation, Papa was still abed when you arrived with Colbert in an official carriage, the banner of the king flying from its corners. I watched through the front window as Master Valin and his wife stepped into the street, their lips curled into a sneer of triumph as they surveyed the royal workshop. Cold fire shot through my veins. I ordered André to stall you while I ran to Papa's room to rouse him.

The air in the room reeked of wine and bile, and I gagged. Empty bottles littered the floor around the bed. How had he gotten so many? I had instructed the servants not to give him bottles, but he was still master of the house. One bottle, tucked into the crook of Papa's arm, had spilled a deep red splash across the sheets. Papa's guts had spilled their contents too, on the floor and across his pillow. His cheeks and hair were matted with vomit.

I swore under my breath and snatched up a cloth, wetting it in his washbasin. There was no time to clean him up properly, but I had to do what I could. Frantically, I wiped his face and hair, kicking every bottle I could reach under the bed as I did. Papa did not wake. He only muttered and tried to push me away.

Growing more and more desperate, I shouted at him to wake up. He muttered again and opened his swollen eyes a slit.

"Juliette? What is it?"

"Papa, you must get up," I said, shaking him. "Master Valin—"

Before I could finish, the bedchamber door burst open and Master Valin came storming through, his smirking wife on his heels.

"Jean Pitau, get up!" he bellowed, sending Papa's bed shivering with a hard kick to the footboard. "Get up, you stinking, putrid pig!"

"How dare you!" I shouted, and I lunged to push him away, but Madame Valin darted forward, quick as the snake she was, and grabbed my arms, wresting me away from the bed. Then Jean-Baptiste Colbert stood in the hallway, and behind him you, René, your face white with horror.

"Get up!" Valin roared, with another kick that rattled the bottles on the dressing table.

Papa groaned and sat up. The room went still for a moment, all eyes on him as he swayed. Then he leaned over the side of his bed and vomited a deep, claret stream of wine and bile onto Valin's shoes. I might have laughed if the world hadn't been crumbling to ruin around me. Or if Monsieur Colbert hadn't stepped through the doorway, with you shuffling reluctantly forward in his wake.

Colbert paused, looking at Papa. If he felt any sympathy or

regret, it did not show, except perhaps for a quick pulse of muscle at his jaw. He drew himself up straight in the power of the king.

"Master Jean Pitau," Colbert said, addressing Papa in a stern, formal voice that carried more menace than the shouts of Valin. Papa looked up, his eyes hollowed out by despair.

"Please, Monsieur Colbert!" I cried. "Papa has done nothing! André and I are at fault!"

"An apprentice and a girl?" Valin scoffed.

Colbert held up a hand to silence us both. He pulled something from his pocket and tossed it toward Papa. It flashed gold in the sunlight before it landed in the mess at Papa's feet. It was the fleur-de-lis, though all the precious stones had been removed from their settings. All that remained was the intricately formed golden lily and the ring of glass gems André and I had made in the night. They had been smashed to dust, every last one of them, and Papa's beautiful goldwork twisted and warped in the process.

I pulled against Madame Valin's grip again, but she only tightened her hands until her fingernails bit into my arms.

"Please, Monsieur Colbert," I begged. "The cut glass was my idea, and I put them there without my father's consent. I—"

"Silence!" Colbert barked. "A master is responsible for all that comes out of his workshop."

Paul Valin nodded in affirmation, while his wife beamed with triumph and gripped me like she wanted to snap my bones.

"Jean Pitau," Colbert repeated, "by authority of His Majesty Louis XIV of France, you are hereby relieved of your position as crown jeweler. Henceforth, all work of this workshop and the oversight of all apprentices and works herein will be under the authority of Master Paul Valin. You will turn over all works, plans, and papers of this workshop to him immediately."

Papa said nothing, only sagged a little further as he sat on the bed, gazing down at the ruined jewel.

Valin glowed with triumph. He had long coveted Papa's secrets, and now, through my own rash actions, I had delivered them up. As if Papa had not suffered enough from the deaths of Maman and Georges and my survival in their place. Now I had given away his most guarded secret to Paul Valin.

I sank to my knees, sobbing, and Madame Valin let me go. She didn't mind releasing me for my abasement. I crawled to Colbert's feet in one last effort, begging again that he punish me instead of Papa.

"Mademoiselle, please," he said, and at last, a slender thread of sympathy ran through his words. He extended a hand and raised me to my feet. "It is the king's command. It is not for me to change it."

He released my hand, nodded once to Master Valin, and took his leave.

Perhaps you did not see much of this, René, for you had kept your eyes averted, perhaps wanting to spare me my humiliation, or perhaps too pained to witness it. But you raised your eyes before you followed your master, and muttered simply, "*Je suis désolé*, mademoiselle." Four simple words in the shape of "I'm sorry." But underneath, I knew they meant goodbye.

"That is not what I meant!" René protests. "How can you think me so callous?"

I shrug helplessly, wrung out by all I have recounted. "Who would want a connection with the daughter of a man so debased? A girl who had so debased herself? I did not think you callous, René, only prudent."

"I was heartbroken," he says, his tone still full of reproach, "and angry at your father. But I offered only my sympathy to you."

"Papa did not deserve your ire," I say, drawing my legs up and hugging them to my body, knowing that I do.

"Of course he deserved it! Don't forget that I saw him that morning, lying there in his own vomit and filth, stinking of ruin. I saw him walk away from the king the night before rather than stay and defend the king's honor. I saw him drunk when he should have been working all those times too." His hand is clenched around his quill, and his eyes are fierce. "You take far too much blame on yourself, Juliette. . . ."

I begin to uncurl, but the sympathy dissipates from his eyes too quickly into regret.

"If only you had gone quietly from the royal workshop and set up a respectable business elsewhere, I would have come to you. I wanted to take you away from all the suffering your father in-flicted on you. I would have asked for your hand, even if it meant leaving Colbert's employ."

There is a lump in my throat too big to swallow. If I had only known, how easy it would have been to turn away from all the bitter politics of court. How different the last year might have been. We could have been married by now, living peacefully somewhere far away, perhaps with Papa nearby in a new workshop of his own, the horror of disgrace forgotten. All that squandered.

"But your wounded pride wouldn't let you go quietly, and so here we are." We are back once again to the very core of his grievance, the sense of betrayal that, like a parasite, will not let him go. "That day, as you begged for mercy for your father, that is the last I saw of the girl I fell in love with. The one I danced with at the Twelfth Night ball. After that, you grew cold and manipulative. You only cared about glorifying your father and, by extension, yourself, about bringing the Valins low."

I feel my temperature rise, as it always does at any mention of the Valins. "How do you know what I cared about? You weren't there, being humiliated and abused by the Valins, so you have no right to judge what I did."

He holds up his hand, as if to ward off my rage. "I am not your judge, Juliette." As if I need a reminder. As if the fear ever unwinds its stranglehold on my heart. He waves a hand over the pages spread out across the table. "It's all here in your own words, all your contrivances, your manipulation."

He leafs through my account, reading back the most scathing passages, painting me the villain. My anger flares again, launching me across the room to slam a hand down on the pages and stop him. I realize my mistake the moment my burned skin strikes the paper. The pain of it buckles my knees. I pull the blistered hand back and cradle it against my body as I fall gasping onto the stool.

The color drains from René's face as he stares in horror at the bloody, puss-streaked mess I've made of his neatly written page. Then, without a word, he strides to the door and knocks, and when the guard opens it, he leaves without a word of parting. I am left alone, holding my throbbing hand and regretting yet another decision with too little thought behind it.

As the pain subsides, I realize the enormity of what I have done. I have driven away the one person who could have given me the chance to live; offended the person I wanted to live for. I look at the bloodied, rumpled page before me. There is so much more I need to explain to secure the king's pardon. I try to grip the pen, to take up the narrative myself, but I cannot bear the pain. I drop it again before I can write a word.

I look at René's beautiful, looping script on the page and the terror of the noose overcomes me. Darkness closes in from the corners of my vision. I drop my head to the table and let it come.

I don't know how much time passes before the door clangs open and brings me back to myself. I do not look up. I am too afraid of whom, or what, I will see. But there is only a gentle touch on my injured hand, a touch I would know anywhere, and my heart feels like it will burst. He has not forsaken me. I raise my head as René sits and takes my injured hand into his lap. On the table he sets a roll of clean linen bandages and a pot of goose fat salve. Wordlessly, he begins to spread the soothing salve onto my hand, pausing whenever I flinch. He is wrapping the bandages onto it before either of us speaks.

"Why?" I ask. It is, of course, a bigger question—a question about futility and hope, and things too big to be spoken that still cry out for answers.

One shoulder rises in a simple shrug as he keeps his eyes on his work. "You are bleeding," he says.

"That's not what I meant . . ."

His eyes flicker up to mine and then away again. "I am not heartless, Juliette."

I say nothing, and he stays intent on his task, unaware that I am drinking in the lovely contours of his face.

He ties the bandage, not too tight. The task is finished, but his fingers and eyes linger on my crippled fingers. I raise my good hand and brush my fingertips along his cheek. He stills, his eyes closing. For a moment, I think he will curve into my touch, but then he straightens, remembering himself, and the connection is broken.

"What did you do after Colbert left that day?" he says, taking up his quill.

I swallow down a growl of frustration. Every time I pull him closer, he slips away like a fish. He means to draw me back to my confession, but when I think about his question, a tight curl forms on my lips. If he hasn't figured it out yet, he will see that I am not one to give up easily, no matter how elusive the prize.

"I could not silently walk away when my actions had so unjustly brought Papa low," I say. "So when Valin demanded that my father turn over all his papers, I grabbed Papa's keys from his dressing table and bolted out the door and down the stairs.

"By the time I heard Valin's feet pounding down the stairs in pursuit, I had the cabinet open and Papa's precious papers in my hands—all his notes and drawings and painstaking calculations. As Valin burst into the workshop, I threw them into the forge, where they burst into flame, reducing Papa's words and calculations to ash."

René is looking at me in horror. He must think I had lost my mind to destroy the very work I had fought so long to protect, an impression no doubt enhanced by the fact that I am still smiling.

"Don't you see? I destroyed the only record of the Mazarin cut, except, of course, the one carried in Papa's head. They would need us now. But as my eyes met Paul Valin's, I knew it would not be a gentle alliance."

SIXTEEN

My plan worked, at least so far as it kept us in the royal workshop, but the consequences were heavy. The Valins took over our apartments above the workshop—which Maman had seen finely appointed with the patronage of the king—right down to our silverware and table linens. Papa and I were sent to live in the tiny apprentice rooms at the back of the workshop near the servants' door, where the stink of the alley seeped in night and day.

André did a little to try to make us more comfortable, and at least had the grace to pretend not to notice our disgrace, though he avoided me now, often looking away when I tried to catch his eye and scurrying to do his new master's bidding. He still showed deference to my father, though there was a new coolness there too. I suppose he wanted to avoid sharing in our ruin, and I cannot blame him for that. He was in an awkward position himself.

Madame Valin wasted no time in dismissing all our servants, including my lady's maid, so that I had to give up my fine clothes and hairstyles. She forced me to work as a servant in my own house—to earn my keep, she said, though we both knew it was to humiliate me. She also barred me from taking my mother's gowns and jewels, though they were rightfully mine.

I begged Papa to do something about it, but he would not. He was either too despondent or too drunk to do anything but sit on the small, hard cot in his room, his head in his hands. My only consolation was that his despondency kept him from telling Valin the secret of the Mazarin cut. As long as Papa alone knew the secret, he might have a chance to redeem himself in the king's eyes. To do so, he would have to solve the dual problems of the Tavernier Violet's shape and the difficulty of cutting with precision. I knew that, overwhelmed by despair as he was, he would never look for the solutions to those problems on his own. But, I reasoned, if I could resolve one problem for him, he might be inspired to find a solution to the second problem. So I returned to his original plan: to find the master who cut Mazarin's diamonds.

As far as I knew, the great Mazarin diamonds had never belonged to anyone other than Cardinal Mazarin and, now, the treasury of France. That meant that the cardinal had to have been the one to commission them, or at least he had acquired them directly from the gem-cutter who produced them. If I could find someone who had known Cardinal Mazarin well, they might know something of the unknown gem-cutter.

I knew of only two people who had been close to Mazarin. One was the Dowager Queen Anne, who as regent had relied on him through the king's youth. There was no way I could talk to the dowager now, after the insult we had dealt the king.

The other would be even more impossible. I didn't want to think of it. Instead, I asked Papa, over our meager supper, if he knew of anyone else.

"Do you think me such an imbecile that I haven't thought of that, Juliette? The king let me see all of Mazarin's papers that had anything to do with the crown jewels. There is nothing there about who cut his diamonds."

I recoiled from the sting of his words, but I wasn't willing to give up. Not when our situation was so dire and our very livelihood depended on it. "What about Monsieur Fouquet? Would he know where the cardinal acquired the gems?"

Papa's eyebrows rose, and he laughed, a short, bitter laugh that sounded nothing like my father. "I wouldn't be fool enough to ask," he said.

"But he might know, mightn't he?" I persisted. "He or perhaps some of his friends?"

"Fouquet has no friends, Juliette. Not in France, anyway."

I knew Papa's words for the warning they were. Nicolas Fouquet had been Cardinal Mazarin's right hand during the regency but aspired to too much power after the cardinal's death. Within a year of the cardinal's passing, Louis had arrested Fouquet for treason and imprisoned him for life, despite the lack of evidence at his trial. Eight years had passed and still no one dared admit to sympathy with Fouquet. It was said the king still forbade him visitors.

I could not stop thinking about Fouquet as I scrubbed floors and dusted furniture for Madame Valin, but I knew of no way to get to a prisoner so well guarded. There was one person who had weathered Fouquet's fall well, despite her closeness to the man: his mistress, Suzanne de Bruc de Monplaisir, the Marquise du Plessis-Bellière. The king had ordered her confined to her home for two years during the trial, yet in the end, she came through unscathed, a feat that assured her fame and popularity among the elite of Paris.

If anyone could get to Fouquet, she would know, and there was one certain way to get to her. Her salon was the most celebrated gathering place in the city. Every night the finest wine, keenest political philosophy, and sharpest gossip flowed freely among the city's most ambitious social climbers.

I had neither the social standing nor the brash manners necessary to gain an invitation, but I was determined to find a way in. Gradually, a plan formed in my mind through those days of drudgery, but the very idea of it terrified me, and I could not muster the nerve to act.

Not until I was propelled to do so by a humiliation of my own. Madame Valin, smug in her victory, ordered me to clean the fireplaces, the dirtiest job in the house. I was on my knees, leaning into the fireplace in the salon, scraping soot and ash from the tiles above my head, when the door opened behind me. I pulled my head from the chimney and turned my filthy face to see you, René, come to confer with Master Valin.

You stared at me for so long, your face a mask of horror, your mouth hanging open in shock while my cheeks flooded with mortification. I wanted to melt away into the floor.

"You had no reason to be embarrassed," René says. "I tried to tell you."

I nod, remembering how he stuttered out my name before Madame Valin appeared in the doorway, smirking, and I knew she'd planned for this to happen. Even now, the humiliation of it is so acute my cheeks are burning.

"I could not talk to you, René. I could not bear the humiliation of what we'd become. That is why I fled."

"I should have done something," René says, the condemnation in his voice no longer aimed at me. "The Valins had no right to treat you so. I should have stopped them, but Colbert was furious, and I didn't dare complain to him. I was a coward. I am sorry, Juliette."

At these unexpected words, my eyes prickle with tears, but this time they are tears of relief and joy. I want to melt into him, but I don't dare—not yet, anyway. What I have to tell him next is the hardest thing I have to say, the one that he may never forgive. I consider leaving it out, but secrets have nearly destroyed us; they've certainly destroyed me. I must set this right.

I was brimming over with rage when I left the salon that day, and that's what gave me the strength to take back my mother's gowns and jewels. Claiming I meant to change the bed linens, I went to Madame Valin's bedchamber, which, of course, had been Maman's before.

I laid a sheet on the floor, then carefully arranged all of Maman's gowns on it. Next, I searched the room until I found my mother's jewelry box, hidden in a bureau drawer. I put the box on top of the gowns, then folded the sheets over all and carried them from the house, right under Madame Valin's upturned nose. Once downstairs, I locked the gowns and jewels into my trunk. I strung the key onto a ribbon around my neck, and I waited.

Madame Valin, no doubt basking in her victory over me, did not notice until the next morning. The moment of discovery was heralded by a loud shriek that echoed from the apartment overhead shortly after the men had begun their work in the workshop. She came thundering down the stairs, demanding that her husband do something. I did not wait for her to come find me. I stepped out into the workshop to face her, and to keep her away from my trunk.

"You little thief!" she shouted, jabbing a bony finger at me.

Everyone in the workshop stopped working and stared.

"You should have put her out on the street, husband! You were too softhearted, and now she has stolen from us! Gowns and precious jewelry, all gone!"

Master Valin looked between his wife and me, but it was Papa who spoke.

"Is it true, Juliette? Have you taken Mistress Valin's things?" he asked.

I raised my head and challenged the woman's accusing glare with a steady gaze of my own.

"I have not," I said.

"Liar!" she shrieked. "Search her quarters, husband! You will find them!"

I turned and faced Master Valin coolly. "They are my mother's gowns and jewels. Any number of witnesses at court can attest that they were hers, as she was much admired when she wore them. When she died, my father bestowed them on me, as was his right."

Valin glanced at Papa, who nodded that this was true, even though he had never gotten around to dispensing with my mother's things. "They were to be her dowry," he said.

"The girl needs no dowry," Madame Valin scoffed, crossing her arms. "I am mistress of this house now, and all that is in it!"

I held Master Valin in my gaze, straightening to my full height. "Where in the guild's rules does it say that a man's family forfeits their personal possessions when another master takes over his workshop?"

Paul Valin's eyes narrowed as he tried to stare me down. I did not blink. I did not look away.

"Those gowns and jewels are rightfully mine," I said.

Slowly, Valin nodded. For all his faults, he was a stickler for guild rules. He had to be. As the guild master, it was his duty to enforce them.

"Paul! She stole those jewels! Have her arrested!" Madame Valin demanded.

"Let the girl have them," he said, turning dismissively back to his work. "You have fine things enough of your own. I'll buy you the most fashionable gown in Paris when the blue diamond is cut."

I turned a cold smile on the mistress before retreating triumphantly to my room and closing the door behind me. That night, I found a better hiding place for Maman's jewels. Though the madame continued to whine and cajole her husband, he held firm to his decision.

I now had the wardrobe I needed to put my plan into motion. I had the opportunity too. Madame Valin banished me from her apartments, leaving me with fewer chores and therefore more time to work out my plan. With the help of one of Madame's disgruntled servants, I dressed in my mother's most stylish gown, a slate-blue brocade with a pale-pink underskirt and wide ruffs of lace on the sleeves. I styled my hair in a mound of ringlets, bound with Maman's pearl bands. I powdered and perfumed my face, my throat, and between my breasts. Then, while my father drank himself into an oblivious stupor, I set out for the salon of Madame Suzanne du Plessis-Bellière.

Seventeen

"Madame du Plessis-Bellière may have the most popular salon in all of Paris," René says, "but it is also the most infamous. You were foolish to go there alone."

I nod. It is true that I took a terrible risk going there, but a greater threat is before me now, as what I have to relate is likely to awaken the demon of jealousy in René's heart. André no doubt took great pleasure in embellishing this part of his testimony, and I must tread carefully to avoid corroborating his lies. Before I decide how to continue, René speaks.

"I came looking for you after that dreadful day when you ran from me. I came more than once, but André told me . . ." He pauses and swallows, averting his eyes from me. I suddenly realize how blind I have been, and how long André has been lying.

I thought that René had stayed away, avoiding me after seeing me as a servant. André never told me that René had come looking for me. And he must have told René that I was powdering and primping and going to Madame du Plessis-Bellière's salon because I was flirting with the vile men who frequented the place. I let out a few choice curses under my breath.

"Tell me truthfully, Juliette," René says, and I can see in his clouded face how much hinges on my answer.

"I found no pleasure at the salon, I assure you." Even mentioning the place sends a shudder of distaste through me. The marquise's salon attracted the worst sorts of social climbers: young men who strutted like peacocks and merchant's daughters with rouged nipples, hoping to become the wives or mistresses of wealthy men. They spilled out into the avenue and coffee houses for two blocks around the marquise's grand hotel. There was no safe passage into or through such a crowd for a naive and single girl such as myself.

I don't want to speak of such an unsavory crowd or admit that I went willingly among them, but he has asked for honesty and I must give it to him. I owe him that much. Still, dread tightens in my throat, making it hard to speak. His rage and jealousy have all but gone. I am so close to winning him back. The truth about what I did with Suzanne du Plessis-Bellière, though, could well destroy all that progress. The truth he says he wants may drive him away for good. I close my eyes, feeling myself sway in the balance. Will his love be like our quest with the diamond itself? Am I destined to come so close once again and then lose all?

A lie that could preserve us forms in my mind—a story that would exonerate me and spare René. The temptation is strong, but when I open my eyes, he is looking so earnestly at me that I know I cannot do it. I will honor him with honesty and pray it is not my parting gift.

"I did smile and flirt with men at the salon, René, but only to gain entrance. Once I'd been escorted inside, I disappeared into the crowd and avoided them the rest of the evening."

"So you admit you used them to get what you wanted," he says. Already I am losing him.

"They were nothing to me, and only meant to use me too." I reach for his hand. "You are nothing like them, and what we had between us was entirely different. You alone hold my affections."

His brow bunches, but there is no flare of anger. I take heart and continue.

"I knew I was taking a risk," I admit. "But I had to redeem Papa in the king's eyes. After all, I had risked—and lost—my father's good name when I tampered with the Twelfth Night jewel, so risking my own in return seemed only fair. I assure you, I took no pleasure there."

Getting in took every ounce of courage, but I soon realized I would have to be braver still if I wished to talk to the marquise herself. Suzanne du Plessis-Bellière was the center of a great orbit of influential people. I could not simply drift close to her. On that first night, I never even got in the same room as the marquise.

I went out every night I could for the next few weeks, despite André's disapproving looks and Papa's vague, wine-soaked warnings about my virtue. I hoped that if I went often enough, I would eventually be noticed by the marquise, or at least might hear something of use. But while I heard much gossip, none of it was useful. No one spoke of Fouquet, whose fall from grace was much too far in the past to be of interest.

It was evident that Madame du Plessis-Bellière favored a handsome young officer who was ever present at her elbow. Her attentions toward him were noted by many, who discussed his pedigree, which was scandalously beneath hers. I cared little for that. What caught my attention was when I heard he was a captain of the guard, with duties extending to the Bastille. I could think of only one reason why a captain so below her station had gained the favor of Suzanne du Plessis-Bellière: he must be her contact with her imprisoned lover, Nicolas Fouquet.

Still, I could not get near him, and night after night my frustration mounted as I watched Suzanne du Plessis-Bellière whisper in his ear while he smiled and nodded.

My chance came at last, when I was retrieving my cloak to leave and saw a movement in the corridor leading off the entry. A closet door creaked open, and a gentleman thrust his head out, glancing around. I shrank back into the shadows to avoid being seen. He emerged and left the house with a smug expression. A moment later, a chambermaid slipped out and scurried away down the corridor, her cheeks pink and her cap and apron askew.

I had a sudden idea, and before cowardice or common sense could stop me, I snatched my cloak from the cloakroom and hid in the closet. It was still warm and stank of the sweaty groping that had only just ended. I was revolted, but I held my place until the house grew quiet. Once all the guests were gone, I intended to emerge, find Madame Suzanne, and beg her help.

After an hour or so, I crept from the cupboard and looked cautiously around, my heart hammering. Most of the candles and lamps along the hallway had been extinguished, and I could hear no voices. I drew a deep breath and began down the dim corridor toward the salon, moving carefully to keep the sound of my heels and starched skirts from echoing off the marble walls.

I stopped before the large, gilded salon doors, which stood slightly ajar. Soft voices purred beyond them, punctuated by quick, sharp peals of the lady's laughter. She wasn't alone, after all. I bit my lip and considered the door. Should I knock? Enter? Wait until her guest was gone?

I put my eye to the narrow opening. Suzanne du Plessis-Bellière was reclining on her fainting couch, her skirts and petticoats carelessly rumpled up around her knees, her rouged nipples bursting over the rim of her bodice. The young captain knelt on the floor beside her, his hand sliding up her silk-stockinged leg while his lips nibbled at her breast. My cheeks flamed with embarrassment, but I couldn't move. I had thought Madame du Plessis-Bellière had favored the captain because he could get her to her lover, not because he *was* her lover. I was a naive fool, and I had no idea what to do. I could hardly burst in and ask her to help me while he was making love to her. Instead, I stood frozen, my eye to the door.

"Mademoiselle! What is the meaning of this?!"

I jumped and spun around. The butler was standing behind me, glaring down his long nose in anger. Involuntarily, I stepped back from him, bumping the salon door. It swung open, exposing me to the couple within.

"I—I was only—I didn't mean to—"

The butler caught my wrist in a viselike grip and jerked me back around to face the marquise.

"I caught her spying at the door," he announced, giving my arm a shake, as if she couldn't see me perfectly well as it was.

Madame du Plessis-Bellière still reclined on the fainting couch. She pushed her skirt back down to cover her legs, but otherwise showed no embarrassment at our intrusion. I, however, felt enough for both of us, and lowered my eyes quickly, trying for humility.

"Explain yourself, girl," she demanded, in a tone that all but froze the blood in my veins. I opened my mouth to answer but only managed a tiny squeak.

"Look at me," she demanded.

I did not move. Every muscle in my body seemed to have frozen in mortification.

"You are Jean Pitau's girl," she said. The surprise of that made me look up at last. Her lips were curling into a smile, and her eyes sparkled with amusement. The captain had moved to sit beside her on the fainting coach and was glaring at my interruption.

"My name is Juliette." I dipped into a curtsy as if it were a proper introduction, feeling a complete fool in the gesture.

"How old are you, Mademoiselle Juliette?"

"Seventeen in May, madame."

"And your father? Does he know you are out?"

I dropped my eyes to the floor again as my cheeks warmed.

"No, of course not," she purred. "He wouldn't, in his condition."

The young captain laughed, and she joined him, with high, sparkling notes that rang like crystal bells. I gritted my teeth, waiting for them to finish.

"Well, Juliette Pitau," she said at last, "what brought you to spy at my door this evening?"

I cringed at her words, but I gave as bold an answer as I could. This would be my only chance to gain the access I required. So I curtsied again, with an apology, and with my request. "*Excusez-moi*, madame, I did not mean to spy. I came to seek your help."

Her eyebrows peaked, and she waited for me to go on.

I swallowed. "I must find a way to speak with Nicolas Fouquet." The words burst out before I could lose my nerve.

She laughed again, but not so prettily as before. This sound could have cut crystal. "Nicolas Fouquet is the king's prisoner, not mine. You should be lurking at Louis's door, *ma chérie*."

"No one speaks to Nicolas Fouquet," the captain added. But I ignored him and kept my eyes on the marquise.

"I thought—I hoped—you might have access to him?"

She cocked her head and one side of her Cupid's bow mouth tipped upward in a sardonic smirk. "Have you forgotten, the king kept *me* a prisoner in my own home for two years while Fouquet was on trial? What makes you think I would be at liberty to visit him now?" she said.

I looked down again, shuffling my feet despite my effort not to squirm. Seeing my plan through her eyes, I felt like a complete fool. But I was a desperate fool, so I continued.

"Every night you whisper with this captain, and I thought—"
I swallowed again, not daring to look up. "I thought you
might have found a way into the Bastille to see Fouquet. He
is your lover, no?"

"You are a cheeky girl!" she snorted. "I am a married woman.
What makes you think I keep a lover locked away in the Bastille?" Again, the young captain laughed, and stroked her leg in
a blatantly intimate gesture, as if cuckolding the marquis was an
honor.

I blushed to the roots of my hair. All of Paris knew of her long
affair with Nicolas Fouquet. It had not occurred to me that del-
icacy was needed when it was common knowledge. I was out of
my depth. But I could not back down, either, so I stood dumbly,
my very presence a plea for help.

Suzanne du Plessis-Bellière lazily ran her hand through the
captain's hair as she continued to consider me. "What would a
child such as yourself want with Nicolas Fouquet?"

"I cannot tell you exactly," I said.

She wagged a finger at me, as if I were a naughty child. "Nicolas is an enemy of the king, mademoiselle. If you want my help
reaching him, you must tell me why," she said.

I hated her more than ever then. I hated her condescension,
her mockery, her immoral behavior. I even hated the rouge on
her cheeks and the pretty bounce of curls around her face. I
would have run from her elegant house but for that last phrase:
if you want my help reaching him. The implication was glaring:
she could help me.

But at what cost? I could not tell her the truth—not all of it. I swallowed nervously before offering a carefully considered answer.

"I must ask him what he knows of Cardinal Mazarin's diamonds," I said, which was as much of the truth as I dared. At once, by the curve of her smile, I could see I had said too much.

"Of course. So your papa might cut the Violet and redeem himself to Louis."

I tried to neither confirm nor deny her statement, but I could not hold her gaze. Then she turned to the captain and they began a whispered conversation, casting glances at me all the while. I was nearly sick with nerves. Had the butler not been holding me firmly by the arm, I might have wilted from fear.

I could see the captain was growing nervous too, even protesting, but with an indelicate hand on his thigh and sweet words in his ear, she soothed away his concerns. At last, he gave a weak smirk and nodded, unable to resist her charms. The marquise smiled too, a cunning smile that sent a shiver down my spine as she turned her eyes back to me.

"Very well, mademoiselle. We will take you to Fouquet, this very night. You can release her now, Gaston," she added to the butler as she and the captain rose to their feet.

The butler glanced quickly between me and the marquise before letting me go. But as soon as the madame and captain had swept from the room, he caught me again. I glared at him, but he cast me a dark look of warning.

"Don't trust her, mademoiselle," he whispered, but I shook him off and followed the marquise and her paramour. He needn't have spoken—of course I didn't trust her, but I followed her all the same. What choice was there but to quell my fear and step into her waiting carriage, which would sweep me away through the dark streets of Paris, to the gates of the Bastille.

Eighteen

I pause, risking a glance at René's face. Storm clouds have gathered, but so far the storm has not broken. And yet the worst is still to be told. I've never told anyone until now, and would give almost anything to keep it that way. The mere thought of it sickens me, and I wish I had not wolfed down so much bread and cheese earlier. Again, the temptation rises to concoct some lie, but it would be one more betrayal, and I can't do that. Besides, this confession is for the king. He has already questioned Suzanne du Plessis-Bellière, and while I doubt she has told the whole truth, I cannot be sure of what she has said. I cannot risk any part of my story being discredited. So with the fear of losing René constricting my throat, I choke out my darkest secret.

The great stone fortress loomed black against the midnight sky as the marquise's carriage clattered over the bridge and drew to a stop. A freezing mist rose from the icy puddles of rainwater in the ditch and whispered across the paving stones before the gates. I shivered and pulled my cloak tighter around me as I descended from the carriage and looked up at the impenetrable walls.

"Have you changed your mind, mademoiselle?" the captain said, his breath hot in my ear.

I squared my shoulders and my resolve. "Of course not."

He offered me his arm, and while Madame du Plessis-Bellière watched from the carriage, he escorted me to the gate. He spoke to the guard for only a moment, issuing a few brief commands, and we were admitted. We continued through several more locked gates and doors. At each, the guards came to attention and we passed through without question.

We climbed a long flight of stairs to the very top of the fortress. In the last guardroom, he dismissed the guards, telling them to take a few hours for supper. I was surprised that they obeyed him, and that we had so easily penetrated the heart of the prison. The captain apparently held more authority than I had realized.

Once the men were gone, he retrieved a ring of keys from a hook behind the desk. He led me through three more locked doors, deeper and deeper into a maze of corridors that grew narrower and darker with each turn. At last, at what seemed like the very center of the maze, we came to a hallway that ended in a single door.

"This will be your only chance, mademoiselle, so make the most of it," the captain said. Then he handed me the single candle he had brought and unlocked the heavy door.

"Knock when you are finished." He gave me a little push forward into the cell and swung the door shut behind me.

My blood pounded in my ears as I peered around me. The cell was large, and in the dim candlelight I could not see to the far wall. I heard the rustle of bedclothes and took a faltering step forward. A table emerged out of the gloom as my eyes adjusted, and I set the candle on it to prevent my shaking hand putting it out.

The cell was far from the bleak pit I had imagined. The room was large and warm. In addition to a sturdy table and chair in the center of the room, a mahogany wardrobe, its doors delicately carved with flowering vines, stood against one wall, and a brightly patterned carpet spread across the center of the room. Along the far wall, just barely visible in the dim light, was an elegant canopied bed, and on the bed, Nicolas Fouquet, squinting in my direction. I could not see him well enough to make out the details of his face and hair, but he could see me.

"Who are you?" His voice grated like an unused hinge, and yet his words carried command.

I dropped into a curtsy. "My name is Juliette Pitau," I said.

"Whom do you represent? Who sent you?"

I curtsied again. I couldn't help myself. Even sitting on his rumpled bed in the dim light, he gave off an air of great authority. As if he were still the most powerful man in France, as he once had been.

"I come on my own, and on behalf of my father, Jean Pitau, crown jeweler to the king."

Fouquet rose then and walked slowly toward me. At last, I

could see him clearly. He was tall, but too lean for his height, and his elegant, lace-trimmed nightshirt hung on him like a great sack. Though he was not old, streaks of gray ran through his long black hair, marking his years of incarceration. His eyes, however, held me in the commanding, haughty gaze of one used to wielding power. He stopped only a few feet from me and scrutinized my face.

"And what could Jean Pitau want of me? Has that fool Jean-Baptiste Colbert brought the kingdom so close to ruin that it has come to this? Sneaking in to get advice from a prisoner?"

"No, monsieur. Neither Colbert nor my father know I am here." I swallowed then to push down the rising terror that came with the admission. I was alone and unprotected in the bedroom of a strange man. Not just any man, but the king's most feared enemy.

His thin lips twitched with a smile, and I knew he had read my thoughts. "How did you get in?" he asked, seeming genuinely curious.

"Madame du Plessis-Bellière helped me. She—" I paused, searching quickly for what I might say that would soften him to my cause. "She sends her regards."

Another twitch, but this time the smile lingered. "She does, does she? My delectable Suzanne?" There was something of longing in his words, and something of irony.

"Please, monsieur. What can you tell me about Cardinal Mazarin's diamonds?"

His eyebrows rose. "For this, you risk treason?"

I swallowed the lump in my throat. "I must know where he acquired them."

He laughed. "The Mirror of Portugal came from Portugal. The Sancy from Queen Henrietta of England when she couldn't pay her debts. It's all recorded."

"But who cut the brilliant ones? Some say Mazarin invented the cut, but a master gem-cutter would have done the work. We must find him."

"Must we?" Fouquet said dryly, one eyebrow arching higher. He considered me a moment longer, then pulled the chair out from the table and sat. I remained standing before him, like a peasant seeking audience from a king.

"And why this great urgency?" he asked, casually folding one leg over the other. "What is young Louis up to now that he requires such information?"

I hesitated. Louis forbade Fouquet visitors in order to keep him ignorant of politics. But what harm could news of the diamond do?

"The king has commanded my father to cut another diamond in that style," I said.

"Your father has overreached, has he? Or has the king asked too much?"

I shifted my feet and lowered my eyes again. He could read me too well. I had to be more careful.

"Our young Sun King thinks nothing of overreaching, *n'est-ce pas*? Tell your father, a wise man does not fly too close to such a sun."

"Do you know who cut the Mazarins?" I persisted, refusing to play his game of pretty words and diversions.

He leaned back in the chair, examining his nails as if they had been freshly manicured. "*Mais oui,* I enabled the transactions. After all, the cardinal was busy with matters of state. France was governed well during the regency."

"France was at war in the regency," I pointed out.

He tipped his head and looked at me in the way amused adults observe naive children. "As long as there have been kings, there have been wars. And as long as there is a Sun King, there are men in his orbit who will get burned. We are all Icarus, with our vanity and our wax wings. Is that what you would have for your father?" He gestured around him at the cell. "Do not think a simple craftsman will fare as well as I after his feathers have been scorched. You should read Ovid, *ma chérie*. Unless it is too late and you are already burning."

I crossed my arms and glared at him. I didn't want eloquent warnings. I wanted answers. I took a deep breath and tried again, sugarcoating words that wanted to be sharp with impatience. "Please, sir. If you know who cut Mazarin's diamonds, tell me. It will save my father from disgrace. It is for the glory of France."

"What do I care for the glory of France?" he spat. "Louis can wear a pauper's crown for all I care."

"Then for the sake of my father. Please. Take pity on us, monsieur."

"I have no pity for free men of France," he said, his smooth voice now laced with poison.

"I can pay," I said. "Name your price. I have jewels. Gold."

He only laughed. "It may surprise you, mademoiselle, but I have nothing on my social calendar at all this season, so my need for jewels is rather limited."

"What have you need of, then?"

"A pardon from the king."

Of course that's what he would say. "You know I cannot offer you that. But if you help us, my father will make sure the king knows of your cooperation."

He laughed again. "Come, child. Neither of us is that naive. Louis fears me far too much to pardon me for a mere bauble."

"What, then?" I said. "Please. I'll do anything."

His eyes ran the length of my body, lingering at my breasts, as a slow grin bloomed on his lips, freezing my blood. I had not meant to offer myself, but the words were out. I could not take them back.

"How old are you?" he asked.

"Sixteen, monsieur," I said, my voice quivering.

"Sixteen," he repeated. "How delicious." He licked his lips as his eyes traveled my curves again. "And you'll do anything, you say?"

My heart stopped for a moment, then set off again at twice the speed. With each frantic beat I could feel the command course through me: *Run! Flee! Escape!* I clenched my fists and held my ground. I would not give up now. Not when I was so close to the answers I so desperately needed.

He stood and stepped closer.

I willed my feet not to budge, but they edged backward of their own accord.

When he was only one pace away from me, he reached up and dragged his rough fingers across my cheek.

"Please, monsieur. I am still a maid," I said, the words barely a whisper in my tight throat. My foot stuttered backward another step.

"You want my help to please the king who locked me away, *ma chérie*. Did you really think my aid would come cheap?"

Inside, I cursed my naivete. It was all suddenly clear. What else could I have offered him? Of course, Suzanne du Plessis-Bellière and the captain had known—that's what they had whispered about. The butler had tried to warn me.

My stomach lurched with fear, but I forced myself to be calm. The captain waited just outside for my knock at the door. I could probably escape. But if I did, I would lose my only chance to learn what I needed to save my father. And who but me should pay the price of his disgrace?

My eyes burned with tears. I squeezed them shut. I squeezed shut my heart as well and gave a single nod. I could scarcely believe I was agreeing to this, but I'd gone too far now. "If you will help my father, I will do what you ask."

He pressed moist lips to my neck and trailed his fingers down to my breasts. "A noble deed, mademoiselle," he murmured, his hot breath smelling of rotting teeth. He nibbled and teased, his tongue flicking along my ear. "The man you seek is a Jew," he whispered, the harsh stubble on his chin scratching at my neck. "Does that frighten you?"

I winced, but not at his words. He gave my ear a nip, and a whimper escaped me, which made him laugh. Repulsed, I tried to push him away, but he gripped my waist and pulled me hard against him. My trembling knees could not resist his strength. I squeezed my eyes tighter and gritted my teeth, as his arms and his unwashed stench enveloped me.

His voice was in my ear again, as he stepped back, pulling me with him toward the bed. "He is a Jew, from Portugal. It was the cardinal's private little sin, preferring the work of a Jew above any other." Between each word he placed a kiss a little farther down my neck, the crown of his lice-riddled head now in my face. I wriggled to free myself from his arms, but they were tight around me while his experienced fingers loosened the laces of my gown and his feet moved us closer and closer to his bed. His last words were breathed into the curve of my breasts as we stood against the canopy. Then his tongue slid out, like a slithering eel, into my cleavage.

The shudder of revulsion shook sense back into me at that. No position at court, no humiliation that Papa had suffered, was worth this.

"No," I cried, and with a great heave, I pushed him off me and darted toward the door, putting the table between us.

Fouquet laughed. "You would have me hunt you, *ma lapinette*?" he said.

"I've changed my mind," I said, my voice thin despite myself. He lunged to one side of the table, but I darted to the other, hoping I could be as quick as the rabbit he had likened me to.

He paused and considered me, perhaps realizing that catching me might be harder than he thought. "The man you seek is in

Paris, you know," he said, casting out a little more information to reel me back to his bed.

"You lie! There are no Jews in Paris. It's against the law," I said, eyeing the door, wondering if I could get the captain to open it before Fouquet could catch me. I doubted it. I had to keep him talking while I thought of a plan.

"There are Jews everywhere," he said, "but Paris is a big city, mademoiselle. If you want to know exactly where he is, you must come back to me."

"I'll find out somewhere else," I said, inching toward where the wardrobe stood on the wall adjacent to the door.

He laughed. "No one else knows, do they? You wouldn't be here otherwise. Come. Let me whisper his name in your ear." He lunged again into the corner by the wardrobe, and while he was off-balance, I darted to the door. I pounded hard, but of course, as I feared, the captain took his time about opening it. Before I heard the first bolt, Fouquet was upon me, dragging me by a handful of hair and bodice back toward the bed.

Now I could hear the bolts sliding, but I doubted the captain would interrupt Fouquet. After all, this was the obscene little joke he and the lady had imagined all along.

Rage boiled through me, and I spun on Fouquet, gouging and clawing like a baited bear. Somehow, he managed to get his arms around me, but only for a moment. I jerked my knee up, catching him hard in the groin, and he doubled over. I bolted for the door just as it opened. Swearing, Fouquet made one last grab for me. As I lunged for the door, fabric tore, but I didn't pause. I

launched myself through the doorway, putting the startled captain between me and Fouquet.

A stream of curses followed me out. "Next time, tell Suzanne
du Plessis-Bellière to visit me herself, or send me a proper whore.
Not that there's much difference," Fouquet yelled before the captain, laughing, slammed the door tight and locked it.

Only then did I realize my bodice was torn off my shoulder
and my right breast exposed. I pulled the bodice back into place
but had to hold it up as I scurried along behind the captain all
the way back to the marquise's carriage. I had risked all this danger, suffered all this shame, nearly lost my virtue—and for what?
A Jew from Portugal supposedly in Paris? It had to be a lie.

Back outside the Bastille, I scrambled into the carriage. The
captain, holding the carriage door for me, trailed a finger along
my bare shoulder, then followed me in, grinning.

Suzanne du Plessis-Bellière looked me up and down. "Tell
me, mademoiselle, has Nicolas a comfortable bed?"

The captain laughed, while the blood pulsed in my ears. I
wanted to fly at them and claw the cruel smirks from their faces.
But now that I was out of the prison, I began shivering too vio-
lently to do anything more than huddle against the seat of the
carriage.

"And did you learn what you came for?" the marquise asked
with pretended politeness, though she could not keep the mocking smile from her lips.

Rage flared in me. I would not play along while she took sport
in my humiliation. So I raised my chin and looked her in the eye

with a hard smile of my own and boldly said, "I did."

Her eyebrows shot up, and her smile faltered in surprise, but only for a moment, before it grew again at another chance to taunt me. "He told you about Abraão Benzacar? Prison has made him generous," she purred, her eyes hungry for my reaction when I realized that my ordeal had been unnecessary.

I am afraid I rewarded her more than I wanted to. A wave of shock and anger rolled through me. At first I couldn't breathe— couldn't even move. I don't know what horrified expression came over my face, but they both laughed again.

"Girls who spy at keyholes must be taught a lesson in the art of politics," Suzanne said.

"Not to mention the art of love," the captain added.

Fury coursed through me, but victory too. They thought themselves clever in their cruel games, but I had gotten the name without paying the price they had intended.

So I smiled and thanked my awful companions. Let them think what they would of me; I never planned to see either of them again. Though the coachman had urged the horses to a trot, I opened the door of the carriage and leapt out, preferring a broken neck to another minute in their company.

My feet hit the uneven cobblestones with such force that my knees buckled and I bloodied my hands and knees in my land- ing. Ignoring the pain, I scrambled to my feet and limped away. Suzanne du Plessis-Bellière's sharp peals of laughter filled the night behind me, while a strange name, a Jewish name, a dan- gerous name, pulled me forward toward home.

NINETEEN

"*Mon Dieu!* The bastards!"

It does not surprise me when the words explode from René's mouth. In truth, I expected them before now. I've been huddled on my cot, struggling to hold myself together, the sensation of Fouquet's disgusting touch all too real on my flesh. I haven't been able to look at René for some time, so though his outburst is expected, I still flinch when it comes, and it takes a moment before the actual words he spoke sink in. When they do, my eyes fly to his face in wonder.

"The bastards!" he repeats, his clenched fist slamming the tabletop so that the pots and cups rattle. "The heartless cowards, to use an innocent girl's desperation for their own sport!"

My ears were not mistaken. He is not raging *at* me; he is raging *for* me. I am filled with so much hope that I come to my feet, meaning to go to him, but my knees are still watery and I am obliged to sink abruptly back down onto the cot.

Seeing me collapse, René comes to my side and wraps a strong arm around my shoulders. I lean gratefully into the shelter of his broad chest.

"My poor Juliette," he says, in a soothing tone that liquefies my joints and my resolve still further. The tears I refused to show Fouquet or Suzanne du Plessis-Bellière now stream down my cheeks.

René makes no protest against the damp mess I'm making of his shirt, but holds me for as long as it takes for the tears to subside and my composure to return. When it does, I can't help but feel embarrassed, and eager to reassure him.

"I never would have gone to Fouquet if I had thought . . . if I had known . . ."

"Going to Fouquet was foolish," René says, more in agreement than condemnation. He rises from where he sits beside me on the cot and offers me a hand. "Come. A cup of wine will settle your nerves."

I follow him to the table, barely believing the calmness of his manner. It persists as he pours the wine and holds the cup out to me. This, at last, is the René I know and love, but when I least expect it.

I take three sips of the wine before the spell breaks. With growing agitation, René begins to pace, and I can see the tension bunched in his shoulders. He reaches back and rubs his neck. "Why didn't you go to the king and request an interview with Fouquet?"

"The king has let no one speak to Fouquet in eight years. And besides, how could I approach the king with Papa out of favor?"

"You found a way into the Bastille. Surely you could have found a way into the Louvre."

"Fouquet would have told me nothing if I'd been there in an official capacity. He would take great sport in frustrating Louis."

"Better than letting him take sport in you!" René says, turning back to face me with burning eyes, his arms stiff at his sides as he clenches his fists.

I flinch back from this flare of temper, and at once it dissolves into a look of almost helpless desperation. "By all the saints! I keep telling myself I should hate you for all your deception. So why do I want to tear them apart to defend you now?"

"Oh, René—"

"All I can think as I write is how I might soften your words to see you spared." The desperation in his eyes shifts to resignation. "To see you returned to me."

Nothing can keep me from him now. I am across the room and in his arms before I know what I am doing.

We meet like water and parched earth. His arms close around me and he becomes my universe. I am crying and laughing and breathing him in, and he is holding me to him like I am the missing piece of his soul and he means to meld me into his essence. He tilts my head back and presses his lips to mine, kissing me hard, with all the passion the past year has denied us. My lips, my whole body responds in kind. I run my hand though his hair. A strand comes free from the ribbon to brush softly against our faces. When his lips finally release mine it is with reluctance. He pulls my cheek to his chest as we catch our breath, his heart thumping solidly against my ear.

"René," I whisper. His name comes out in tears of joy, relief, and gratitude. His arms tighten around me, and I feel his lips against my hair as he makes my name into an endearment.

I want to stay like this forever, but too soon, he leans back to look into my face. I try to press back into him, to hold on to the moment, but he cups my cheek gently with his hand and holds my gaze.

"How are we to save you?" he whispers. His gaze lingers on mine one delicious moment longer before his hands release me and he strides purposefully back to the table to scrutinize my confession.

My heart protests, but I see what he is doing. The only thing he can do.

"Write that I was driven by a desire to see Louis glorified," I say, putting my hope in the power of his words. Surely if he can see the good in me, he can make the king see it too. "Write that I knew Valin would ruin his most precious possession, and I only meant to protect him."

"Yes!" René says, suddenly invigorated with the task before us. "Louis must understand that everything you did—the sacrifices, the deceptions, the conspiracies—it was the only way to achieve what *he* wanted. We must appeal to his vanity."

I move to the table and perch on the stool, for the first time daring to hope for salvation. He rolls up his sleeves and cuts a fresh quill with purposeful strokes. Before he dips into the ink, he pauses and looks at me, his eyes serious. "If we survive this, promise me you'll never do anything so dangerous again."

A little bark of laughter escapes me, surprising us both. "If I survive this, I will gladly be a quiet little mouse to the end of my days."

A mischievous glint comes into his eyes and he looms over me. "*My* quiet little mouse?" he asks.

"Only yours," I answer, and lift my lips to nibble his ear.

"Very well then," he says, poising his nib over a fresh leaf of parchment. "Let us make your words shine brighter than the king's great diamond."

TWENTY

It was closer to dawn than to midnight by the time I limped home, and the workshop was locked up tight, so I waited on the stoop until dawn, huddled against the icy February drizzle in my torn dress, my knees bleeding. André found me in the morning, before Valin arrived in the workshop.

"Where have you been?" he demanded, his eyes full of censure as he looked me up and down.

My teeth were chattering so hard I could not answer. He sat me beside the forge, and got me a blanket to warm myself.

"I've finally got some information of use," I said when I could at last speak. My voice shook, betraying the horrors of the night. An eager light came into André's eyes, and he leaned in to hear more, but before I could continue, we heard a tread on the stairs, and the voice of Master Valin berating Papa in the harshest of terms.

"Go, before the master sees you in this state," André said,

pushing me toward the apprentice quarters. "I will tell Master Pitau you are home."

I was happy enough to comply. I didn't want either Papa or Master Valin to question my virtue or my whereabouts. In my tiny room, I stripped off my wet gown and stockings, my corset and petticoats. I pulled on my warmest nightgown and slipped under the blankets on my bed. Soon I was asleep, and did not wake until Papa roused me at lunchtime. Valin had retreated upstairs for his midday repast with his wife, and Papa and André brought a meal back to my room, away from the two new apprentices Valin had brought to the workshop.

"Where were you, Juliette? I was worried sick when you did not come home!" Papa demanded.

I lowered my eyes and mumbled an apology before blurting out my news. "I've learned something of the Mazarin master at last, Papa! I have a name."

Papa's lips parted in an expression of disbelief, though a tiny hope flickered in his eyes.

"He's in Paris, Papa. Or at least he was ten years ago."

Just like that, the hope snuffed out. "Impossible. I know every guildsman in the city." He began to raise the wine jug to his lips, but I put a hand on his arm to stop him.

"He is from Portugal," I said. "That is why he was not known to the guild."

"Portugal?" Papa said, considering. "I should have thought to look there. Their diamond trade is dwindling, but twenty years ago, thirty years ago . . ."

"His name is Benzacar. Perhaps we can still find him."

Papa frowned at the name, guessing its origin. "There are no Portuguese gem-cutters in Paris, Juliette. Their kind is not welcome here," Papa said.

"His kind?" André said. "Is he Moorish, then?"

"He's Portuguese," I repeated, not wanting to confirm what Papa had already guessed: that he was a Jew.

"Which means he's probably long dead," Papa said with a sigh. "The Inquisition has burned many a gem-cutter in Lisbon, curse them. That explains why he cannot be found."

"I think he can be," I said. "Mazarin brought him to Paris twenty years ago."

"We will not find him," Papa said. "Our time is better spent here, helping Master Valin." Then he pushed my hand from his arm, got to his feet, and stumbled off to his own room, taking the bottle with him.

André watched him go, frowning. "Every night he drinks as much as he can get his hands on. With you out at salons, there is no one to prevent him. I've never seen a man so altered."

Guilt squeezed my heart, but I reminded myself that what I was doing was for my father. If I could put the means of cutting the Violet into his hands, he might shake his despair and recover his position.

I turned to André. "We have to look for this Benzacar if he won't. Mazarin brought him to Paris twenty years ago. We might find him, or at least someone who remembers him."

"Who told you of him?" André asked. "And what else can he tell us?"

My cheeks grew hot at the question. I busied myself slicing off a piece of cheese so I wouldn't have to look directly at him. I told him I had learned the name from Madame du Plessis-Bellière, which, strictly speaking, was true. Then, before he could ask for details, I laid out the plan to find Benzacar that I'd devised during the long, cold hours of the night while I'd huddled on the doorstep. A jeweler might use a forge for gold and silver, so André could seek out information when he went to buy fuel for Master Valin. I would search in the Portuguese district, where foreign merchants and craftsmen made their homes in Paris. Of course, if he was a Jew, he could not legally live in the city, but people there might know of him, or he might be living under a false name.

André agreed to the plan, meager though it was, and a burden lifted from my shoulders. At last I could be doing something to right the wrongs I'd done my father. I thanked André and rose, wanting to go to Papa, to stop him from drinking too much.

André grabbed my hand as I got up to walk away. I turned back to him in confusion.

"I've seen you, you know," he said, staring hard at me. "I've followed you to Madame du Plessis-Bellière's. I've seen you enter on the arms of young gentlemen. Have you prostituted yourself to find the name of this Benzacar?"

I glared at André, who glared back at me with an expression I couldn't fully read. There was anger and jealousy there, but something else too, something that had always been there, underlying everything but now coming to clearer definition. It was a gleam of cunning, and I didn't trust it. I pulled my arm free

from his grasp and stalked away, unwilling to dignify his accusation with an answer.

For the next few weeks I scoured Paris for the elusive Master
Benzacar. My search of the Portuguese enclaves led nowhere, but
that didn't stop me. I wasn't sure how to look for a Jew. I knew
only the unreliable rumors that circulated: they didn't eat pork,
they wore their beards long, they bathed every Friday afternoon
before their Sabbath, and they kidnapped small children for
heinous sacrifices. It wasn't much to go on, and I wasn't even
sure it was true, but I watched at butchers' stalls for patrons
who avoided pork, and I wandered through neighborhoods on
Friday afternoons, watching the wells for anyone drawing large
amounts of water. I asked among the glassblowers on the edge of
town, and among the blacksmiths throughout the city, where I
thought a goldsmith might hide his forge.

Neither André nor I found any sign of the man. Perhaps he
was long gone from Paris, or, as Papa had suggested, dead. Perhaps he had changed his profession or his name, not wanting
to be found. Whatever the reason, the weeks passed and I once
again began to lose hope.

Hope was in short supply at the workshop too. Despite my
efforts, Papa drank himself into oblivion every night, intent on
his own destruction. Each morning, he was sick and disoriented,
and of no use to Valin. He was drowning his memories, his
skills, and his brilliant mind along with his sorrows, and Valin
was growing increasingly abusive in his attempts to pry secrets
from him. I felt a small, mean satisfaction at Valin's frustrated
ambitions, but I saw, too, our precarious position should he give

up on Papa and turn us out. With each passing day I grew more desperate to find Benzacar but was nearly out of places to look.

Easter approached, and all the guilds and churches began their preparations for Holy Week. Papa was disgraced and censured, but he remained a guildsman, so he was expected to participate in the processions of Palm Sunday, Good Friday, and Easter Monday.

The guildsmen's role in the Palm Sunday procession was a simple one: walking through the streets of the city en route to the cathedral, spreading flowering boughs on the pavements for the triumphant Christ. I only had to convince Papa to drink less the night before—no easy task—and to make sure he was shaved and well dressed in the morning when the procession set out. André stayed beside him, but Papa walked without stumbling or staggering. I sent up a prayer of thanks to the Virgin when the procession reached the cathedral without incident.

Good Friday posed a greater problem. While the clergy carried the suffering Christ through the streets, the guilds came behind, bringing the apostles and saints in veneration. As the goldsmiths and gem-cutters ranked highest of all the guilds, it was their honor to carry the sorrowing Virgin, a tall statue of gilded wood robed in blue velvet and bedecked with flowers. She was carried through the street on a grand litter, one man at each of the four corners of the heavy platform.

I was surprised when Master Valin assigned Papa the task of carrying one of the corners for part of the route. I think he saw it as another opportunity for Papa's disgrace to be made public. The litter was heavy, and Papa's months of grieving and drinking had left him frail and unsteady. If he fell or dropped the corner, his humiliation would be seen by all of Paris. Again, André promised to stay nearby, but I feared Papa would be beyond our help.

The procession started at the Monastery of Saint-Éloi, patron saint of our guild. While I joined the women decorating the platform around the Virgin's feet with lilies, Papa wept at the graves of Maman and Georges. When the first set of bearers hoisted the platform to their shoulders and set out, I coaxed Papa away and we joined the procession, my arm through his for support. His hands were trembling, either for want of alcohol or too much grief. I feared his strength might give out at any moment, but he managed to lift his head and walk, straight-backed and dignified among his colleagues. At length, his turn came to bear one corner of the litter. He let go of my arm and took his place, and I was pushed back among the guildswomen, where I could do nothing for him.

He walked steadily under the platform's weight for most of a block, but worry gnawed at me as I watched the increased sag of his shoulder beneath the weight, and the droop of his head as the strain began to overwhelm him. Another twenty steps and he swayed, tilting the Virgin on her pedestal. He stiffened his back, and for a moment, I thought he would balance himself, but his foot turned on an uneven cobble and he stumbled. A collective gasp rippled through the crowd lining the avenue as Our Lady of Sorrows rocked on her platform and lilies tumbled to the pavement. I lunged forward, but Madame Valin caught me and held me back.

Papa fell to his knees. Just in time, André rushed into the gap and caught the litter, righting it before the statue could topple. While the crowd murmured their disapproval of Papa and their praise of his apprentice, my father crawled out of the way and the procession continued without him, André in his place.

I pulled my arm from Madame Valin's grip and hurried to help him to the curb. There we sat while the stream of worshippers passed by, casting us looks of anger, disgust, and, occasionally, pity.

"Are you hurt, Papa?" I asked, looking him over and helping him dust off the knee of his best hose, now torn and dirty. He buried his face in his hands.

"Papa?"

"I am so weary, Juliette. I cannot go on," he moaned.

"You don't have to carry the litter. We can walk at the back."

He looked up at me then, his eyes dull and empty and his face streaked with tears. He hadn't been speaking of the procession.

It is strange how many times a single heart can break. How much pain we can endure, only to endure it all again when we think we can feel no more. Looking into Papa's eyes in that hour, I longed for the world to end. Perhaps the Virgin, who knows herself the bitter sorrow of so great a loss, took pity on us then. Because in that darkest hour of Good Friday, when all hope seemed lost, we were granted a miracle.

As we sat there on the curb and the procession moved away, I realized that the people around us were not like others along the route who had crowded the street to watch. I might have missed it if I had not spent weeks looking for just such people. They looked on with less devotion but more obedience. They did not make the sign of the cross or join the procession at its end. They only stood silently watching until the last stragglers had passed. Then they dissolved away like smoke, down a narrow alley and into doorways, as if they had never been there at all.

All except one boy. A boy poised on the cusp of manhood, all lanky limbs and the soft beginnings of a beard, with bright blue eyes and curling black locks that would have made the king envious. He loitered on the step until the street was nearly empty. Then he gathered the bruised lilies from the cobblestones. Gallantly, he stepped back to an aproned girl watching from a bakery door, and presented her with the flowers and a grin. She was laughing and flirting with him when an old woman appeared from the alley, her head covered in a fringed shawl. Frowning, she called out to him, waving him to her. I did not understand her words. They were not French. I wasn't sure if they were Portuguese, but I knew one thing. She called the boy Isaac. And Isaac, in any language, is a Jewish name.

TWENTY-ONE

René has stopped writing, his brow furrowed in an expression of worry.

"What is it?" I ask him.

"Must we speak of the Jews?" he asks, exasperated. "It would be one less crime to try to justify."

"The king already knows of them. You read the charge yourself: consorting with Jews," I remind him, though I see his point. This may be one place we could soften the truth of my story. An idea strikes me.

"They called themselves *conversos*, or New Christians, when I met them. Do you think that would help?"

His face brightens. "If you thought they were Christians, then you can't be said to have *knowingly* consorted with Jews."

"I did see them at church on Easter," I say. "And they were always good and kind to me." I'm not sure this last part really proves they are Christians after the behavior I've seen from the French nobility, but all my life I'd heard Jews maligned as cruel.

"Yes, that's good," René says, dipping his pen in the ink. "You believed them to be Christian, and if they practiced secret Jewish rites, it was never in your presence, so you couldn't have known."

"I never saw them engaged in Jewish rites," I agree.

René smiles and squeezes my good hand. "Excellent. Go on, then," he says, but the dimple on his cheek as he grins makes it hard to remember where I was. I touch that dimple with my injured fingers, so grateful to have him smiling at me again. I wish I could forget my confession and just bask in his gaze.

His places his hand over mine, and I know he feels the same. He leans forward, his lip grazing enticingly along my cheek, and I think he is going to kiss me—

"You saw Isaac in the street," he reminds me.

"Isaac. Right." With difficulty, I wrench my thoughts, and my cheek, away from his lips.

"I wanted to run after the boy as he followed the old woman into the alley, but of course, I could not. I had a duty to Papa, to the guild, and to God to carry out my Christian obligations. Papa had to rejoin the procession or he would be missed during the Good Friday Mass, which would only heap more disgrace upon him."

"Yes, good," René says, scratching the words out on the page. "Christian obligations."

I might have waited until after Easter, but events of the next day hurried my pursuit of the Jews. I was sweeping the workshop floor when André emerged from his room in his best clothes. Our eyes met momentarily, before his darted away guiltily.

"Where are you going?" I asked, suddenly suspicious.

He pinched his lips between his teeth and glanced nervously toward the stairs to Valin's apartment. "I have to go to the guildhall with Master Valin." He tried to edge past me to continue on his way, but I wouldn't let him.

"The guildhall? Today?"

"Master Valin has called a meeting of the masters of the guild. He has asked me to come along."

"Should I get Papa?" I asked, wondering why Papa had said nothing about this to me.

André rolled his eyes, impatient now at my slow wit. "Don't you see? It is *about* your father. After what happened yesterday, Valin wants the guild to expel him."

I took a step back, my hand over my mouth. I could not remember anyone ever being expelled from the guild. It was an extreme punishment, since it barred a man entirely from practicing his craft in Paris.

André, still avoiding my eye, tried to step around me, but I grabbed desperately at his arm. "They can't expel him, André!"

André glanced at the stairs again. Apparently, Valin was due to appear at any moment, and André didn't want to displease him. André always did know how to look out for himself. "Valin is taking me along as a witness to your father's drinking."

At this my rage spilled over, and I shook his arm, as if he was an errant child. "How could you, after all Papa has done for you?"

"He should have made me a journeyman," André said, his voice cold with the old grievance.

"And for that you will betray him?" I shouted. I wanted to slap him, but he clutched my arm and spoke quickly to quiet me.

He rolled his eyes. "I only meant that if I were a journeyman, I would not be beholden to anyone," he said. "As an apprentice, I have little choice but to obey Valin. Surely you see that. But I will do my best by him. I can give witness to all the good things he has done too."

I relaxed a little, though I was still gripped by panic. "You will protect him, then?"

"There may be little I can do," he said, "as an apprentice."

Overhead, we heard the apartment door open. I seized André's arm, and rising to my tiptoes, I whispered in his ear the only thing I could think to say that might bring him to Papa's defense. "I may have found Benzacar, André."

André's eyes widened, and the spark I had hoped for appeared in them.

"But I need more time," I added quickly. "Stall their decision if you can."

That's all I had time to say before Master Valin turned on the landing and came into view. I went back to sweeping, watching out of the corner of my eye as André fell silently into step behind his new master and departed.

I set my broom aside and checked on Papa. He was still sound asleep. An empty wine bottle on the floor beside the bed suggested he would be for some time yet. I pulled the covers up around him, gave him a kiss on the cheek, and slipped away.

I hurried until I got to the entrance to the narrow alley, and there I hesitated. My heart hammered a rapid beat as I peered down it. I could see no signs of life—no old women mending on doorsteps, no men hurrying to or from work. Only the narrow passage curving off to the left, a still, silent crevice in the city, shaded by unremarkable frame houses. Small windows looked out like blank eyes from the upper stories.

Few people were out on the avenue either. There would be no one to rescue me should evil befall me in the alley. I drew a steadying breath, and with a silent prayer to the Virgin, I stepped forward.

The alley was paved with rough cobbles, but after a short way these disappeared, leaving only a narrow track of dirt. The buildings closed in tighter on either side, leaning in and casting gloomy shadows. Though the walls were dingy and in need of repair in places, I took heart to see the doorsteps were swept and the road free of garbage.

I walked the length of the curving lane, hoping to encounter someone who might direct me, but I met no one. Every house was closed up tight, the doors latched and the windows shuttered. Not so much as a stray dog or pigeon moved.

I rounded the last curve. The passage ended abruptly against the back wall of a sturdy stone structure. I looked back along the alley, debating what to do. Did I dare go door-to-door knocking? What if everyone in this alley was a Jew? What if all the closed doors and windows concealed heretical rituals?

As I stood debating, I realized I was not alone after all. An old beggar woman was huddled on a blanket in a small alcove where the buildings met up at the end of the alley. Nervously, I approached her.

"*Excusez-moi*, madame," I said. She glanced up at me, but said nothing, so I hurried on. "I am looking for a Portuguese gentleman, a Monsieur Benzacar. Do you know where he lives? Which house?"

She waved a vague hand back along the way I had come, then held up a small cup and shook it. I had little money, but I dropped a denier into her cup.

Her wrinkled face puckered as she smiled, revealing bare gums and only two jagged teeth. "Portuguese," she said, hissing on the soft sounds. "*Oui*. Portuguese." She waved her hand more enthusiastically back along the alley, this time her finger raised and pointing.

I thanked her and walked back along the alley, taking a careful look at the houses she might have indicated. Most of them were wood or brick, with doors and windows on both the ground floor and the one above.

One house, however, stood out. It was sturdier than the others, made of well-dressed stone. It had no windows on the ground floor, but only a single, stout door opening into the alley. I paused, examining the door, which was unpainted and decaying, but which had once been finely carved. It was an unusual house for an ordinary family. A jeweler, though, a man with a forge to melt and mold and shape fine metal, his workshop would be stone, for safety's sake. And a man who cut diamonds in secret would have no windows.

Was this the house of Benzacar? Two narrow windows marked the second floor, and as my eyes turned upward, I thought I saw the quick movement of someone drawing back from one of them. My heart stopped for a moment. Who had been watching me? Why had they fled the window?

I waited for the door to open in challenge, but as the moment stretched, nothing happened. So I stepped forward and rapped my knuckles against the solid oak.

After a long wait, the door finally opened. A matronly woman stood in the opening, blocking any view of the room beyond. She wore a simple but tidy dress of black wool. The lines of her face all stretched downward. It was a face that had known grief and grown strong for the knowing.

"Yes?" There was a faint accent to the word, which gave me hope, despite the silver crucifix that hung prominently at her throat.

I realized too late I hadn't planned what to say, so I just stood there in my dirt-smudged work dress, with an empty mind. Who would believe I was a master gem-cutter's daughter?

The woman edged backward, and I knew I had to speak or she would close the door. "I am looking for a man named Benzacar," I said quickly. "Abraão Benzacar."

In a cold voice that gave away nothing, she asked, "For what purpose?"

"On an errand for my father," I said quickly. "Please, does he live here?"

"And who told you to ask for this Abraão?" the woman asked. She pronounced the name deep and full in her throat, and I was sure then that she was not French. Not by birth, anyway. I was sure, too, that the stiff stillness of her face masked an answer I had long been seeking.

I squared my shoulders and looked her in the eye. "A man named Nicolas," I said. "A man in the king's service."

Her eyes widened with fear. "I cannot help you," she said, and closed the door so abruptly I could say nothing more.

I stood for a moment, uncertain what my next move should be. She had known both names, Abraão and Nicolas. And how many Abraãos with a connection to a Nicolas of the king's court could there be in Paris? There was only one answer to that question, and it renewed my urgency. I pounded at the door again.

The woman did not return. I hammered with both fists but was met with silence. At last, I sat down on the stoop, determined not to leave until someone came out. I sat there for nearly four hours, until the alley was draped in twilight and the air grew chill. I was trying to decide whether to stay or go when a deeper shadow fell across me. Someone was standing over me. I shrunk backward, squinting to make out his features.

Then, with a surge of relief, I recognized him. It was the boy who'd gathered the flowers for the girl at the bakery. I smiled, but my smile quickly faded when I saw that he held a large, jagged stone in his hand, and his expression was hostile.

"What are you doing?" I asked, scrambling to my feet.

"What are *you* doing?" he returned. Unlike the woman at the door, his French was perfect, and Parisian.

I swallowed and gestured to the door. "I'm waiting to meet a man who lives here."

"What if that man doesn't want to meet you?" He weighed the stone in his hand, which pulled my eyes down to it. It was easily large enough to crack a skull.

I forced my eyes back up to his face, giving what I hoped was a challenging glare. "Has he sent you to scare me away?"

He stepped closer. Though he was a beardless youth, he was taller than me, and most likely stronger. Still, I held my ground, hoping that a boy who gathered lilies for the baker's daughter wouldn't stone an innocent stranger in the street.

"You are Isaac," I said.

He stiffened a little, and his eyes narrowed. "My name is Étienne."

"Please, I am looking for a man named Abraão Benzacar. I only want to talk to him."

"You are wasting your time."

"I mean him no harm," I said quickly.

He bounced the stone a few times on his palm. The muscles in his arm flexed. "If you want to ensure no harm is done, mademoiselle, you should leave now."

I edged away, keeping my eyes on the stone. "You don't scare me," I said.

He sneered at my feeble attempt at bravado. "Don't I?" He bounced the stone on his palm again and took another step closer.

Goose bumps prickled along my arms, but I kept my eyes on his. "My father will come looking for me if I don't come home," I said.

"I don't think you have a father looking out for you. Otherwise, you wouldn't be here alone."

"Please," I said again, my voice cracking. "I was told Abraão could help me. It's important."

"I believe my mother told you there was no Abraão here," he said.

I took a deep breath. "Then maybe you know where he is?"

"Why would you think that?"

"Because you are named Isaac. And you are foreigners."

His eyes flashed with annoyance, and I realized too late my words had offended. "Do I sound like a foreigner to you? My name is Étienne, and I've lived all my life in Paris."

"But the old woman spoke to you in Portuguese," I said, hoping I was guessing the language correctly. "She called you Isaac."

He raised his eyebrows, but he didn't raise the stone, so I rushed on.

"The man I am looking for—he is from Portugal but came to Paris about twenty years ago. He is a gem-cutter. A true master."

"Who told you his name?"

"Nicolas Fouquet," I said, my tone sarcastic. I wanted him to know I knew things, but I didn't want him to realize I spoke the truth.

Even in the dim light, I saw the pupils expand in his pale eyes. "You lie! Everyone knows Nicolas Fouquet is imprisoned for treason. No one speaks to him."

"I have," I said, crossing my arms defiantly, hoping to press my advantage. If I had one, anyway.

"The only ones who speak to Fouquet are the king's inquisitors," he said. "What would they want with my grandfather?"

"Then he *is* here!" I cried. "Thank God. Please, I must speak to him at once."

But my words were falling on deaf ears. He had turned red as he realized his mistake, and now his whole face was contorting in rage.

"Get away from here!" he shouted, and before I knew what was happening, he let fly the stone, straight toward my head.

I ducked, but I turned my ankle as I did so, and rather than moving out of the stone's path, I blundered into it. It glanced across my temple before shattering with a loud crash against the stone wall behind me.

Dizzied by the blow, I staggered. I could feel the warm flow of blood on my cheek.

Behind me the door opened. "Étienne! What have you done?!" hissed the woman I had spoken to before. Hands grabbed me and began pulling me into the door.

"I threw it at the wall," the boy protested, following us inside. "It wasn't supposed to hit her!"

And then, quite by accident, I had what I had wanted. I was inside the dark, windowless house, with the door closing behind me. And I was reeling with fear.

TWENTY-TWO

I pause. "Perhaps we should leave that part out," I say. "It makes them look like monsters."

"No, I think it is good," René replies, his quill moving along the parchment as fast as he can write. "If you were attacked and dragged inside by them, it isn't your doing, is it?"

"I wasn't exactly dragged." This talk of the Jews is making me anxious. They were nothing but kind to me, and have already suffered too much by my hand.

"We can say you were," René replies, his eyes suddenly bright with an idea. "Dragged in by the Jews, who, when they found out who you were, forced you to participate in their plot."

"*Their* plot? That's not at all—"

"Don't you see, Juliette? This is perfect. That Jewish boy, Isaac, attacked you. They forced you inside. What happened after that—the worst of what you are accused of—it could all be framed as their doing. So far, you have only confessed to a few minor deceptions and to visiting Fouquet, and we can implicate Suzanne du Plessis-Bellière and her captain of the guard in that. If we can convince the king that everything else was a Jewish plot and not your own, you might be spared." René is speaking fast, excited by the new hope of salvation he is laying out, like a rare gift, before me.

I can see why the idea tempts him. He has never met Isaac or his kind grandfather, and like me, he has always heard stories of the wickedness of the Jews. But I have met them, and I could never compound my sins with such a betrayal. I shake my head, adamant.

René gives a frustrated sigh. "They are Jews, Juliette. What are they doing in Paris if they intend no criminal mischief? They have been here for decades, biding their time, waiting to exact their revenge on the king."

"No!" I shout, startling René into silence. "I will not blame them. It was not their plot; it was mine."

"But this is your chance to live, Juliette." He brushes my cheek with the backs of his ink-stained fingers, and a shiver of delight runs through me. "You can go free. We can be married. Don't you want that?"

I close my eyes, fighting the temptation of his words. "More than anything, René. But we cannot condemn innocent people."

"They aren't innocent. They are Jews!" René spits. "They shouldn't even be here."

I push his hand away and straighten my spine. "They are only here because they have nowhere else to go. You wouldn't suggest such a thing if you knew them. They risked everything for us— their home, their livelihood, their lives. And in the end, it was my own carelessness that betrayed them. That betrayed us all."

"But . . ." René hesitates. "You could live." The words quaver from his throat, one last desperate plea that nearly breaks my heart. I take his hand in mine and hold it tight.

"I could not live with that. We will tell the story as it really happened. I am sorry, René."

He nods his understanding, though he cannot mask his disappointment, and we continue.

The woman guided me across the dark, windowless room to a stiff chair.

"Go get water and a cloth. Quickly!" she instructed her son as my knees gave out and I sat down hard on the chair.

While she examined my injury, I glanced nervously around. I was in a small receiving room, paneled with dark wood. It would have been fashionable some twenty years earlier. The furnishings appeared a little shabby and outdated, the leather seats of the chairs polished with wear, the legs of the table scuffed. The room was lit with a fine silver candelabra, but the candles were tallow rather than wax and smoked, darkening the ceiling and giving off a greasy aroma.

"It is only a scrape," the woman pronounced, with a sigh of relief. "You will forgive my son, I hope? He is an impetuous child. He has not yet learned to think before he acts."

Behind her, Isaac stepped into the room with a basin of water. He heard her words and blushed. "She stepped into it," he said again.

"You will apologize!" his mother demanded, and he shrunk a bit. He might be on the cusp of manhood, but she could still intimidate him.

"I am sorry, mademoiselle," he muttered, not looking me in the eye.

His mother dipped the cloth into the water, and gently began to wash the blood from my cheek and scalp. The wound was still bleeding, so she commanded her son to hold the cloth to it while she hurried away to get a salve.

"Please, mademoiselle," the boy said, speaking low so his mother couldn't hear. "Don't report me to the king. My family needs me. I'll do anything if you will just promise not to turn us in."

"Let me speak to your grandfather," I said forcefully, letting the unspoken threat hang in the air between us. In truth, I could never have turned them in, but if he thought there was the chance, perhaps he would help me.

Before he could answer, his mother came back into the room, and he used the opportunity to slip from it. She gently rubbed a salve onto the scrape, which soothed the pain and stopped the bleeding.

"Now let me see, mademoiselle, if you are hurt anywhere else." She lifted my chin with her fingertips, then paused, cocking her head as she took a good look at me. Recognition came into her face.

"You are the girl who helped that old man," she said.

"Old man?"

"In the procession," she said. "The old man who fell."

"That was my father, Jean Pitau. He has been unwell. I came here on his behalf, to find Abraão Benzacar."

The woman's eyes widened. "Your father is Jean Pitau? The king's jeweler? The greatest jeweler in all of France?"

I opened my mouth to agree but, instead, shook my head. "No, madame. Not the greatest. That is why I must speak to Abraão. He is the only one who can satisfy the king now."

"It has been many years indeed since I was asked to satisfy a king," said a parched voice from the doorway. I looked up. Isaac had returned, an old man leaning on his arm. As the old man stepped unsteadily forward, Isaac shot me a dark look.

He didn't have to explain its meaning. It was the same look I had given Madame Valin the day before, when she tried to keep me from helping Papa. It was a look that said, *I'll protect this man with my very soul. Don't you dare hurt him.*

TWENTY-THREE

At last, I had found Abraão Benzacar. He looked nothing like I'd expected a Jew to look, except perhaps that he wore a beard. Beyond that, he looked like any other wizened old *grand-père* in Paris. I was taken aback by his age, though I shouldn't have been. Twenty years had passed since Mazarin had brought him to Paris, and he'd already been a master then.

Now his gnarled hands and his cloudy eyes made my heart sink. But I'd come this far, so I curtsied respectfully.

"What is it you want, child?" he asked in strongly accented French. He gave me a warm smile, which encouraged me. I let my whole story spill out: the king's command to cut the Violet, Papa's fruitless search, the death of my mother and brother, and the king's embarrassment at the hands of the English jeweler.

He stood still, considering for a long moment after I finished my tale. Then he asked, "What can you tell me of this great blue diamond the king would have cut?"

"It is nearly the size of your palm, but flat, and very dark.

To make such a dark thing shine, the cut must be very precise. Could you do it, monsieur? Could you cut such a stone with that precision? Could you make it shine like the sun?"

"The sun is not blue," Isaac noted.

I cut him an angry scowl. Those had been the exact words my father had said to the king, his admission of defeat, and I didn't care to hear them repeated now.

I turned back to Abraão, hopeful and nervous for his answer.

"How did you find me?" he finally asked.

At once, my face colored. I told him the same abbreviated story I had told André, and of how I had seen them a few days before and surmised that they were Jews.

The old man held up a hand to silence me. "We are New Christians," he corrected. "My grandson there was baptized in the cathedral."

Issac cast a nervous glance at his mother, who was wringing her apron. "She will draw attention to us, Father," she said. "We should leave Paris."

"No, please!" I begged. "I've told no one of you." This wasn't entirely true. André knew—in fact, André had been searching too. But I hadn't told André they were Jewish, and besides, I did not think André would betray me. He was ambitious, but we were allies in our quest to cut the Violet.

I turned back to Abraão, clasping my hands beseechingly. "Can you cut the stone for us, monsieur?" I asked. "Can you make the Violet brilliant?"

"To cut this diamond, it is the dream of my heart," he said, and my spirits lifted a little. But I soon crashed back down to earth when he held up his arthritic hands for my inspection. "But these hands can no longer do it."

"Then train my father," I begged.

He shook his head. "Such days are behind me, mademoiselle." With finality, he nodded to Isaac, who crossed to the door and swung it open.

"I wish you peace and many blessings," he said, and turned back, disappearing into the room beyond.

I stayed where I was, looking hopefully from Isaac to his mother. They both looked back at me in silence as cold night air flowed through the open door.

"It is dark out," Isaac said to his mother. "I should see her home safely."

She frowned but agreed. "Just be careful," she said.

Reluctantly, I stepped out into the dark alley, and Isaac followed. I kept my distance from him—after all, he had thrown a rock at my head, so I didn't feel any safer walking with him than I would have alone. We walked in silence all the way back to the Manufacture Royale. He stopped walking across the street from our workshop, and only spoke after I had turned away from him.

"If my grandfather helped you, what would you do for him in return?" he blurted, stopping me in my tracks.

I turned back, opened my mouth, then closed it, considering. I didn't have a detailed answer for him. "The king will pay handsomely for cutting the diamond," I said.

"And how do I know that your father would share that handsome pay?"

I glared indignantly. "My father is a man of honor! If he

collaborated with your grandfather, of course he would share the reward fairly!"

"Begging your pardon, mademoiselle, but our family has been cheated by so-called men of honor before," he said coldly.

I fell silent, taken aback by his acerbic tone. I knew how we had suffered at Valin's hands—how much more had Isaac's family suffered, powerless as their Jewish faith made them in France? "It could be put in writing. A signed contract," I offered. "But if your grandfather can't help, then there is no point."

Now it was Isaac's turn to hesitate, chewing his lip nervously. "Maybe I could be my grandfather's hands," he said at last.

"His hands?"

"His mind is still sharp, and he has taught me much of what he knows."

"You are an apprentice?" I asked.

"Not exactly. He's taught me the ideas; I just haven't had the chance to work. But I could. I mean . . . I would. If your father could help me, we could work together."

It was a last, wild hope, but I caught hold of it with all my strength.

"Tomorrow is Easter Sunday. We will go to church, and then to the guildhall for the great feast. But Papa hasn't been well, I'm sure we could make our excuses to leave early. Could you meet us here tomorrow evening?" I didn't add that the feast would keep Master Valin away and would give me a chance to sober Papa up before he met Isaac. "We can tell Papa our idea, and if he is willing . . ." I didn't know what we would do if he was willing. The Violet was no longer Papa's commission. But one way or another, I was determined to find a way to unite Papa with Abraão, and the two of them with the Violet.

Isaac grinned. "I will be here," he said.

ᴛᴡᴇɴᴛʏ-ꜰᴏᴜʀ

André was not back from the guildhall when I returned, and Papa was fast asleep—probably drunk again—so though I was bursting with news, there was no one to share it with. Neither was there any news of the guild's meeting. I retired to my small room and stretched out on my bed, planning to tell André as soon as he returned, but my exhaustion overcame me. Thus, Easter Sunday dawned without a chance to tell or receive news of the previous day.

I dressed and roused Papa. I wanted to make sure he looked his best, as there was always a feast at the guildhall after services on Easter. It would be the perfect opportunity for him to show the guild he was still respectable. Still worthy of membership.

The air was filled with the joyful ringing of bells as we stepped out into that fresh Easter morning. Every church bell in the city had been silent through the long weeks of Lent. Now they pealed out the joy of the risen Christ. It seemed that all of Paris was in the streets in their finery, walking or riding to the churches and cathedrals to celebrate the promise of Easter. How strange it was to think there were secret Jews in the city who were not on their way to Easter Mass. The thought sent a little shiver through me. I had always been taught to fear Jews. And yet the Benzacar family had seemed kind enough, once they at last gave in to me.

We entered the church amid a crowd of craftsmen and their families, Master and Madame Valin among them, his apprentices following behind. André caught my eyes and raised a questioning eyebrow to my smile. I gave a small nod, hoping he understood that it meant I had good news to share.

The Valins now laid claim to the honored seats that my family had once occupied in the church, so Papa and I stood with the common folk in the back. André silently took up a place beside me. I could see he was as eager to share news as I was, but we had no time before the service began.

I fidgeted through church, my mind far from the priest's monotonous Latin intoning. I was thinking instead of arranging the meeting between Papa and Isaac. I didn't know what to do if Papa refused to talk to him or, even worse, if the guild barred Papa and we were put out of our home and workshop. That possibility was too awful, and I thrust it from my mind.

When Mass ended, André, Papa, and I moved together toward the doors, along with everyone else. To my surprise, I caught sight of Isaac in the crowd toward the back. He stood with his mother, both dressed exactly like everyone else around them. New Christians, his grandfather had called them. I smiled again.

If they came to church and had been baptized, surely there was nothing wrong in working with them. They had probably been here every Sunday for years, just like us, right here under our noses at the Church of Saint-Éloi. I had searched Paris from end to end for them, and they had been so close all along.

"Who is he?" André hissed into my ear, his tone an accusation as his eyes followed my gaze.

"No one," I whispered, quickly looking elsewhere. I didn't dare tell him with the stretching ears of guildsmen and their wives all around us.

André frowned at the answer, so I quickly changed the subject. "What happened yesterday, André? At the guildhall?"

He cast an uncomfortable glance at my father, ahead of us in the crowd, and shrugged, his expression still surly. "They asked me questions about your father, his work, and . . ."

He trailed off. I used the jostling bodies in the church aisle as an excuse to lean in closer to him. "And what?"

"And his drinking. I tried to speak well of him, Juliette. But they didn't want to hear anything but the answers to the questions that Master Valin put to me."

"And what was their verdict?" I asked.

"They dismissed me after I'd answered the questions. I know nothing of their decision," he said, though his refusal to meet my eye suggested he knew things he didn't want to tell. At least not to me.

As soon as we were out of the church and free of the crowd, he slipped away from me and back to his place behind Master

Valin, leaving Papa and me to walk together to the guildhall, through streets filling with joyful people on their way to the many feasts throughout the city. I envied them their carefree manner. Our feast was to be with our guild, and I felt only foreboding.

The gem-cutters' guildhall was a sturdy stone edifice with a large, comfortable hall for feasts and other entertainments. This was where we had come for the Easter feast my whole life. Even after Papa became crown jeweler, he still shared this holiday with his brother craftsmen. But today, the guards at the door barred our entrance.

Papa looked from one to the other of them, his eyes questioning but his lips struck dumb in confusion. The guards stood their ground, though they tried to avoid Papa's eye.

"Martin? Chansey?" Papa said at last, substituting their names for the questions that were too painful to ask.

The guard named Martin answered, his gaze falling somewhere around Papa's knees. "We have our instructions from Master Valin, Monsieur Pitau."

I blinked at the address—*monsieur* and not *master*. They had really done it. They had stripped Papa of his rank in the guild. My gut twisted, but all I could do was step forward and run my arm through Papa's to offer him support.

"We met yesterday to discuss your recent transgressions, Monsieur Pitau," said Master Valin, appearing beside us out of the crowd, his smirking wife on his arm.

"Without giving him a chance to defend himself? To speak on his own behalf?" I said, fierce with indignation.

Valin only turned a cool expression at my anger. "You would do well, Pitau, to teach your daughter to curb her sharp tongue."

Papa said nothing. He only pulled his arm from mine, turned, and began to walk away.

I opened my mouth again to demand our right to enter, but Madame Valin prevented me. "You had better go, Juliette. Your father might stumble, as drunkards do."

I glanced over my shoulder and saw that the crowd around us had parted to clear Papa's path, as if he were a leper. And even as I glanced, as if the madame's words had been a curse, Papa stumbled on a loose cobble. There was nothing for me to do but to go to his aid, exactly as she had suggested.

Behind me, the Valins entered the guildhall for the feast, and the crowd dispersed. Master Hansen, a Dutchman by birth who had apprenticed with Papa before I was born, slipped quietly out of the crowd and, taking Papa's hand as if to shake it, pressed five gold livres into it.

"I am sorry, monsieur," he said quietly. Then he followed the others into the guildhall.

A year ago, Papa would have thrown such charity back in disdain. Now he just stood rooted, staring at the money while a continuous stream of guildsmen flowed around us, averting their eyes. Anger flared in me. They, Papa's friends and associates, had voted to bar him and now weren't man enough to look him in the eye. I seethed and raged and cursed them all—but silently, in my heart and mind. I could not bear to make more of the spectacle.

We stumbled home, our own dark cloud moving through the celebrating streets. As soon as we stepped into the deserted workshop, Papa began searching for a bottle. He found one in the bottom of a cupboard and wrenched the cork out with his teeth.

"*Joyeuses Pâques!*" he muttered before lifting the bottle to his lips and gulping.

All the anger and pain and bitterness I had been holding inside suddenly exploded. "Are you set upon destroying us?" I demanded, wrenching the bottle from his hand.

He reached for it again, but I jerked it away. Overbalanced, he stumbled forward, barely catching his fall at the workbench. He sagged miserably onto the stool and looked up at me with pathetic, rheumy eyes. "Why do you deny me the right to forget, after what I've been through?"

I rounded on him, glaring. "What *you've* been through?" I shouted the words into his face. He flinched, but that only enraged me more. How could he be so selfish? I had suffered too, and he was my father. He was the one who should give me guidance and protection, not the other way around. "Do you forget that I loved them too? I'm the one who watched them die!" And with that, I threw the bottle into the forge, where it shattered, the alcohol flaring in an explosion of flame. The heat of it drove me back beside him, where I stood, watching, my blood hammering in my ears until the flames settled.

"We should leave Paris," Papa said in a voice flattened by defeat. "Find a new start. Amsterdam, perhaps, or Brussels. Or

London—the English have no talent of their own where gems are concerned."

"No!" I snapped, so suddenly that Papa flinched back from me again. I took a breath and spoke more calmly, not wanting to reignite the argument. "I have someone I want you to meet—he said he could come by the workshop this afternoon. He might be able to help us."

"A suitor?" Papa asked.

"A friend, Papa. You'll see. Now let's find something to eat."

We settled quietly by the forge, eating bread and toasted cheese and drinking tea as we waited for Isaac. The minutes ticked by as I waited nervously for him to appear. Perhaps he wasn't coming and my hopes had been in vain. At last, Papa rose from his seat, declaring himself tired, and shuffled off to his room. I did not protest. Rest would do him good. I would rouse him if Isaac came. If not . . . I did not know what I would do if Isaac did not come. Perhaps I would seek him out again. Perhaps I would go to Amsterdam or England with Papa. There was a certain appeal to a new life, but to leave was to hand the victory to Valin, and the thought of that blistered my mind with rage all over again.

It was growing dark before I spotted Isaac in the shadow of a building on the other side of the street. He was watching the workshop with an expression of mingled excitement and fear. I opened the door wide, inviting him in.

He hesitated, glancing around. "Are you sure this is all right?"

"Of course," I said, putting on a welcoming smile, though there were butterflies in my stomach.

He hesitated a moment longer. "Introduce me as Étienne."

"Papa is sleeping, but he will welcome you," I said, praying I was right. I gave him another encouraging smile, not wanting my own misgivings to scare him away.

He straightened, took a deep breath, and stepped into the workshop.

TWENTY-FIVE

Inside, the workshop was quiet and dim, but Isaac's eyes were bright with excitement as he took in the grinders, tools, patterns, and projects of the royal workshop. He ran his fingers lovingly along the tools, eagerly examining any gem, wax model, and drawing on the benches and shelves. He was not like Valin, or even André, who craved glory. His eye was drawn to beauty, much like Papa's, and that gave me a warm sense of kinship with him, despite his Jewish origins.

The last worktable we came to held Valin's calculations for the Violet. Isaac studied the drawing only for a brief moment before he shook his head.

"These calculations are wrong," he said. "It will have no sparkle."

"Then you know the Mazarin cut?" I asked, my heart quickening.

He nodded. "Avô taught me. On paper at least."

"Avô?"

"Grandfather. It's Portuguese."

"And did he teach you how to cut the angles so precisely?" There was little point in continuing if he had not.

Isaac shrugged. "I've never done it," he said. "But I know he still has the tools."

"Would he let my father work in his workshop?" I asked eagerly. I was so close at last.

Isaac looked startled, but there was an eager light in his eye. "Bring the king's diamond to *our* workshop?" He screwed up his face in thought, and I could see he was trying to assess the risk versus the reward.

"Do you want to see it?" I said, hoping to tempt him. I still knew how to open Papa's hidden cabinet. Valin had moved the key, but I had kept Maman's spare key from her ring when I had turned the household keys over to Madame Valin.

His eyes grew wide. "The Violet is here?"

I nodded, ignoring the twist in my gut. I knew never to reveal the hidden panel where the most valuable jewels were locked away. But I had to convince Isaac to help us, and I could think of no better way to draw him in than to show him the diamond.

"Go to the far corner, turn your back, and close your eyes," I said.

When he had done so and I was sure he wasn't peeking, I turned to the secret panel in the wall behind the counter.

Behind the panel was a strongbox, chained to a large iron ring. The chain clattered loudly in the quiet workshop as I freed the strongbox and opened it. In no time, I had the rosewood box out, and I placed it on the counter. I was just pulling the panel shut again when Papa stepped into the workshop. The rattle of the chain must have roused him.

"Juliette?" he said through squinted eyes.

I jumped in surprise. "Papa!"

Isaac spun around, his eyes huge.

"Papa, this is . . . Étienne," I said quickly, remembering the correct name at the last second. "His grandfather served as gem-cutter to Cardinal Mazarin."

Papa's eyebrows shot up as his eyes ran down and back up Isaac's coltish frame.

"To Cardinal Mazarin?" he repeated, his tone full of doubt.

"*Oui,* monsieur," Isaac said, his perfect French revealing nothing of his secret heritage.

"A Frenchman? Parisian no less?" Papa shook his head and turned to me. "You believe such a ridiculous claim? Were you going to just hand the diamond over to this thief? I did not raise you to be a fool, Juliette."

"I am no thief!" Isaac said, his face flushing bright red. "She came to me! If you don't believe me—"

"Étienne wants to help us, Papa!" I said quickly, before Isaac's temper ran away with his tongue. "I was only showing him the diamond."

Papa shook his head, still not believing. I told him again how I had learned a name from Suzanne du Plessis-Bellière. How I had searched Paris for them.

"If you still think I'm a charlatan, ask me anything you want about gem cutting," Isaac said, puffing out his chest with pride.

Papa stared evenly at him, unimpressed, then said, "Tell me the secret of the Mazarin cut."

Without hesitation, Isaac told. As he did, I watched the doubt in Papa's face melt and re-form into wonder. "You have your grandfather's skills?" Papa asked when Isaac finished. "He taught you?"

Isaac hesitated, but nodded. "A little."

Papa gave a snort. "You will need more than a little skill for that thing," he said, gesturing toward where the Violet lay on the counter, absorbing the darkness. He crossed the room and picked it up.

Though still hesitant, Isaac drew close. His eyes were locked on the stone as if it held him enthralled by some powerful magic.

"It's beautiful," he whispered. "So dark."

Papa tipped it on edge. "You see how flat it is? To get the light at the proper angles to really shine—" He stopped speaking and pulled a piece of parchment from a drawer. He traced around the stone, first laid flat and then on edge, so all three dimensions were represented. Then he set the stone aside and began explaining the problem by working through all the calculations he had repeatedly told Valin he could not remember. I watched in amazement, and unexpected joy. Papa was not as far gone as I had believed. He hadn't completely collapsed, and he hadn't given up. I was certain that, given the chance and the means to do it, he would cut the Violet. And I intended to give him that chance. Success was in my grasp for the first time in many months. I had the expertise in Papa, the knowledge in Isaac and Abraão, even the workshop—despite Valin's theft of ours.

While I was imagining our possible bright future, Papa handed the stone to Isaac and instructed him to hold it to the light, first one way, then another, to see how the light was scattered. Isaac was holding it aloft when the door opened and Master and Madame Valin stepped in, André behind them.

Master Valin froze for a moment when he saw us, his eyes moving in confusion from Papa, to me, to Isaac. Then his face went scarlet. Isaac dropped the diamond as if it were fire in his hands.

"What is the meaning of this?" Valin demanded.

Papa stared, his lips working idly, as if the surprise of being caught had once again addled his brain.

"He's a friend," I said. "I brought him here."

"The little thief!" Mistress Valin said, glaring at me. "She meant to steal the diamond! Just as she stole my jewels and gowns!"

Isaac began to back away.

Master Valin pointed menacingly at him. "André, detain that boy!" he commanded.

"No, André!" I cried, but Valin was his new master, and he had no choice. He stepped around Valin and toward Isaac, with a helpless glance toward me.

I grabbed Isaac's arm and yanked him to the back of the workshop and down the narrow hallway that led to the servants' entrance to the alley. André gave chase, but we had a head start, and after Isaac was through the door, I blocked André's way, gripping his sleeve to slow him.

"He's going to help us," I whispered as he moved me aside. "Let him go."

Then André was around me and into the alley, but Isaac had already disappeared. André gave chase, but somewhat halfheartedly, to my relief.

In the workshop, Valin was screaming at Papa, while his wife goaded him on. "How dare you break the king's trust!" he was saying. "How dare you flaunt his most prized possession as if it was your own! As if you have any right to even touch it after the insult you dealt him with your incompetence!"

Papa had regained a bit of his composure. He looked Valin in the eye and spoke with quiet reason. "You know you cannot fulfill the king's request, Paul. Why must you stand in my way as I try?"

Valin glanced at the door through which Isaac had fled, and I saw fear and uncertainty wash over his face.

"Call the king's guard," Madame Valin screeched. "Have them arrested! Theft and treason! The king will deal with them once and for all."

Valin held up a hand to silence his wife. Then, glaring at Papa, he pointed toward the door. "Get out," he commanded.

Papa's jaw went slack.

"I have been patient with you, Jean Pitau, but I can tolerate no more. Pack your things. I want you out tonight."

"Why are you being so soft on him?" his wife screeched from behind him. "Have him arrested! Call the guards!"

"Silence, woman! Go upstairs if you cannot hold your tongue!" Valin roared.

Bright patches flared on the mistress's cheeks, but she did as he said and retreated.

Papa stumbled to his room and began gathering his things into a trunk, with me on his heels, trying to help, to comfort, to somehow cling to some small wisp of the hope that had inflated me just a moment earlier.

André returned a short time later, out of breath, but without Isaac. He tried to talk to me, but Valin forbade it, sending him to his own room until Papa and I were gone. There was nothing for me to do but pack my trunk. I followed Papa outside, into the damp, chill night, and prayed that his fragile, broken heart could withstand this latest blow without shattering irretrievably.

TWENTY-SIX

I shiver, caught up in the chill of that night. The small patch of sunlight that filters through the high window of the cell has long since climbed the wall out of reach. The day is passing too quickly. Dread is thickening around my heart.

René uses this pause in my story to stand and stretch, flexing his hand, which has been recording my words for hours. I had hoped by now he had forgotten his earlier plan to blame my Jewish friends, but he has not. He suggests it again, noting that it would be corroborated by the testimony of the Valins after seeing Isaac in the shop that night.

"They will say, too, that I was there, conspiring in the theft," I point out. "We don't want to validate that testimony."

Seeing me shiver, he takes his coat from the back of his chair and drapes it around my shoulders, then sits beside me. I close my eyes, breathing in the scent of ink and parchment, feeling his solid strength, like an island of hope in the stinking prison.

He puts an arm around me and speaks, his voice urgent in my ear. "This is our chance, Juliette. I will get a position with a bookbinder, or keeping accounts for a merchant somewhere. We need never look back."

He kisses my neck, and I give myself over to the comfort of his arms and the softness of his lips. I press deeper into his embrace, turning my lips to his. He is all I want, and the dream of being far from here with him, leading an ordinary life, spending every night held in these arms, is almost more than I can bear. I ache for this life, but I know it can't be. Not at this cost.

"If we must implicate someone else, it should be the Valins," I say. "If they hadn't been so grasping, if they had left Papa in peace to grieve and to find himself again, none of this would have happened. Had they been kinder, Papa might have even taken Paul into his confidence and shared what he knew. They were intent on ruining him, and so ruined all of us and nearly ruined the king's diamond."

"Yes," René agrees, "the Valins have much to answer for, and we will be sure the king knows of it. But as they have the king's favor right now, and you do not, we would have to provide evidence to implicate them."

It is all too much. I can see no way forward, and panic begins to grip me. I push it down with deep breaths, but a residue lingers in my throat like sour milk.

René picks up his quill again. "What did you do after Valin threw you out?"

I force my mind back to my story, though my voice is unsteady at first. "Eventually, we found a cheap room to rent, and sold my mother's jewels one by one. But that night, we would have slept on the street if it hadn't been for Isaac and his family. He found us trying to carry our trunks through the street, though Papa could hardly carry himself, and he took us to his grandfather's house. And though his family was afraid that our presence would expose them, they took us in that first night. The next morning, Papa and Master Benzacar met at last, so I suppose Valin did us a favor."

"We won't say that to the king, though," René says as he writes. "It must have been a great meeting between two masters who have served the royal court."

"It should have been," I agreed. "But once again, Papa was too mired in defeat to see the opportunity for what it was. Abraão, however, appraised my father with a long, keen gaze, the way I'd often seen one craftsman assess another."

"Monsieur Pitau, I'm told?" Abraão said.

Papa nodded once. "*Oui*. We thank you for your hospitality, monsieur."

I stepped forward quickly, eager to make the introduction. "Papa, this is Master Benzacar. Master Benzacar enjoyed the patronage of Cardinal Mazarin," I reminded him again.

A ghost of humor flits across Papa's face, though it's been a long time since he found anything amusing. "I have traveled the world in search of you while you were here in Paris the whole time. What a fool I have been."

"But, Papa, we've found him now," I said, in what I hoped was an encouraging tone, trying to get him to come out of his melancholy and discuss business, master to master.

"You have the means to cut a diamond with the precision to put the sun in its heart?" Papa asked, looking past me to Abraão.

Abraão smiled and inclined his head in acknowledgment, a proud light in his eye.

Papa nodded and turned toward the door. "Well, I thank you, sir, for your hospitality in our misfortunes. I have little I can offer you in payment, but I will pray for your health and good fortune. Come, Juliette."

"But, Papa—"

"Come, Juliette!" he barked. "I require your obedience."

I glared at Papa, my hands balling into fists. He wasn't even trying. He was just going to walk away, after all I had done to get us here.

"I have shown your drawing to my grandfather," Isaac said quickly to Papa's retreating back. "He thinks it's possible."

Papa paused, his hand on the door. He did not turn around. "What is possible?"

"To cut brilliance into the Violet without reducing it to nothing," Isaac said.

Papa remained frozen. We waited in silence. Then he took his hand from the door and turned.

"You have my drawing?" he said to Isaac.

Isaac looked a little guilty but produced the page on which Papa had traced the Violet the night before. The drawing was smudged and the parchment crumpled, but it was still legible. "I wanted to show my grandfather."

Papa looked from him to the old man.

Abraão smoothed the paper onto the table before him. "You can save more of the stone if you give up on the idea of symmetry." He took a stub of charcoal from his pocket, and drew several quick, deft lines across the page. Papa stepped closer despite his reluctance.

"Seventeen facets on the crown, like so. And an open culet instead of a point, like so . . ."

"Sacrifice the center to save the rest?" Papa said. "That just might work."

Bright hope fluttered in my chest at his words. I smiled and slipped my hand into his. "Just think, Papa! It would be beautiful," I said.

"That it would," Papa said. "But you forget one thing, Juliette. Cutting the Violet is no longer my task." He looked up at Abraão. "Seek out Master Valin, at my former workshop at the Manufacture Royale. He can use your help. He has the stone. *Adieu*, monsieur. Come, Juliette." And with that, he turned again and we walked away from the only man in Paris who could save us.

TWENTY-SEVEN

"Perhaps your father should take the blame," René grumbles. "How could he be so obstinate after all you had done for him?"

René simmers with the frustration that has plagued me these many months. But now, looking back on it, I can see a little better my father's view of things.

"Perhaps Papa was right. Perhaps it would have been better to give up," I say. "The responsibility was no longer ours—what business was it of mine if Valin made a mess of the king's blue diamond?"

"Do you really feel that way?"

I consider. "I don't know. I didn't at the time. Even now, knowing what will happen tomorrow . . ."

"Might happen," he corrects, but it does nothing to ease my curdling stomach.

"Even so, I am proud of what we have done, and I won't be sorry to see Paul Valin embarrassed when the king sees what Papa achieved that he could not. I know I must find some humility and forgiveness in my heart before I go to God, but I cannot just now."

"Valin hardly deserves your forgiveness," he says. "He is a vile man."

"Perhaps if I had walked away with my father that day, I would have seen him fall into the same ruin as Papa, and I could be living comfortably somewhere far from here, building a new life."

"You could not have known that at the time," he says sympathetically.

"I was desperate to set right what I had done. We were so close, or so it seemed at the time. Make sure the king knows that."

René makes a note on the page. "So what exactly did you do?"

"I followed Papa to a cheap room in a decaying boardinghouse and paid the landlady for a week. Papa wrote letters to his friends in Amsterdam, Antwerp, and Lyon, hoping to find a position, but I slipped back to the Manufacture Royale to consult my only ally, André."

"You had me," he says, sounding a little hurt.

"I have you *now*," I say, smiling and caressing his cheek. It is rough with stubble, reminding me again how much time has passed, and how little we have left. "But then I thought I had lost you, and anyway, I needed someone with access to the diamond, which was at Valin's workshop. You see, I had an idea."

I returned the next day to the Manufacture Royale, and when André went out on a task, I caught him and asked him to meet me in a café where I could explain my plan. André, always eager for any opportunity that might advance him, agreed. That evening I encouraged Papa to go to bed early. It was not hard to do. Despair and cheap wine soon had him snoring.

I slipped out and across the river, to the appointed café. André was waiting for me in the corner. Quickly, I explained to him about finding the Mazarin master, and about Papa walking away.

"Maybe you should bring this Benzacar to Master Valin's workshop," André said.

My blood boiled over at the very suggestion. "After what Valin's done to us, you cannot be serious," I said, pushing my chair back and standing to leave.

André clasped my hand and pulled me back toward the chair, his expression sympathetic. "I'm sorry for what's happened to your father, Juliette, truly I am. But only Valin has access to the diamond, or the king's permission to cut it. What good does it do us to know where this man is if we can't get him to the diamond?"

"He has his own workshop, with all the tools he needs for the Mazarin cut. If we can get the diamond to him—"

"Have you gone mad?!" André said, lowering his voice and glancing nervously around, as if even my suggestion of it might get us arrested. "We cannot trust this man with the king's diamond!"

I lowered my voice too, suspecting he might be right. "What if he cut a model to prove he could do it?" I suggested. "Then would you help me?"

"A model?" André's expression, which had been set against me, now softened, and a light came into his eye.

"Make me a glass model of the Violet, and I will have him cut it," I said, filling my voice with confidence, though I had no right to make such a promise on Abraão's behalf. But a glass model was not too great a request. Most designs were tested on glass first. He had said his hands could no longer do the work, but he had Isaac. Surely between them they could achieve the simple task of a glass model.

André shook his head. "I can't cast a model without raising suspicion."

"Then make me the mold. I can find a glassworks that will pour the glass."

André considered for a long moment, then nodded. "If Valin has gone to bed, I can make a mold yet tonight. Meet me here at the same time tomorrow."

The next night, André returned with a simple clay mold, as promised. I, meanwhile, had found a seamstress who would buy my mother's gowns for a good price. I took the money and the mold to a glassworks, where neither I nor Papa was known, and paid them to create a replica in blue glass, telling them nothing of what it was.

I hadn't been back to the Benzacar house since Papa had walked away a week before, so I was nervous as I returned now, glass model in hand. Would Isaac and his grandfather be willing to cut it after the way Papa had behaved? For all I knew, they had fled Paris after having been discovered.

I breathed a sigh of relief when I spotted Isaac leaning against the doorframe of the bakery, flirting with the same shopgirl, who was arranging pastries in the window.

"*Bonjour*, Étienne!" I called from the street, still a few steps away.

Isaac burst into an exuberant grin when he saw me. The shopgirl's dimples disappeared, but I didn't care.

"I have something for you," I said, then lowered my voice to a whisper. "In private?"

He led me down the curving alley, the girl frowning after us. I thought he would invite me into his house, but instead we continued past it. Unlike during my Holy Saturday visit, the alley was alive with activity. Houses and small shops opened onto the narrow path. Tables and blankets displayed shoes, yards of fabric, containers of wood and tin, meat pies, hanks of brightly dyed wool, hair ribbons, buttons, braided rugs, and rag dolls. Shoppers, probably also New Christians, haggled and bartered noisily. Through open windows and doors, I saw cobblers mending shoes, women washing laundry, children playing games. A few people glanced my way with wary, even fearful looks, and I understood. It was a secret community of Jews hidden away in the heart of Paris, where Jews were outlawed. Yet it seemed like any other neighborhood: ordinary people doing exactly what their ordinary Christian neighbors did.

Isaac paid no attention to suspicious glances cast in our direction. He pulled me along until we came to the alcove where I had encountered the beggar woman. Isaac pushed me into the narrow space and followed behind. There, I took the glass model from my pocket and put it into his hands.

"*Mon Dieu*, Juliette! How did you get this?" he said, turning the false gem this way and that to catch the light. It was both a deeper and brighter blue than the real stone, but the same size and shape.

"Never mind that," I said. "I've talked to André—"

"André?"

"Papa's apprentice. Well, Valin's apprentice now."

"You didn't tell him about us, did you?" Isaac said, alarm in his voice.

"I only told him you could cut the diamond. He wants to help get the Violet cut, but he wants some assurance first."

"Assurance?" Isaac was looking skeptically at me. I understood his concern. His family was in a precarious position, and cutting this glass model would be unpaid work that might lead to a commission—or to their discovery. André wasn't the only one who needed some assurance.

"That your grandfather's idea will work," I said, keeping my tone easy and reasonable. "Do you think you could cut a model of the Violet? André would help us get the diamond to your grandfather, if he had this assurance."

"If he likes it, he would convince his master to let our workshop cut the Violet?" he asked eagerly.

"That's the idea," I said, though I still didn't know how to get Abraão and the gem together in one place. I'd work out the details later.

"And what of the king?" Isaac asked.

"What of him?"

"If my grandfather does this for him, what reward will we receive?"

He had asked this question before, but I still had no answer for him. I knew the king's payments were generous. We had always had the finer things through his patronage.

"What payment has he offered your father?" Isaac persisted into my protracted silence.

"He's offered Papa a title," I said.

Isaac gave a snort. "That's not something he would ever give us. We'd settle for just being allowed to live in peace without hiding."

"It's not impossible," I said. "Many of the German princes have court Jews, you know. The Archduke of Austria even brought his court Jew with him on a visit a few years back. Thought he was too valuable to leave at home."

"Or too untrustworthy," Isaac said. "We are regarded with suspicion everywhere."

"It would be better than being in hiding, wouldn't it?" I said. "It would be a comfortable life, with the king's patronage and guarantee of safety."

A dreamy look came over Isaac's face as he thought of life at the king's court.

"Will your grandfather do it, do you think?" I asked. "Can he cut it?"

Isaac nodded, his eyes bright now with excitement. "I can talk him into it. I'm sure I can!"

I wanted to throw my arms around him in gratitude, but of course, I did not. I merely thanked him and told him where Papa and I were staying. Then I returned to my father, each step buoyant with my success.

Cutting even a glass model takes time, and so for the next several weeks I waited, trying to be patient. It wasn't easy.

Papa wrote more letters and drank more wine. Much more. A third week came and went, and I sold two more of my mother's lovely dresses to pay our rent and buy food. Papa's drinking was going through our money fast, but there was little I could do to stop him. When I hid the money, he simply bought his bottles on credit, sending me around later to settle his bill.

Finally, nearly a month after I'd given him the glass model, Isaac arrived at our door one evening. I ushered him in on a wave of relief.

"Do you have it?" I asked, when he was inside with the door shut tight. Papa was snoring on the cot, so I pulled Isaac to the far side of the room where we wouldn't disturb him.

He grinned and pulled me close to the small lamp on the table. There, he opened his hand to reveal the newly cut model on his palm.

For a moment, I couldn't breathe. I knew it was only glass, and yet it was such a thing of beauty. It was heart-shaped, every surface, top and bottom, carved into facets that shimmered and sparked as the lamplight caught and danced inside it.

"Will it do?" he asked, but his grin told me he knew the answer.

"Oh, Isaac!" I took it from him, barely able to contain myself.

The design had surpassed my expectations; surely it would do the same on the diamond. Success seemed within my grasp.

"Now what?" he asked.

"Now I show André. He will know what to do," I said.

René groans and rubs the back of his hand across his eyes. "I wish you had come to me then and left André out of it entirely." I scrutinize his face, trying to decide if he is envious or if he truly believes he could have kept me safer. It is such a fine, open face. He would not have made a good conspirator with such honesty in him. If there is one thing in all of this that I did right, it was not involving René. He, at least, is safe, and for that I am grateful, though I do not want him to think I did not trust him.

"André was already involved by then," I remind him. "And anyway, we did bring it to you, when the time was right."

René's face darkens. "For all the good it did."

I lay a hand on his knee to reassure him. "Colbert was the one who failed me. Or the king, or André. I don't know." I shrug. It is exhausting and futile, trying to find someone to blame when the fault was mine all along. René squeezes my hand, the encouragement I need to continue.

"Anyway, I hadn't thought of petitioning the king. That was André's idea. 'If Master Pitau were to present this model and promise to cut the diamond according to this design, the king might relent and reinstate him,' he said, admiring the model as he spoke.

"But André had a request too, should Papa succeed. He made

me promise that Papa would take him back on when he had the commission. Of course, I had to agree. He had done me the favor of the mold, and he had served Papa for years. I could see no harm in it."

"So how did you get your father to agree, after he'd already walked away from Benzacar once?" René asks.

Early the next morning I took the last of our money and I bought fresh pastries, a wedge of good cheese, and the finest fruit I could find. Then I gently shook Papa awake. He had eaten very little in the past month since we'd been put out of our proper home, and he looked thin and pale.

"I have something special for you," I said in a soothing voice as he reluctantly awoke. "Come see, Papa."

"What is so important that you can't let a ruined man sleep?" he grunted. The shadows beneath his eyes, dark as bruises, gave me a shock of concern, but still, I persisted. I lifted a cup of tea from the table and brought it to him, hoping a few sips of the strong, hot brew would brighten him.

"I have a special breakfast for you. All your favorites. Shall I bring it to you in bed?" I asked, as if he were reclining in luxury and not sprawled on a thin, filthy mattress.

He propped himself up. "I am not hungry," he said, but he took the teacup and lifted it to his lips. There was a faint tremor in his hand, and my stomach clenched. Had I let him go too long—left him to the clutches of drink until he was irretrievable? No, surely I could pull him back—back to his work and away from the brink of despair before it destroyed him.

"Papa, you remember the Portuguese gem-cutter who cut the Mazarins?"

"The Jew?" He perked up.

"Do you remember how he modified your design a bit, and you said it might work?"

Papa took another sip of his tea.

"You were right, Papa. Look." I held up the model, and though it was only glass, and the light in our room was flat and dull, it sparkled with promise.

Papa stared for a long minute, in which neither of us drew breath. Then, slowly, he reached out for the gem, his fingers both hesitant and hungry.

"André made a mold for us, and I had the glass model cast. Abraão cut it, and Isaac brought it to us. Now we need you to do your part, Papa."

He was examining every facet, turning it in his hands, his eye close to its surface. At first, I thought he hadn't heard me, but after turning the model over two more times, he spoke without taking his eyes from it. "What part is that?"

"You must take it to the king."

His eyes snapped up to my face. "After the humiliation I dealt him? Louis would never grant me an audience."

"Then take it to Colbert. Colbert is a reasonable man. When he sees what you propose to do—"

"What *I* propose?" He shook his head vehemently. "I have not cut this stone."

"Abraão has agreed to work with you, Papa. His hands are not good; he cannot cut the diamond himself. But you and he together—you could do this, and in the process, you would learn the one thing you don't know: how to achieve the Mazarin cut on a diamond. Imagine all that you could do once he has shared that secret with you."

A light came into Papa's eyes at the thought. "He must have a machine. An ingenious device to achieve such precision. To see such a thing . . . to use it!" Still turning the cut glass between his fingers, he lifted a pastry from the plate. He took a bite and chewed, thoughtfully.

I waited, excitement growing inside me as I watched my father's spirit reawakening.

"I no longer have a right to even be cutting a model such as this. There is a chance that even Colbert will not meet with me," he said. Perhaps he was trying to protect me from getting my hopes up. Perhaps he was trying to protect himself.

"The king is impatient to see the Violet cut. He will forgive all when he sees that you alone can fulfill his desire," I said, refusing to let him squelch my hope.

Papa nodded. He couldn't refute my point. "Very well. I will go to Colbert and petition to steal the commission back from Valin." He looked again at the glittering gem of blue glass in his hand. "Have my best suit cleaned and pressed and tell the Jew to be ready."

TWENTY-EIGHT

"I am ashamed of what happened when you came to see Colbert," René says, unable to look at me. "I cannot help but think that without our part in this, you would not be here now."

I know what he is feeling. I have been feeling it myself all day: the regret and shame of all those moments we might have made different had we had hindsight. Seeing René so racked with guilt inspires an overwhelming urge to wrap myself around him and try to ease his mind, but of course, we must keep working. We have too little of the day left. So I step behind his chair and gently massage his shoulder. "For your part, you have nothing to be ashamed of," I assure him. "In fact, seeing you that day gave me hope again."

"Hope?" he asks, laying a hand over mine where it rests on his shoulder. "How could it have given you hope?"

"Well, we waited for more than a week for a response to Papa's letter and received none, so we thought Colbert had refused us an audience."

"He had," René says solemnly. "As soon as he saw the signature on the bottom of the letter, he refused to even read it."

"Papa was going to just give up. And he would have, if not for you."

He shrugs, still looking down at his papers, embarrassed by my praise. "I did not do much."

His modesty charms me, and I feel a rush of affection for this gentle, kind soul whose love I am lucky enough to hold. "You got our model to Colbert, even when he refused us."

René laughs suddenly, and I am relieved that he is no longer glowering. "I was surprised to see you at Colbert's office, but I shouldn't have been," he says. "I didn't know then how persistent you can be."

This makes me laugh too, and I release his shoulder and return to my stool to address him with mock indignation. "You mean stubborn."

"I saw you right away that day in the corridor, waiting to see Colbert along with so many other craftsmen. You were sitting at the end with your father. The space was filled with the black-robed lawyers, artisans in their white smocks, craftsmen in their brown woolen breeches, and there you sat in their midst, in a gown of peacock blue, glowing like Venus herself in a sea of mortals."

Now it is my turn to be embarrassed, to blush and lower my eyes. He smooths his hand along my hair, then draws me toward him until our foreheads touch.

"I thought, 'Lo! A muse of the ancient world has descended here to earth to outshine all the works of man!'"

I pull back from our embrace, laughing again. "You did not! You stole a quick glance our direction, made a face like you were being strangled, and practically ran the other way."

I mean for him to laugh as well, but instead his smile fades and he grows serious once again. "My behavior that day was deplorable. My heart all but stopped when I saw you sitting there. So much had happened between us, and André had told me months before that you had met a gentleman at Madame du Plessis-Bellière's salons and no longer cared for me. When I saw you sitting there, looking so vulnerable and afraid, I wanted to rush to your side and make you feel safe, but I didn't dare. I swear, Juliette, if André hadn't told me—"

"Shh. Never mind," I say, pressing my fingers to his lips to silence him. We have very little time left together, and I don't want to spend one moment more airing our grievances. "I was embarrassed too, after our last meeting." When he had seemed horrified at the sight of me covered in soot.

"I didn't know what to do," he continues, his boyish uncertainty melting me a little. "I had been sent out by Colbert to take the names of all those waiting for an audience. There are always so many on Wednesdays. It is a tedious job."

I nod. Of course, it would be. Papa and I had known that anyone could seek an audience with Colbert one Wednesday a month. That had been our only recourse when the letter had gone unanswered.

René pours a cup of wine as he continues, as if remembering that tedious day requires a drink. I use the break to stand and stretch, feeling much the same fatigue I had felt that day, the long wait settling into my bones. I had understood perfectly why we had been ignored for so long as we sat in that corridor, even after all others had been admitted or dismissed, even after Papa started doubting himself and insisting that he would be better served leaving Paris and seeking work elsewhere.

"Would you have ever admitted us if I hadn't accosted you and forced the model into your hand?" I ask.

He looks embarrassed, and when he answers, I note that it isn't exactly an answer to my question. "When you put the model in my hand, it stopped my breath."

I beam, allowing myself to feel pride for our accomplishment, but René is still looking uncomfortable and fidgeting with his quill. I stand still, to give him the space to say whatever is bothering him. At last, his fingers still playing along the shaft of the feather, he speaks. "I was a coward that day. I took your name to Colbert right off, but he absolutely refused. I couldn't bear to come tell you. That's why you waited so long. I was hoping you would give up and go away." He looks at me at last, nervously meeting my gaze. "Can you forgive me?"

I return at once to his side. "There is nothing to forgive. You got our model into Colbert's hands in the end."

"When I saw it, I knew he couldn't reject it any more than I could. But how are we to explain it in your confession?" René says. "The king doesn't need to know any of this."

"Perhaps he does. He should know of my persistence. He should know how hard I tried to do everything right—to follow the rules of the court. I knew we had the means to make him happy when Valin did not, and I was not going to go away and leave him to be disappointed. You can write that."

"Yes, that's good," he says. "You came to petition the court, entirely according to protocol. You knew your father had the skill to cut the diamond that Valin did not. That of the two, only your father could cut the Violet in a way that would do glory to our *Roi-Soleil*." He is writing as quickly as he can as he speaks. It moves me beyond words to see him trying so hard, and all for me. I don't dare interrupt him, so I sit by, watching his elegant hands, the way his intense concentration presses his brows down ever so slightly over his eyes. The way that unruly wisp of hair has come loose once again from the tidy ponytail at his neck. It is all I can do to keep from reaching out and curling it around my finger.

"So," he says, oblivious to my admiration, "when you were turned away, you forced the model into my hands."

"And you had the prudence and the artistic eye to recognize what you were seeing."

His quill pauses and he looks up, eyes shining. "It was like holding blue fire. Is the real diamond so magnificent?"

"Ten times more."

His eyes glaze with a look of awe. "Your model made Valin's design look like the work of a child."

I smile, still unable to resist the pleasure of an insult to Valin. "Be sure and put that in the report," I say.

He rolls his eyes at me.

"All right," I concede, "but you must convey the beauty of what you saw, the vast superiority of it over Valin's version."

"The king knows that," René says. "He saw them both, the model and Valin's drawing."

Of course. Since I hadn't been there, I had forgotten that part. I never saw Valin's drawing. I only know that when I thrust the model into René's hands that day, his eyes nearly popped out of his head. That's when I knew it would please Colbert, and by extension the king. And I had been right—it took only minutes for us to be admitted to see Colbert after René showed him the model. That's when he assured us he would take the model and Valin's competing design to the king, and would send word to us of the result.

"I left the palace floating on a cloud that day," I tell René. "I knew our model must outshine whatever Valin had submitted. I knew the king would have to choose it, no matter how angry he was at Papa. But more than that, I'd had the pleasure of seeing you, René. You had touched my hand and reawakened in me the hope that if Papa could just succeed in this chance, your affection for me might be rekindled. That, as much as pleasing the king, kept me going."

Papa's spirits were not as high as mine as we left the palace. In fact, he seemed troubled, and this annoyed me. I wanted him to be happy with the new opportunity, but he seemed determined to wallow in misery.

"Come, Papa, this is the opportunity we've been waiting for!" I said.

"I don't know, Juliette." He combed a hand through his matted hair. "Perhaps it is best that I am done with the king's workshop. I'm so tired."

"Nonsense, Papa. You know Valin will ruin that diamond if he gets his hands on it. You don't want that, do you?"

He sighed—a deep, weary sigh. "Of course not," he conceded, but without much enthusiasm.

"This is our chance, then. Surely the king will give the diamond to us!" I said, my voice rising on my sense of the impending victory. "Think of the glory, Papa! Think of the opportunity."

A bit of the old spark came into his eyes at that, and I could see his old passion still there, just buried by all the suffering of the last year.

"So you will come with me to Master Benzacar's house and tell them of the news?" I said hopefully, slipping my hand into his.

Papa sighed. "I've sent letters to friends in Antwerp and Lyon, you know. If I hear of a position for me there before we have a decision from the king, I will take it."

"But—"

Papa held up a hand to silence me. "I want a fresh start, Juliette. But if we receive this commission, I will work with your Master Benzacar and see that the stone is made glorious."

"Oh, thank you, Papa!" I sang, and rising on tiptoes, I kissed his cheek with so much enthusiasm that it made him smile.

"We better go see them, then, and tell them the news," he said.

At the Benzacar house, Isaac opened the door when we knocked. The morning's events tumbled from my mouth so eagerly that he could scarcely understand, but he smiled at my joy.

"I must confer with your grandfather," Papa said, interrupting my babble.

Isaac's smile faltered, and he glanced nervously toward the unseen rooms where his family lived.

"What's the matter?" I asked.

"I'll get him," he muttered, though he hesitated a moment more before retrieving him.

Papa swept into a bow when Abraão entered the room, the women of the house trailing behind him, curious. "Master Benzacar, I congratulate you. It is with the king now. If he chooses the design, I beg you to allow me to work with you to complete the commission. I was too despairing before to see the possibilities in such a partnership. But your persistence and that of my daughter have persuaded me."

Abraão stared silently at Papa, his lips parted in a blank expression. When Papa fell silent, his eyes shifted to me and then to Isaac. Isaac's gaze was fastened tightly to a smudge on the floor.

Abraão looked back to Papa. "Am I to understand you took my drawing to the king?"

"Not your drawing," Papa corrected. "Your model. We have left it with Colbert, who assures us it will be presented to the king."

Abraão's expression darkened, so Papa continued quickly.

"Do not be alarmed. We have not betrayed you," Papa rushed on. "The king believes it is only my work. But if you agree to help me achieve this commission, I will see to it that the king rewards your efforts handsomely. You have my word."

Abraão did not respond to Papa. Instead, his eyes turned to his grandson. Even in the dim light of the windowless room, I could see the bright red flush of Isaac's neck and ears.

"What is this model he speaks of, Isaac?" he said.

I turned to Isaac, suddenly apprehensive. What had he done?

He squirmed under the scrutiny and answered in a meek voice. "I knew your design was good, Avô. Juliette brought me the model, and I knew you would protest. You had already turned her away."

"But how? When?" Isaac's mother asked.

"At night. After the family was all asleep."

Abraão frowned at Isaac, and when he spoke his voice was stern. "Diamonds are not glass, Isaac. You know nothing about cutting them."

"But I thought if you could help me!" Isaac said. "Your hands and eyes are not as bad as you say. I know they're not."

"Isaac! Speak with respect to your grandfather," his mother scolded. He ignored her.

"I know you could teach me, Avô," he said again, clasping his grandfather's hand in a beseeching gesture. "Master Pitau needs your help. Surely with him and me, you could do this job."

"And me," I added. "I can grind and polish. I've helped Papa before."

Abraão looked at Isaac for a long time, then at me, before finally addressing Papa. "It seems our children have gone before us, mon-

sieur. It is up to us now to rise to the occasion of their dreams."
He extended a hand to my father, who shook it. Then he turned to
Isaac. "As for you," he said, "it is time your training began."

Two weeks passed before we heard from the palace. Two weeks
of excited anticipation and frenzied activity. Abraão had begun
to put Isaac through the trials and tests of apprenticeship, and
Papa spent many days assisting in the workshop, though drink
still pulled him astray too often. I did my best to pull back, and
Papa's mood brightened with each passing day. He was returning, bit by bit, to his old self. He was pleased with Isaac too. Papa
had rejected many apprentices for inattentiveness to detail or the
inability to see or appreciate beauty, but Isaac had none of those
downfalls and Papa delighted in his work.

After two weeks of waiting, you came to us with your message, René.

"Must we write of it?" René says, looking up at me, his eyes
troubled. "The king already knows of his decision."

I grit my teeth. "He knows of his decision. Now he must know
of the suffering it caused."

"I just wish I could rewrite my part in your suffering," René
says, taking my hand and unclenching the fist I hadn't realized I
was making. He smooths my palm against his until my breathing slows back to normal.

"You had no choice," I remind him. "I should have recognized that at the time. I was returning from the workshop when I saw you on the doorstep that day. My heart soared as always at the sight of you, but I was embarrassed, too, that you would see the squalor of our situation."

"You shouldn't have been. I know what it is to come from humble origins."

"I didn't know that then," I reply, giving in to temptation and turning the unruly strand of his hair onto my finger. It is soft as a kitten, and the richest, warmest shade of brown. "Even with my embarrassment, I was happy to see you."

He looks more distraught than ever. "Because you thought I was bringing you a commission from the king." He rubs a hand across his eyes, leaving a smudge of ink on his forehead. "That was the longest walk of my life, bringing that news to your house that day. I kept thinking, there must be some way to soften the blow. There must be some way to tell her so she won't hate me forever." He pauses, looking down at his hands, and I can still see the hurt I dealt him, like a raw wound in his eyes. I reach forward and wipe the ink from his brow with my thumb, then kiss him in the clean spot left behind.

"I was angry, René, but how desperately I regret the hard words I spoke, when you were the last person on earth I wanted to hurt." He closes his eyes and wearily leans forward, resting his forehead against mine, and we hold each other up, even as the storm wails around us, as I see again in my mind's eye that painful meeting.

"What is it, René? What has happened?" I asked, seeing your pained expression, though I was weary of bad luck and bad news.

You drew a deep breath. "The king favored your design . . ."

"But that is good news," I said, worry sinking into my chest.

"So he gave your model to Valin and ordered him to cut the Violet in that form."

My mouth fell open. I couldn't help it. I couldn't find words, only shock.

"I am so sorry," you said, wringing your hands anxiously. "I swear, Colbert did not mean this to happen."

I sunk onto the steps. I had been so sure the king would give us the commission, but of course, just because he liked the design did not mean he had to give it to Papa. Why hadn't I foreseen this danger? To steal another master's design was the lowest form of treachery, but it was not beneath Valin, not with the king's patronage at stake. I had delivered Papa's most precious secret directly into the hands of his enemy.

"But . . ." I could not finish. There was nothing more to say.

"I am sorry, Juliette," you said again, lowering yourself to the step beside me and trying to take my hand. But I pulled away. My bewilderment had condensed into impotent rage and was brimming over.

"I thought Colbert was an honorable man!" I said, all but spitting bile. "How could he betray us? How could *you*?"

You flinched at my accusation. "It is the king's command, Juliette. We had no choice." You reached for my hand again, but I pulled away once more. Even then I knew I was being unfair, but all I could do was lash out.

"Go!" I shrieked. "Leave me."

You opened your mouth to say something more, then closed it again, your jaw clenching. I saw at once how I had hurt you and I regretted it, but I could say nothing. I could only drop my face into my hands in despair.

Across the city, Isaac, Abraão, and Papa were hard at work on Isaac's training, filled with the eager fire of hope. How would I tell them of this? It would break their hearts. Once again, ruin had come upon us. And despite the cruel things I had said to you, words that I regret as much as anything I have ever done, the only person I could blame was myself.

TWENTY-NINE

"What did you do after I left?" René asks.

"What could I do? I couldn't bear to disappoint Papa and the Benzacar family. They had all been brought back to life by the project, and I would have to go to them and destroy all that."

Seeing my despair, René pulls me into his lap and cradles me in his arms, but I can feel tension in him.

"How I hate all these petty machinations of the court!" he says as he holds me. "If the king hadn't been so childish, acting on his hurt pride . . . If he had done the sensible thing, no one would have been hurt."

I draw back and press my fingers to his lips to silence him, my heart tight in my chest. To speak so of the king is treason, and anyone could be listening in the king's prison. René at least must come through this unscathed.

He kisses my fingers before pulling my hand gently from his lips. "I've lain awake at night thinking how things would be now if just one thing had been different about that day."

"I was wrong to lash out at you," I say.

"I was hurt, I admit," he says with a shrug, "but who wouldn't lash out after such a betrayal? I should have stood up for you and your father. The king never should have given his model to Valin."

"But truthfully, René, what could you have done? They were the king's orders."

"Well, at the very least, I could have stayed to deliver such dreadful news to your father."

He still looks forlorn, so I lean in close to his ear and whisper, "I know one way you could make it up to me."

He takes my face gently in his hands and gives me a kiss so sweet and slow that I forget there is anything to forgive. I kiss him back, drawing him closer, parting my lips and letting his tongue explore between them. It is some time before either of us remembers the confession we are meant to be writing. At last, with a few tender nudges at the corner of my mouth, his lips leave mine.

I wait, holding my breath, my eyes closed, not wanting to break the spell. He is silent too, but soon, he coaxes me back to my stool. Without a word he takes up his quill and pours himself back into the confession.

"What are you writing?" I ask.

"After I brought the news of the king's betrayal to you—"

"The king's *decision*," I correct. "We must not anger him further."

"You relayed the king's decision to your father and the

Benzacar family, and that is when they hatched the plot to steal the diamond, and forced you into silence. You tried to dissuade them but could not."

I snatch the paper away from him, breaking the tip of the quill with the force of it. "You cannot write that," I say, crumpling the paper in my hand.

"The king doesn't care about truth!" René says. "He only cares about his own glory and making someone pay for his embarrassment."

"But—"

"Don't you see? Your father and the Jews have already made their escape. This way you can be pardoned, and you will *all* live," he says, trying to grab the paper back from me.

I tear it in two, and then again. "They are still in Paris, René. They will be caught and burned at the stake."

A look of annoyance comes into his eyes, and he opens his mouth to argue, but I stop him with a look. I have to make him see the disastrous consequences that could result from this plan. "If we let the king blame these Jews now, what's to keep him from punishing every Jew he encounters from now on? Do you really think there would be an end to it in the king's eyes, just because the Benzacar family slipped through his grasp?" By now I've torn the page I took from him into tiny bits, and as he watches, I feed them into the flame of the candle. Together, we watch them flare up, then disintegrate into ash. "It is a death I would not wish on anyone, René. It is too much to risk."

"I can see why you want them spared," René concedes, "but I

can't see why you call them innocent and take all the blame on yourself. They had the king's diamond in their possession for months—they had to know it was stolen, even if they didn't steal it themselves."

"I did not return to the workshop that afternoon after you brought me news of the king's betrayal," I say.

"*Decision*," he corrects.

"Decision," I agree. "I waited until the next morning, when I would be going with Papa anyway. I intended to tell them then, when they were all together before starting work. But when we stepped inside, the workshop was warm and comfortable and filled with the sounds of family. Isaac's grandmother was in the kitchen, singing while she worked. Miriam, Isaac's mother, smiled when she saw us, and poured us each a cup of strong black coffee while she scolded Isaac for forgetting to bring in the wood for the kitchen fire. He was not listening. Eager to start another day of lessons, he was oiling the grinder.

"I could not tell them, René, not when their happiness depended so heavily on cutting the diamond. So I took the offered coffee with thanks, and together we began the day's work, as if the king had not yet decided."

"When did you tell them, if not then?" René asks. I hesitate, nervous about how he will react. But I have to tell him sooner or later. And the king must know, if he's to pardon Papa or my Jewish friends.

"I never did," I admit, then pause, expecting a protest from René. He remains quiet. "The truth is, the longer I waited, the more outraged I became at the injustice of the king's decision, and that outrage hardened inside me into something it shouldn't have. You are right, René; I should have told them that day. Things might have been different then. There might have been another solution, other than the dangerous one I settled upon."

"To steal the diamond," he says, his lips tightening in a grim line.

"That evening, when Papa was abed, I went in search of André. My anger by then had made me reckless and bold, and I knocked on the back door of the king's workshop, not even caring if it was Master Valin himself who opened the door."

"Was it?"

"It was André, as I hoped it would be. He grabbed his coat, and together, we made our way to a café, where a table in the back corner allowed us to talk."

Once the waiter had brought coffees to our little table and André had passed him a few coins, we were alone. I bent in close, so that we would not be overheard.

"Valin was crowing when he returned with the model from the palace," André said.

"Did he suspect you of getting the model to my father?" I asked, worried that we might have been discovered.

André shook his head. "He was too excited at having stolen your father's design to dwell on how it came to be in the first place, though his wife has asked. But then he spent all day today trying to understand it, and it confuses him. So many facets, and on both faces. There is the problem of holding the diamond steady and with enough precision to create so many even, perfect facets."

"The same problem that plagued Papa," I said, feeling no sympathy at all for his plight, despite its familiarity.

He nodded once. "And that, it would appear, your father has solved."

"So what is he going to do?" I asked. "Do you think he will ask for Papa's help?"

André took a long sip of his coffee, then shook his head. "The idea of it galls him as much as it does you," André said. "Valin is going to Antwerp, in hopes of finding an answer there. He may continue to Amsterdam or Lisbon if he must."

"And so history repeats itself," I said, without a hint of pity. "What will he do when he finds no help?"

André shrugged. "Perhaps then he will seek out your father."

I considered. I hated the Valins, but perhaps I could let go of my bitterness if it meant some small redemption for Papa.

"Perhaps I should tell Papa what has happened and send him to Valin."

André shook his head. "He should not come to the workshop. As I said, Madame Valin is suspicious. She think your father may have stolen the mold, or one of the glass castings, to make the model. She might have him arrested if she sees him near the workshop, afraid he might steal the diamond itself."

I smiled at his words—a cold, hard, humorless smile. You see, the idea was already forming in my mind.

André started to say something more, but his words petered out as his face registered alarm. "You aren't really thinking of stealing it, are you?"

I suppose I wasn't. It would be an impossible task. And yet . . .

"If only there was a way, but it would take months to cut. The diamond could not go missing for so long without being noticed," I said. "And you just said yourself, Madame Valin suspects us. We'd be arrested immediately."

André tipped his head, considering. "Valin is likely going to be away for months. He plans to return the stone to the king before he goes, just as your father did."

"So, you see? It will only be more impossible." But even as I said it, an idea came to me, more dangerous and rash than any I had had so far.

At first, I pushed it aside, terrified at the thought. But as another week passed and I continued to watch hope work its magic on Papa and Isaac's family, the fear of a crime against the king began to pale in comparison to the fear of destroying that hope. With Valin absent from the city, the king's diamond would lie untouched in the king's treasury, no one examining it. If there was ever a chance of getting the stone away from Valin long enough to cut it, this would be it.

I had let my mother and brother die, and I had brought ruin upon my father. I knew the consequence of taking the diamond: public execution, if I was caught. But as I lay awake in the night, thinking of crushing my father again with this latest betrayal, thinking of Valin strutting about in luxury, knighted by the king for a design that was not rightfully his, my resolve crystalized. And when I told André of my plan, he agreed to help me, on one condition.

"If I help you get the diamond, will you promise to let me help cut it?"

I hesitated. I knew it wasn't my promise to make—I had no right to say who could come or go from Master Benzacar's workshop. But it seemed a reasonable bargain. After all, André was taking a great risk for us, and he deserved some part of the reward. Surely I could convince the others to include him. "If we get the diamond, we will need all the hands we can get to complete it before its absence is noticed," I said, resolving to myself as much as to André.

I gave him a confident smile, which he eagerly returned. "Then we will do it!" he said.

So I returned to the glassworks, choosing a craftsman who had no connection to the king, carrying the mold and a sample of color André had provided. In exchange for a pair of my mother's earrings, the glassmaker colored one sample of glass after another until he matched the steely blue of the diamond. Then he made a new replica of the stone, which I ground and buffed and oiled and polished until it could be mistaken for the original by an untrained eye. I went to a cabinetmaker in the Marais district and presented him with a drawing of the rosewood box, knowing Papa would be suspicious if he received the diamond without it. The craftsman fashioned it without question. After all, all the gentry often sought to replicate the finery of the royal household.

André alerted me when the gem was due to be returned into

Colbert's keeping and Valin was to set out on his voyage. The night before, I waited in the darkness across the street from the workshop until all was still and silent. Then once again, I crept to the servants' entrance in the alley. As promised, André had left it unlocked. I eased it open and slipped inside, my heart hammering until I feared it would wake Valin's household.

André was waiting for me in the workshop. I paused as I stepped into the space, overcome for a moment by a wave of painful nostalgia at the smells of airborne dust and hot metal that lingered there.

"Juliette," André whispered through the darkness. "Hurry!"

I crossed to where he waited for me, near the secret panel. Even through the darkness I could see the tight, tense lines of his face, made more vivid by pale fear.

"Have you got the key?" I whispered, for Valin had taken mine the night he threw us from the workshop.

He held it out to me. He had removed it that afternoon from Valin's key chain. If Valin saw it was missing, he would come looking.

With shaking hands, I slid open the hidden panel, and while André held a candle to illuminate the dark niche, I opened the strongbox.

The great blue diamond lay in its rosewood box, cushioned on red velvet. I lifted it carefully out. It caught the moonlight and swallowed it. I laid the glass model on the velvet cushion, making sure to press it into the indent left by the real stone. Then I shut the box again, leaving no trace that I'd been there.

André extinguished the candle and closed the panel. Overhead the floorboards creaked. André pushed me toward the back passage. A door opened somewhere above us. I quickened my pace and eased open the door to the alley, willing it into silence. It gave a faint creak as cool air poured in from outside.

André gave me another little shove, and then closed the door hastily behind me. I pressed myself against the wall, afraid someone might be looking out the windows overhead. After a long, frozen moment, I inched toward the street. Once there, I set off as fast as I dared toward home, trying not to think about being alone at night on the streets of Paris with the greatest treasure in France in my pocket.

Returning to our room, I buried the diamond deep in the straw of my mattress while Papa slept, oblivious, across the room. Then I lay down and stared into the darkness for the rest of the night, unable to still my racing heart. The enormity of what I had done seemed to grow until it nearly suffocated me. More than once I rose from the bed and paced the room, fighting the urge to return the stone before I was found out, but each time I went back to bed, as afraid of returning it as of keeping it.

The next morning, I told Papa I wasn't feeling well and sent him off to the workshop without me. I sat alone, listening for the sound of horses in the street. If the theft was discovered and soldiers came to arrest me, I was determined to confess my crime and see Papa spared.

But they did not come. Not that morning, and not the next. The only one to seek me out was an errand boy from the cabinetmaker I had commissioned, with news that he had completed the box. That night after Papa fell asleep, I cut red velvet from the hem of one of Maman's gowns and sewed a cushion, then set the diamond in the box. The next morning, I sent Papa ahead once again. After an hour, I put the box in my shopping basket and ran for the workshop.

I was out of breath when I arrived at the Benzacar house. I rushed inside, flushed and panting. Papa was teaching Isaac to see the planes in a stone in order to cleave it, and Abraão was bent over calculations, refining the design for the diamond in every detail. They all stopped what they were doing to stare in surprise.

"Juliette!" Papa said, his voice anxious. "What is the matter?"

I smiled, though my heart was hammering in my ears. "I have it, Papa! Look!"

I opened the box quickly and removed the diamond, putting the box away before Papa could notice any differences from the original. The air shuddered as Isaac, Abraão, and Papa all drew in a breath at the sight of the gem lying on the workbench before me. Their eyes were no longer on me, which made my lie easier.

"René delivered it an hour ago. The king has given us the commission!"

A sudden cheer burst from all three men, rattling the tools where they hung along the wall, bringing the Benzacar women from the back of the house to see what the fuss was about. Abraão grabbed his wife and danced her around the room. Isaac followed suit with his mother, while my own father reached for me and held me to him in a warm embrace.

"*Mon petit bijou,*" he crooned. Tears sprung into my eyes at the pet name he had not uttered since Maman's death. "You have done this. You have made this all possible."

He held me there, my head pressed to his chest, his heartbeat strong and vibrant against my ear. But my eyes were on the great diamond where it lay, gathering darkness to it.

THIRTY

"So your father truly knew nothing of the theft?" René says. He is looking at me with something between amazement and horror in his eyes.

"Nothing," I say, looking down solemnly.

"Nor the Jews?"

"They are all innocent. I calculated my deception carefully, counterfeiting the rosewood box as well as the stone, rushing into the workshop midday, as I think we had all imagined I might when word at last came from the king. And they were taken in completely. I deliberately kept them in the dark."

"To protect them?"

I nod, but I know in my heart there was more to it. I was afraid that if Papa or Abraão knew the truth, they would not consent to the deception. A wave of guilt washes over me as I acknowledge this. If I had not reached for glory, or wanted so badly to keep Valin from that glory, Papa and I would be together now, perhaps in Amsterdam or London, rebuilding our lives, and the Benzacar family would be as they were before, poor but safe from the wrath of the king.

"But André knew," René says. "André even suggested it, did he not? So André should take his share of the blame."

"Yes, André knew," I say, and the thought makes me want to grind my teeth. "Be sure the king knows that. He is culpable. As is, I suppose, whoever accepted the diamond back into the treasury. That was the greatest risk in our plan, and why I waited at home, expecting the counterfeit to be recognized and the king's men to arrest me."

The color drains from René's face and his eyes widen with shock. A whispered curse escapes his lips.

My breath catches in my throat, and I cover my mouth as I realize the significance of what I've just said. Of course, Colbert would have assigned a clerk to record its return to the palace, and he has relied on René throughout this business.

René leans his elbows on the table and buries his face in his hands. "*Merde!* How is this going to look to them? Colbert knows of my feelings for you."

I am at his side, my hands on his arm, beseeching. My heart is pounding in my ears with this new fear. "You must write nothing of your accepting it. Leave yourself out entirely."

"That will do no good. All they have to do is look in the ledger and see my handwriting there."

"Destroy that page of the ledger," I demand, determined to keep René above suspicion. I could not bear it if I brought him down too.

"That would look even worse."

"Then tear the page from the ledger and record that it was some other clerk who received the stone and inspected it. Surely there is someone in Colbert's employ who is careless and who would raise no suspicions if they made this mistake."

He shakes his head.

"René, you must!" I say, gripping his arms, my voice now shrill with panic. "If Colbert knows you have feelings for me, they will think you knew of the deception. That you were in on the theft. You can't let them—"

"Shh! Juliette, stop," René says, taking my face in his hands and tilting it up to his. I search his eyes desperately, hoping to see a plan there, but all I see is the candle reflected in warm amber and a tender kindness. He gives me a small smile as he holds my gaze.

"Just as you cannot lay the blame on others, I cannot either," he says. "We will simply leave it alone, making no mention of what happened when the stone was returned, and if the king seeks out further conspirators, I will answer honestly and hope for the best."

"But—"

He stops my words with a gentle kiss to my forehead. "Quiet your thoughts for once," he says. "Your mind is always running ahead like this, getting you into more trouble to try to find a way out of the current dilemma. How often has it gotten you out of one trouble only to get you deeper into the next?"

I draw a shuddering breath and do as he says, forcing my frenzied thoughts to still. It is a gentle benediction, this pause in my constant striving. I close my eyes and let my cheeks rest in his palms.

"There now," he says. "Perhaps nothing will come of it. But André—we will be sure to show his role in this whole affair."

"Where is André now?" I ask. "I saw him in the king's chamber this morning. Does the king hold him to blame at all?"

"André pointed his fingers at everyone he doesn't like, but not at himself. He painted you as quite the villain, the scoundrel." René's hands, now back on the table, are curling into fists.

My blood is pounding in my ears as I think of André's role in my downfall, but I try to think clearly. He must have been convincing in his testimony, judging from how René was raging when we started. If I am going to cast some guilt back on him, I must frame it carefully. "We must tell the truth of it," I tell René. "If we embellish his role, it may be too easy for him to worm his way free, and then our account will only look false. And anyway, the unadorned truth is enough to damn him. He helped me steal it, and he knew I had it all along. He deceived his betters just as I deceived mine."

"You would have him hang beside you?" René asks, and strangely, the old jealousy is back in his voice, as if dying beside me is an honor.

"I would have you write that what we did, we did for the honor and glory of the king," I say. "That is our best defense. André knew as well as I that Valin could not do the job. That he would ruin the stone. If pressed, he will surely confess that much. And neither of us wanted to see the stone diminished. It was vital that the king shine like the sun. That the Tavernier

Violet be forced to yield to the king's bidding. That he be made the most magnificent sovereign in the world."

René smiles and places another peck on my forehead. "Yes, that is what we must tell the king."

He takes up his quill, dips it in the ink, and once again spins out my story into artful words upon the page. Words to make *le Roi-Soleil* outshine the sun.

THIRTY-ONE

The next day, our work began in earnest. The initial shaping of the stone would be like any other. Abraão's secret knowledge would not be needed until the final stages, when we cut the facets. I relayed this information to André, and we agreed it would be safest for him to stay away until that stage began.

For a week, Isaac practiced his hand at the grinder on plain stones while his grandfather and my father consulted and worked out calculations. By the end of the week they had a plan to cleave and grind the stone, but decided not to do so until the following Monday.

Now that we had the diamond, leaving early galled me. I was afraid that the theft might be discovered, and I longed to urge my innocent accomplices to haste. But to admit my urgency would give away my secret, and I wanted to do nothing that would implicate them in my crime. Papa, sensing my impatience, smiled and patted my shoulder. "We will all benefit from the rest, and no doubt from a few prayers for the success of our project. Monday will be a big day."

Knowing that Papa would need a steady hand to cleave the stone, I consented to leave early and rest through both the Jewish Sabbath and our own. The task would take strength and concentration. An error at this stage could destroy the stone forever. By Sunday night, however, I realized that the rest had been a mistake. It gave time for the enormity of the task to grow too great in Papa's mind. By Saturday evening, he was pacing nervously around the room.

His agitation only increased on Sunday, and after supper he told me he needed some air. Foolishly, I let him go. He staggered home much later, reeking of wine, a half-full bottle tucked under his arm. I do not know where he got it on a Sunday, but I suppose a drunkard can always sniff out a bottle. Angrily, I pulled the bottle out of his grip. He swayed and slumped into a chair.

"I can't do it, Juliette," he slurred.

I resisted the urge to scold him, assuring him he'd feel better in the morning.

"I won't," he insisted. "Don't you see? I'm a cheat. A charlatan! I can't cut the king's diamond. I can't."

"Nonsense, Papa! That's the wine talking," I said, helping him out of his coat and onto his bed. I slipped his stockings and shoes off and laid a blanket over him. "Get some sleep."

"I can't," he muttered again, but soon after he did succumb.

In the morning, he was wretched. Sick and shaking, he refused to come to the workshop.

"You must!" I insisted. "Today we begin, remember?"

Papa shook his head. "I can't, Juliette."

"But—"

"Isaac can do it. He's been practicing," Papa said. He rummaged around the room until he found the bottle he had bought the night before, and lifted it to his lips.

I pulled it away from him. "Isaac hasn't the skill, Papa. You are the master! You must do it."

He shook his head, tears shining in his eyes. "I'm sorry, Juliette."

He was shaking all over, like a wet cur caught out in the rain, but after all I had risked to get us to this moment, I was too angry for sympathy. Without another word to him I stormed off to the workshop.

Abraão and Isaac were waiting for me when I stepped inside. The Tavernier Violet was waiting too, lying on the workbench, marked in chalk for cleaving. I looked from Abraão to Isaac and back, my gut clenching.

"My father won't come. He is—" I swallowed. What could I say? I was angry and disappointed, but he was still my father. "He is not well today."

Isaac's face fell. "Perhaps tomorrow, then?"

"I don't know," I said, shrugging helplessly.

Abraão looked at me for a long time, with eyes that, though dim with age, seemed to see right through me. At last he turned to Isaac.

"You have demonstrated a good knack for the hammer," he

said, laying his hand on Isaac's shoulder. "Perhaps you should cleave the stone."

Isaac's face lit up. "You think I'm ready?"

My gut dropped so fast I thought I might be sick. My father's cowardice meant a novice would break the king's diamond. If he erred, there was no correcting it.

Abraão smiled and nodded. "You have cleaved the stones in your tests successfully. I have marked the stone, according to all the calculations Master Pitau and I made. All there is to do is the hammer work."

Smiling cautiously, Isaac retrieved the hammer and chisel. I tried to catch Abraão's eye with a silent protest, but he only gave me the same mild, encouraging smile he had given Isaac. Then he watched while Isaac, a mere boy of sixteen, an apprentice with only the lightest of training, set the chisel's sharp edge on the largest blue diamond in the world. I put a hand to my mouth. I couldn't breathe.

Isaac shifted his hand on the handle to get a comfortable grip. Abraão muttered a quick instruction in Portuguese, or perhaps it was a prayer. Then he kissed Isaac on the forehead and stepped out of the way.

Isaac swallowed. Our eyes met, and he flashed me the smallest grin, though beads of sweat glistened on his brow. I turned away. Shut my eyes.

A rush of air marked the passage of the hammer, and a sharp crack echoed through the room, like the heavens rent apart on Judgment Day. Then silence.

I turned back, my breath still captive in my throat. Isaac was wiping the sweat from his forehead with the back of his sleeve. The king's diamond lay in two pieces, the long, ungainly point at the end neatly removed, the remainder now more symmetrical and even, with a new, smooth face where the chisel had caught its plane. A perfect cleave. My breath rushed out with a force that left me dizzy.

Abraão examined the stone and praised Isaac. Then he handed the stone to me. I gave it a quick inspection before returning it. I didn't want him to see the way my hands were shaking, but he did.

"Sit down, mademoiselle, and recover yourself," he said. "Of course, you were frightened. It is a great deed we undertake, and no great deed is done without risk. But the worst is over now."

I gratefully sat, my knees nearly too weak to support me.

"Perhaps when you feel better, you should go home. Tell your father of our success. It will make him feel better, I am sure."

I looked up into his eyes and saw that he understood everything. Of course he had seen through my father's "illness," and of course he had seen my own fear too. My cheeks filled with hot blood. I was hardly better than my father, falling apart so easily.

Abraão spoke again, very quietly, so that Isaac could not hear. "Your father is not a coward, Juliette, but a wise man," he said. "That is why this was a better job for Isaac. Cleaving a stone that is well marked is not so hard, and he is still young and foolish enough to feel little fear. Go home now and tell your father it is done. Our real work is ready to begin, and I need him."

I thanked Abraão, and when my wobbly legs would support me, I did as he said and walked toward my home.

As I walked, a cool breeze revived me, drawing me back into the world. Trees along the river and in the gardens of the gentry were brightening: amber and ruby and shimmering gold. I realized the date then: September 29—Michaelmas, the Feast of the Archangels. A fitting day indeed. With Isaac's courage—or foolishness, whichever it might be—we had spread our wings and leapt into the sky. Whether we would soar like Saint Michel himself or melt and fall like Icarus remained to be seen. But we had leapt, and the Tavernier Violet was no more.

In its place, the Blue of the Crown was born.

Thirty-Two

René has been dutifully recording my words for hours now. What little sunlight we had is gone. The square of sky visible through the high window is a darkening, dusky blue, and the stones of the prison are giving off a clammy damp. Twice, he has had the guards bring us extra candles. I have moved my stool closer to René's for warmth and comfort. From time to time he has paused and read back a passage so we can carefully select our phrases. Raised by a jeweler, I am accustomed to fine crafts-manship, but I marvel at his skill with words. With each stroke of his pen he spells out our dedication to the king, to the glory of France, until I myself forget the dark anxiety of those days in the workshop.

When we come to Isaac cleaving the stone, he leaves that out.

"The king would not like to think that the master gem-cutters took their charge too lightly," he says. "He will want to believe that the greatest treasure of his hoard is the work of the greatest masters in the land."

I nod and give him an encouraging smile. "Two masters worked for a full day on their calculations and examinations of the stone, and from such work came the perfect cleave."

René rises from his seat and stretches his back and neck, then flexes and unflexes his hand. I pour him a cup of wine, and he takes it with a grateful smile. He savors two long sips before he passes it to me.

"Of course," he says, a mischievous smile coming to his face, "there are other ways to think of a perfect cleave."

He moves behind my chair as I sip at the cup of wine. A tingle of anticipation runs through me as he lays his hands on my shoulders. He leans down, his lip beside my ear, so that his breath warms me, even before his whisper.

"Is not a man to cleave to his wife?"

"He is, but that means to cling together, not to split apart."

His lips nibble at my ear, emboldening me. I take his hands in mine and slide them downward.

His hands glide comfortably over the curve of my breasts. "Now *that* is a perfect cleavage."

I laugh, though I am tingling at his touch. "I'm glad you find it so, monsieur," I say, releasing his hands to explore on their own while I reach my arm up and around his neck, entangling my fingers in his hair. I pull free the ribbon holding it back and it falls around his face. His lips are now working down from my ear, along my neck, growing hungrier as his fingers toy with the strings of my bodice.

I have only once before been touched so intimately by a man, in those terrible moments in Fouquet's cell. This wanted touch is nothing like that. My muscles tense below his fingers, and my back arches me up toward him of its own accord. I skip a breath as his lips reach my collarbone, where the shoulder of my bodice bars his progress. I reach a hand to pull the cloth away, but he stops me, grabbing my hand and resisting my advances.

"We must not," he says in one gravelly breath.

I turn, wrapping both arms around his neck and leaning my head against his chest. "I want to, René."

He lifts my chin, his thumb gliding over my lips. "We still have work to do, and it's growing late."

"What if we're wasting our time?" I say, giving voice to the fear that, as darkness gathers around us, is harder and harder to push down. "As Colbert said, I challenged the king in front of the court. Even if we can convince him that all I did was for his sake, there is little chance he will spare me." I tighten my arms around René's neck, as if he is the last solid thing in the world. "I do not want to die tomorrow having squandered the time we have left when it could have been spent in love."

I try to pull another deep kiss from his lips, but he unhooks my arms from his neck and pulls gently away.

"We must try, Juliette. Now tell me, what more is there to cutting the diamond?"

It is a very unromantic question. I am still craving his touch with every inch of my body, and the last thing I want to think about now is the long, dull, dusty hours of shaping a stone.

"Come on," he coaxes. "We have to demonstrate your usefulness."

"My usefulness?"

"You helped your father, did you not? The king must know that you are needed to ensure that future diamonds are also cut as he desires."

The word *desire* is almost too much for me, but I try to focus on what he is saying. "Once the cleaving was done, we began the long hours of bruting."

"And what is bruting?" he asks, emphasizing the word as if it implies something risqué.

"It is the grinding process by which the facets are shaped. The stone is held for long hours on a spinning wheel to wear it away. Like this." I smile, place my hands on his chest, and begin moving them in a circular motion.

He responds to my explanation by reaching his hands around my waist, his eyes crinkling with mischief. "Long hours?" he says, leaning into me. Emboldened, I untuck the tail of his shirt so I can reach a hand underneath, to feel the soft fuzz on his chest. His eyes flutter shut, and he lets out a long, slow breath.

"Did you know that only a diamond can cut a diamond? Nothing else is hard enough—not steel or stone. So the diamond must be worn away against another diamond, or against a wheel coated with a grit of diamond dust."

"Mmm," he says, his eyes still closed. We are rocking now with the movement of my hand. "That does sound slow."

"Tedious," I breathe, stepping in a little closer and running my hand around his back to explore along the muscles there. "The slow progress drove me nearly to distraction."

He bends his head, returning his lips to my neck, and I use the opportunity to draw him closer to me again, so that our bodies press against each other for the first time.

"I can understand your urgency," he says, and I know he is speaking the truth, for I can feel his own urgency now pressed against me. I turn my eyes to the narrow cot in the corner, wondering how I might maneuver him to it. I shift my weight forward and he takes a step backward toward the bed.

"I urged the others to work every hour they could. Papa thought me overly impatient, but never thought to question the reason for my impatience."

René abruptly pulls back from me, and I admonish myself for mentioning my father to him at that moment. What was I thinking? He paces away, running a hand through his hair, trying to get hold of his excitement. We are both breathing hard.

"Yes, your father," he says in a flush. "We must continue." He turns back to the table, and taking a wide step around me so that I cannot recapture him, he regains his chair and quill.

"Everyone . . . worked . . . long . . . hours . . ." he says as he writes the words on the page.

I sigh and return to my own seat. Of course, I know he is right. We must remain focused on our task. It is evening, and we are running out of time.

For many weeks, the diamond was pressed against the grinding wheel from sunrise to sundown, the four of us taking turns at the work so that it might continue uninterrupted. I reminded Papa as often as I could that the sooner we completed the work, the sooner we could be returned to the king's favor and our rightful home. I reminded Papa weekly of our dwindling resources in hopes of instilling urgency in him. Isaac was my confederate in this. Though he did not know my reason for haste, his own desire for his family to claim their due of fame and fortune drove him to work hard, and to hurry to take his grandfather's place whenever the old man grew weary.

In the evenings at least once a week, I met with André to learn any news of Valin or events at court that might bring our deceit to light. Valin's venture to the northern cities in Belgium and Holland kept him away for a month. He returned with very fine sapphires, which, he proposed, would make elegant shoe buckles for the Christmas feasts.

"Wasn't the king outraged?" I asked André, when he told me of it in the small café that had become our regular meeting place. "When Papa had proposed anything other than the Violet, Louis would have none of it."

André nodded. "He wasn't entirely pleased, but the sapphires are very fine, and Louis saw that Valin was offering him the stones at a mere fraction of their worth to appease him. The king is eager for his diamond, but he's eager to expand his collection too. So Valin has bought himself a little time."

"That is good," I said. Every minute Valin bought for himself was another minute he bought for us.

"But, Juliette, I have better news," André said, his face alight with excitement. "He's made me a journeyman. I am no longer a lowly apprentice, forever under a master's thumb."

I tried to look pleased, though his choice of words annoyed me. He had hardly been under my father's thumb. Papa had been kind and had treated André like one of the family.

"Will you be leaving Valin's workshop, then?" I asked, as it was customary for new journeymen to leave the workshop that had trained them.

André shook his head. "I am working on the sapphires. He is shaping the stones while I design the gold work. I have three of Valin's apprentices to assist me. I wouldn't find such a good job elsewhere."

He leaned in closer. "Besides, I have to stay with Valin until your job is done. Otherwise, who will warn you—protect you—should something happen?"

For this, I truly was grateful, and my annoyance at his careless words slipped away. I laid my hand over his and smiled. "We are working as hard and as fast as we can. Already the stone is taking shape."

"And when you get to the faceting, you will let me come help," he reminded me.

"Of course," I said, though my gut tightened. I hadn't secured that reassurance from Abraão yet.

"After the sapphires, what will Valin be doing? Will he recall the Violet from the treasury?" I asked, eager to turn the conversation away from the promise.

"He's thinking of going to Portugal." André grinned. "I might have mentioned that I'd heard a rumor through Master Pitau that a Portuguese master had cut the Mazarins."

"André, you're a genius!" I cried, and in my relief, I embraced him before I departed.

The conversation reminded me of my promise to André, and the problem it posed. I hadn't told Papa or the Benzacars of it. After all, the secrets of Benzacar's workshop were not mine to reveal. Still, after all the seemingly impossible things I had accomplished, I was sure I could get Abraão to let André join us when the time came. To prepare, I mentioned André whenever the opportunity arose, praising what a good apprentice he'd been, how trustworthy he was, and how he'd been part of Papa's work with the Blue until now. Abraão listened, but made no suggestion to bring André into our fold, as I'd hoped he might.

We worked feverishly, barely aware as the year cooled from fall into winter. We added layers of clothes as we took our turns for long hours at the grinder. October gave way to November, then to damp, gray December, while the diamond slowly shrank and took shape. André met me in the evenings and told me of his sapphires, and I told him of the Blue.

Master Valin delivered his sapphire buckles to the king on Christmas Eve. They were the talk of the Christmas season, to André's great satisfaction. Excitedly, he told me of the flood of orders to jewelers across the city, the wealthy eager to join in a new passion for blue gems.

This stirred a new anxiety in my gut. If everyone was wearing blue gems, Louis was bound to think again of his diamond. Why couldn't Valin have returned from Antwerp with rubies or emeralds?

I shared my new concern with my companions in the workshop a few days after Epiphany. "He is going to want his diamond soon," I said. "With everyone donning sapphires to match his, he is going to want a greater stone than all the others."

"Perhaps we should tell him he may have it by Easter," Abraão said.

Every eye turned to him as every mouth fell open.

"Easter!" Isaac said. "That is scarcely three months away. Could we finish so soon?"

Abraão smiled. "I think the bruting is all but finished. We can begin to refine the facets very soon now."

A thrill ran through me. This was the great secret of the Mazarins—the skill Papa had not been able to replicate. Abraão's great secret.

I looked at Papa. He was looking at Abraão in silent entreaty.

Abraão nodded solemnly. "All these long years I've taught no one this secret. When Cardinal Mazarin brought me to Paris, I thought he would present me to the king. I thought a new time was coming, when Jews would be welcomed in France. But the cardinal kept me all to himself, wanting his share of that glory too. I bided my time, thinking that when Louis came of age, he would seek out the man who could put the sun in the heart of a stone, and I was right. But to my dismay, a Parisian master, Jean Pitau, stepped forward claiming the skill.

"What could I do? I was a Jew in a city where Jews were banned, and by then Louis had married the infanta of Spain, and as we Portuguese know, every Spanish princess demands the death of Jews as her dowry. And so, with the cardinal's passing I did not rise, but became trapped here, without papers or protection. With no chance of winning the king.

"But now God has brought that very same Jean Pitau to me. For this, I will give thanks to God and teach you."

"What about André?" I said.

"André?" Abraão said, surprised. Apparently, all my hints had not hit their mark.

"We could use more hands if we are going to finish by Easter," I said. "He was Papa's apprentice, and he's eager to return to your side, Papa."

"I think he's more eager to remain at *your* side, Juliette," Papa said.

Color rose in my cheeks. "I don't know what you mean!"

Papa grinned. "Do you think I haven't noticed the way you constantly praise him, or that you sneak off to meet him in the evenings?"

I had no answer to this—at least not one I could give Papa, though he took my blush as an answer.

"It needn't be a secret, *ma chérie*. It would not be such a bad match. I know your mother put thoughts of a titled marriage in your head, but the wife of a gem-cutter is a good life too."

"We aren't courting, Papa!" I said, but he only laughed.

"If he is working in this Master Valin's shop, I will not have him in mine," Abraão said. "If the guild master of the Paris guild learns my technique, all of Paris will soon know. That was not part of our agreement."

Papa nodded. "You have every right to protect your workshop, Master Benzacar. André will understand."

André would not understand; of that I was certain. I had given him a promise, and I knew, even before I met him in the coffeehouse a week later, that he would be livid. He was in high spirits when he arrived, reporting to me that Valin was en route for Portugal, and would be gone at least a month. I hated disappointing him when he was this happy, so, hoping I might still change Abraão's mind, I told him Abraão was hesitant but considering his request. I told him, too, of Papa's belief that we were courting. I expected him to laugh. Instead, he reached a hand to rest atop mine.

"Would it be so bad if we were?" he asked.

I stared at him, my mind blank with surprise. Before I could formulate a response, he frowned and pulled his hand back.

"I am so grateful for all you have done for us, André," I said, trying to appease him. He fell into a pout, so I changed the subject. "Papa thinks we can finish by Easter, but we still have the problem of getting the stone to the king. If the king believes it has been in the treasury all this time, we can't just show up with it."

"I suppose you want me to retrieve it, or to convince Valin to request it. I take all the risk and for what? Am I going to meet this Master Benzacar or not?" André said.

"You can't blame him for being cautious with someone who works for the guild master."

André's face reddened. "So I've put myself in danger for nothing? I won't do it again, Juliette. I'm not taking any more risks until I see how the facets are cut."

I tried to soothe him, but André remained surly, and I left him, filled with misgivings. Somehow, I had to get Abraão to relent. André *had* to retrieve the false gem from the king. I re-doubled my efforts to praise André to Abraão, but he showed no signs of yielding.

"So your praise of André and all those meetings with him . . ." René pauses, his question left unfinished in his doubt.

"Was only to get what we needed to cut the Blue," I assure him.

He nods, but I can see a hardness coming back into his jaw. "He said in his testimony that you had seduced him. That you made promises but spurned him when you thought you no longer needed him."

"Ridiculous! I never did anything to encourage his affections. And he never felt anything for me, I promise you that."

"But you just said—"

"Has it occurred to you, René, that men can play games as well? Women are not the only ones who try to use their charms to achieve their ends."

"So you were tempted by him, then?"

I throw my hands up, annoyed by the tenacity of his doubt. "Just because he tried, René, does not mean I succumbed. André never appealed to me, and he certainly never cared for me."

I can see René believes me, but he is still glowering, so I give him an alluring glance from beneath my lowered lids, and I slip the fabric of my bodice down a little to reveal the white flesh of my shoulder. "Shall I prove my devotion to you, René?" I ask him.

He lifts an eyebrow. "That will hardly convince me you aren't a seductress," he says, but his eyes are glued to my bare skin.

"I offer only out of love, honestly and forthrightly," I say in a coquettish voice.

He laughs, and I realize I've laid it on too thick, but I hold the pose a bit longer, all big eyes and innocence.

"We have work to do," he reminds me again, tapping a finger to the page. It comes away ink-stained, and, leaning in close, he presses a fingerprint onto my bare shoulder. "To mark my place for later," he whispers, then steals a kiss that leaves me breathless.

"Go on," he urges, grinning at having gained the upper hand. "Benzacar revealed to your father his means of cutting the stone?"

I nod. "Yes, but I do not think we should describe it in the report to the king."

"It would assure him of your cooperation," René points out.

"If we don't reveal how the stone was cut, if we keep the secret, then there are still only a handful of people who know how to do it. Papa, Abraão, Isaac, and me. And if Abraão and Isaac can't be found—and I hope they can't, for their sake as well as mine—well then, if the king were to execute me it would only be Papa left who knew the secret. And everyone knows Papa has had trouble with drink. Perhaps we can convince the king that Papa needs me to keep him from drinking, and Louis needs me to ensure that future diamonds can be cut so brilliantly."

"Yes," René says, and I can see a new spark of hope in his eyes. "Yes, that just might work. So should we remove what we've written so far, about the grinding and the cleaving?"

"Any gem-cutter knows how to do that. It is only the fine control necessary for the very precise final facets that are hard to achieve. As Papa had guessed in his early experimentation, controlling the angles and achieving small, precise facets took a special apparatus that could be attached to the grinder. That is the secret that Abraão revealed to us, and that all four of us used as the weeks went by, from Epiphany to Easter."

"And André?" René asks. "Did he work on it too?"

I shake my head. I will come to André's role soon enough.

Within a few weeks, the entire pavilion, the lower portion of the stone, was done, and we had begun the smaller facets on the crown. There were seventeen of these, and they required greater skill and greater precision than the larger ones of the pavilion. With each day of cutting, the stone gave off a little more light. Whenever we wiped away the slurry to assess our progress, another surface sparked to life. It was as if the diamond was being drawn out of its melancholy with each passing day. Spirits were running high in the workshop, driving us harder and harder as Easter approached.

Ash Wednesday arrived in the cold, wet depths of February, and the Lenten fast began. To Papa and me, it was barely noticeable, so meager were our resources. Still, we worked on, with cold fingers and aching bellies.

"Do you think we can finish in time?" I asked one evening, three weeks before Easter.

Papa nodded, though his brow furrowed with concern. "We

must. So much rests on this, Juliette. If the king wears it to church on Easter Sunday, it will strike amazement in the hearts of the court—like a new miracle on the day of miracles. And the season of Easter feasts will allow him to be seen by all the nobility of France. It will be a great advantage."

"Then we will need not only to cut it by then, but to set it as well," I said.

"Setting it is nothing. It needs only the simplest of mounts, just enough to suspend it," Papa said.

"But we have no gold," Abraão said.

Papa thought for a moment. "Juliette, you have your mother's jewels, do you not?"

"I've sold most of them for food and rent," I said, "but I still have her pearl buttons and the ruby brooch."

"The brooch will do," Papa said. "We can take the stones out and melt down the setting. It is very fine gold."

My heart constricted. "But it was Maman's favorite." I had held the brooch to the last, the single memento that reminded me most of her.

"I know, *ma chérie*," Papa said. "But if we please the king now, we will have a great reward, and I can reset the brooch."

"How great?" Isaac asked. We had seldom spoken of money while we worked, but of course we all needed it.

Papa raised the Blue to the light, admiring the work we had done so far. It sparkled and glinted and stole my breath. "I shouldn't wonder if it is more than ten thousand livres."

Isaac gasped. "And how much for Avô?"

Papa smiled at him, then at Abraão. "The work has been

yours, monsieur, and the workshop. The greater share of the sum shall be yours."

"Well then," Isaac said, stepping to the grinder, "let's finish by Easter. We have no time to waste."

We redoubled our efforts then, taking the work in turns for long hours so that the grinder never stopped in its slow, steady task of carving out facets. Meanwhile Abraão, whose gnarled fingers would not serve for long hours at the grinder, began work on the setting.

Two more exhausting weeks, and the major facets of the crown were complete, with only the smallest left to cut. I *had* to get the false diamond back from the king. I needed André's help, and there was only one way to get it. I hated the idea, but seeing no other choice, I went to André and struck a bargain.

"If you can get the stone from the king, I will take you to Master Benzacar's workshop," I told him. "I will show you his cutting device and how it works." My heart squeezed painfully at the betrayal, but I could see no way around it. And I believed André deserved the chance, after all he had done for us. Without his help, we never would have had the stone to start with. Surely Papa and Abraão would not begrudge him this, if they knew the truth.

"You promise?" he asked.

I nodded.

"Then I will get it," he said.

THIRTY-THREE

Now that he was committed to his task, André wasted no time getting the rosewood box and its forged contents back from the king. Valin had just returned from Portugal a week before, so Colbert did not question the request. It was now a little more than a week from the start of Passover, two from Easter. The gem was nearly finished, but time was running out. The women of the Benzacar household were adamant that no work would be done during Passover, so we had to finish even sooner than Easter. I told André he would have to wait, and I avoided meeting him, which was easy enough to do. We were working around the clock to finish the diamond in time, which left me little time to meet him, and no time in which I might sneak him into the workshop without being seen.

The day before Passover arrived. The workshop buzzed with excited anticipation, despite everyone's exhaustion. As the sun neared the western horizon, Papa stopped the grinder and rinsed the slurry from the stone one last time. We all stared as he held it to the light of a candle. Blue sparks of light danced along the walls. The stone itself was almost too glorious to look at.

Papa breathed out a long, shuddering breath. "We have done it," he said. There was a moment's silence, then Abraão, Isaac, and I all burst into giddy laughter. We embraced each other with joy and relief, and more than a few tears.

Miriam appeared in the doorway to tell her son and father that it was nearly sunset. Time for them to prepare for Passover.

"In a moment, Miriam. Right now, bring us wine, for a toast!"

She soon reappeared with glasses and Isaac's grandmother, who poured out small cups of sweet red wine for everyone.

"To you, Master Benzacar, and to the great Tavernier Violet," Papa said, raising his glass.

"No, it's no longer Tavernier's," Isaac said.

"The Benzacar Blue?" Papa suggested.

Abraão shook his head. "I've learned my lesson about pride."

"We have shaped it for the glory of France," I said. "It will be the crown among the crown jewels."

"It will be the Blue of the Crown," Papa said.

Isaac raised his cup again. "The Blue of the Crown. May it soon shine like the sun on the breast of the Sun King."

"Though the sun is not blue," I added with a smile, and we drained our glasses. Papa paused before he raised his glass, a cloud passing across his features, and I immediately regretted the words. But then he drained his wine with the rest of us, and I thought no more of it.

Papa and I took the diamond home with us that night. Passover prevented the Benzacar family from working over the next few days, but the stone still needed its final polish, which I could do at home with goose quills and rags. Then, when we could return to the workshop, it would be ready to set in its mount.

When we arrived at our rooms, André was waiting for me on the doorstep. I smiled at him and clasped his hand. "Wait until you see!" I said, and pulled him inside. Once in our tiny room, we showed him the diamond, which glowed all the brighter for its shabby surroundings.

"*Incroyable!*" André whispered, after a long, speechless moment. "Master Pitau, you have done the impossible!"

Papa only chuckled contentedly.

"Let's celebrate!" André said.

"I am too tired. You young people go," Papa said, with a wink that annoyed me. He still thought André was courting me.

I was tired too, but I saw my chance to keep my bargain with André, so I kissed Papa good night and we set out.

"As soon as it is dark, we can go to the workshop," I told André as we stepped out of the shabby building and I turned him toward a better street. I hoped I was right. I wasn't sure how Jews celebrated Passover, but I had heard Isaac say something of a meal with neighbors, and I hoped that meant they would be away. At the very least, they would be in their house and deep in their celebration, and not in the workshop itself. Isaac had cut the glass model at night without them hearing, so surely I could sneak André in.

André was more impatient than ever as we walked the few

blocks to the hidden Jewish alley, and the key to the workshop weighed heavily in my pocket. Abraão had trustingly given it to Papa some weeks before, so that we could come and go as we needed to work our long hours. I had taken it from Papa's coat pocket without his knowledge, betraying both masters at once. But I assured myself that André could be trusted. That my luck had held this far and would hold a bit longer to get us through to success.

The lights glowed faintly through the drawn curtains in the upstairs window of the Benzacars' house. André was gazing all around, open curiosity on his face. I fitted the key into the latch on the sturdy oak door and turned it as quietly as I could. As I had hoped, the workshop was dark and empty. André and I tiptoed inside. André lit a candle in the embers at the forge and turned to the grinder.

The hinged arm that had held the stone securely was still there. In fact, everything had been left as it was when we had finished. The workshop needed a good cleaning. But the grime and dust went unnoticed by André.

At once, he sat down at the grinder and examined it, running his finger along the arm and the hinges, noting the arc of metal that measured the precise angle. He began asking questions about how it worked. As I explained, I forgot myself, at least until a lantern bobbed into the room, casting us into a bright circle of light.

"Juliette?" It was Abraão, holding a lantern aloft, looking at me with a knitted brow. He was dressed for the Passover celebration in an embroidered robe and cap, his long beard trimmed and combed, smelling of soap and looking every inch the Jew.

"Master Benzacar!" I said, jumping to my feet, trying to hide André behind me, though it was impossible. "I—I forgot my tools. For polishing the stone."

He looked past me to André. "Who is this?"

"This is André," I said. "You can trust him. If only I could explain—"

"You had my decision on this matter, Juliette," he said, and his eyes were so full of disappointment that it nearly melted me into the floor. I backed toward the door, pushing André with me.

"I am sorry, monsieur. Truly, I meant no harm." We were to the door now, but still the useless apologies were on my lips, and I repeated them again as we slipped out of the house and fled down the alley.

"You did not tell me they were Jews," André said when we were a block away. "Is that why you have kept me from them?"

"It is why he is fearful of meeting you," I said. "He could be arrested just for living here."

André nodded. "That explains why the guild did not know of them."

"You won't betray them, will you?"

He reached through the darkness and took my hand. "I have seen his work," he said. "He is a great artist, and I greatly admire what he has done. What you all have done."

"We couldn't have done it without you," I said, and I gave his hand an appreciative squeeze.

We walked on in silence. The air was warm and fresh, the first confident breaths of spring drawing through the city. Holy

Week was only a few days away, then Easter, and all the promise of resurrection. I had never felt that promise as keenly as I did now. This Easter we would celebrate not just the resurrection of the Lord, but of my father's good name and position. My guilt at betraying Abraão's trust fell away, and I was filled to brimming with contentment and gratitude, thinking the dangers and the work were behind us.

Perhaps they would have been, if I had not spoken those fateful words to my father in the toast, or if André had not spoken his next fateful words to me.

"At last, Juliette, our happiness will be complete," he said. "With our shares of the king's payment for the diamond, we will be able to afford a fine apartment of our own, and with your dowry we will furnish it with all the best."

I stopped walking and turned to him, my brow drawn down in confusion.

André smiled and took my hand again in his. "Your father has given his consent, Juliette. Will you marry me?"

I stared, my mouth hanging open. I had never thought of André as a husband, not in all the months I had worked beside him or made plans with him. Perhaps that was my own foolishness. Looking back, I can see how we had grown close after my mother's death, and we had come to rely on one another as a married couple might, but I swear to you, René, not once in all that time had I ever wanted or encouraged a proposal from him. And the matter-of-factness, the bluntness of his proposal, devoid of all warmth, convinced me that I was nothing more than another reward of his apprenticeship due to him. As he stood there, holding my hand and smiling, the shock of his proposal began to settle into a pool of dread in my gut. "Marry you? André, I had thought . . ."

His jaw tightened. "Of René Relieur?"

I shook my head, but my heart leapt at the name, and André's eyes narrowed, that unsettling gleam coming into them. "You were just a toy to him, Juliette. He has higher aspirations. I've seen him at court and can assure you, he's forgotten all about you."

"He was lying, Juliette—I swear it!" René cries out, interrupting my narrative, his fists clenched so tight his knuckles are white. He jumps out of his chair, and makes it to the other side of the cell in three long paces.

"You see?" I say, and though I am surprised by his sudden anger, I can't help but feel a little satisfaction now that the tables are turned. "He told me the same thing he told you, trying to drive us apart."

"Surely you knew of my feelings," André said, annoyed by my reaction.

"I've only been thinking of the diamond. Of staying safe. I . . ."

He lifted my hand to his lips and kissed it. "Of course, you want time to think."

"I am very tired," I said, by way of apology, and to give myself time to formulate a rejection that wouldn't hurt him too deeply.

He gently took my arm and led me back to my home, where he kissed me on the cheek. "You will give me your answer soon, *mon coeur*?" he said.

I nodded, wondering when I had become his heart. His workmate, his friend, his associate, his master's daughter—I had been all those things. But his heart?

When he was gone, I opened the door as quietly as I could, expecting my father to be asleep. Instead, he sat at the table with paper and ink, so absorbed in his work that he didn't hear me enter. I leaned over his shoulder to see what he was doing. He had traced the newly cut diamond and had drawn lines and marks across it, and now he was working feverishly on a series of new calculations.

"Papa, did you know that André wants to marry me? He says you have given your consent," I said.

He didn't even glance up. "Never mind that. Look! We can do it, Juliette! We can do it!"

I glanced at the drawing, then at his face, wondering if he had been drinking. "We *have* done it, Papa. It's finished."

"No! It's as you said: the sun is not blue. And Louis demands the sun. We have to go back to Abraão tomorrow, Juliette. Don't you see? It's not finished! We can still capture the sun in the heart of the stone!"

THIRTY-FOUR

René groans. "Do you mean to tell me that it was done weeks ago, and your father passed up the chance to give it to the king then and be done with the whole thing?"

I nod. Given where I am, I know Papa should have done just that. But knowing what the stone looks like now . . . how much more we have achieved . . .

"Papa is a true master. He cannot be done until he is sure he has created an unsurpassed splendor. Despite the beauty of the stone, in his heart of hearts, Papa saw that it could be more."

"I wish he had not seen that," René mutters.

"When you see what he has done, you will forgive him. And we must be sure to include this in your pages. This is the difference between Papa and a man like Paul Valin. Valin will settle for the easiest solution, but a man like Papa truly brings glory to the king. Write that down."

He smiles. "As you wish, mademoiselle," he says with a little bow. "And pray, what shall I write was his grand idea?"

"He revealed it when we returned to the workshop the next morning, which I was loath to do after my blatant betrayal of Abraão's trust. I felt terrible. How could I explain why I needed to let André into the workshop without revealing the extent of my deception?

"Of course, I was preoccupied by André's proposal too. I had never considered André as a marriage prospect, but did I dare refuse him? I wanted to trust André—after all, he'd been my compatriot in most things since my father had gone to Italy— but there had been a surly defiance in him in recent weeks that worried me."

"Did Abraão tell your father what you had done when you arrived there that morning?" René asks.

I shake my head. "Papa was in the grips of inspiration and noticed nothing amiss. He banged hard on the door, and when Miriam opened it, he pushed past her, shouting to Abraão to come at once, ignoring her objection about their holiday."

"And?" René prompts, his eyes wide and bright with curiosity. I smile and pause, savoring his boyish eagerness, before giving in and continuing with the story.

Abraão gave me a dark look when he entered, but Papa did not see. He was already laying out a stack of papers on the table.

"We haven't finished!" he declared, still fumbling with the papers. "Look! It's what Juliette said last night—what we have all said. The sun is not blue, but the diamond is! We can still put the sun into the stone."

He glanced around at all of us. Isaac had entered the room along with his grandmother, and they all stood staring at my father with their mouths open, as if he were a madman.

He pulled out the sparkling diamond and set it atop the papers, then waved Abraão over to it. "Look through the very center of the stone, where we left a large culet. We had to sacrifice the light there for light everywhere else, *n'est-ce pas*? But look into it there! What do you see?"

Abraão looked, then raised questioning eyes back to Papa. "Nothing."

"*Exactement!* Nothing! No color! Where the light passes straight through, it is not blue!" He pushed the diamond aside and jabbed his finger at a new sketch of the stone. "So if we cut shallow facets between the facets already there—seven shallow facets around the culet—they, too, will appear colorless, you see? And then we mount the stone in gold, with a solid gold surface beneath it." He picked up the stone and held a gold livre up behind it, and I saw what he meant. The culet, the flat circle at the center of the cut stone, gave off a burst of gold surrounded by glittering blue. I looked at the drawing and realized the new facets would form a sun. A golden sun, gleaming in the heart of the king's great blue diamond. My breath caught in my throat.

"*Que isso!* Jean Pitau, you are a genius!" Abraão said, thumping Papa on the back. Then he rushed off, shouting for Isaac to follow. In a matter of moments, they returned, dressed for work, overriding the women's howls of protest. At once, the stone we thought we had finished was again mounted in Abraão's miraculous apparatus, the first of seven new facets being ground on the pavilion, along the fine, clean lines where the existing facets met.

I watched as Papa and Abraão threw themselves into the work, my stomach knotting. We were more vulnerable than ever now that André had retrieved the box from the king. And what would I tell André? I had already arranged to meet him on Good Friday. He was to bring the real rosewood box with the counterfeit stone so that we could replace it with the real one to present to the king. But I could tell them nothing.

I met André on the steps of the church a few days later after Good Friday service. He looked at me with a hopeful smile. He was expecting more than the completion of our long work. He was ready for an answer to his proposal as well as a finished diamond. It seemed I would have to disappoint him on all fronts. I prayed he would understand.

"You won't believe what has happened," I said as he took my hand, trying to sound as excited and passionate as Papa had when the idea had come to him. I launched into an explanation before André could reply. "So, you see, it will be a few weeks yet before we present the diamond," I finished.

André was scowling. "This is foolish. The diamond was beautiful as it was. And now the king won't have it by Easter."

"But it will be so much better, don't you see? He's asked for the sun, and that's what we mean to give him. It is better to give him something perfect late than something less than perfect on time, isn't it?"

"I cannot hold Master Valin at bay forever, you know," he said, losing patience.

"Just a little more time. It will be worth it, I promise," I said, squeezing his hand, meaning only to reassure him. I remembered too late his proposal and how he would undoubtedly interpret the gesture. I never meant to lead him on, or to use his affections against him, whatever he may believe.

He put his hand over mine, somewhat softened. "And you, Juliette? Surely you've had enough time to think. About us?" he asked, his eyes searching my face expectantly.

I shifted my eyes away from his, afraid he would see my answer too clearly. "I haven't—" I began, but I didn't have time to finish.

André dropped my hand and stormed away without another word, taking the diamond's box with him. I watched him go with unease. I wasn't sure what he would do in anger, but I reassured myself that he would not betray us. After all, to do so would implicate himself, since he had been my conspirator since the beginning.

I didn't see André again for two weeks as we worked night and day, making the Blue of the Crown more brilliant still. The new facets were small, so the work went quickly, but in my heart, I knew our time was running out. Whenever the others rested, I stepped into the void, keeping the grinder turning.

We finished the last facet about three weeks after Easter, and just as Papa predicted, the stone now had an almost colorless sunburst at its center. All we had left to do was polish it and refashion its setting with a panel of gold beneath the sunburst for the full effect. It was late, so Isaac agreed to do the polishing, and sent me home to sleep in my own bed.

I was half-asleep on my feet as I approached our boarding-house, so I didn't see André waiting for me on the stoop until I was nearly upon him. He stood, and I smiled at him.

"André! We've finished!"

"At last!" he said. "Do you have it now? I can take it and put it in the box."

"It still must be polished and mounted. But soon. Another day or two."

André's jaw clenched and unclenched. "I thought you said it was done."

"It is," I said. "Bring the box tomorrow, and we will take it to the king."

"And what about you, Juliette? Do you have an answer for me?" He leaned in like he might kiss me, and I could smell the strong odor of wine on his breath. After nursing Papa through months of drunkenness, the stench repelled me and I took a step back.

"I have no dowry. I've sold my mother's jewels to feed us this past year," I said, hoping to put him off the idea. André had always had an eye for profit.

"Your share of the king's reward for the Blue will be dowry enough," he said with a smile, grasping my hand and staggering a little.

Again, I pushed him away. "Please, André, I am very tired, and you're drunk. Can you bring the box tomorrow and we'll talk then?"

"Say you'll marry me, and then I'll bring you the box," he taunted, like an errant schoolboy.

I was too tired to be teased, and I let my annoyance show on my face. Instantly, his face twisted in anger and his grip tightened on my hand. "Your father promised me I could have you," he said, his words slurring into each other.

I pulled away but couldn't break his grip. "My father only gave his consent," I said. "He would not make me marry if I did not consent as well."

"So that's it then? Your answer?"

"André, let go of me!"

"What other promises have been lies? The diamond, perhaps? Does your father intend to keep that for himself as well?"

"Of course not!"

"For himself and that Jew?" The word *Jew* came out in a contemptuous spray of spittle.

"André, you're drunk," I said again, trying to keep my fear from my voice. "Go home and go to bed."

"Have you bedded that Jew boy? Given yourself to a filthy heretic?" He pulled me up tight against him, so that his eyes burned into mine, and I saw more than alcohol there. I saw cold, hard calculation. "I have the power to ruin them all, you know. One word from me and your father and the Jews will all be arrested."

"You would only get yourself in trouble too," I said, trying to keep my voice steady and calm. "And me."

He laughed at that, and a clever gleam came into his eyes. "Not me. I have been acting under orders from my master."

"Your master?" Slowly, I realized he meant Valin. A slow boil of rage bubbled within me. All I had done—cutting the model, presenting it to Colbert, stealing the diamond—André had plotted alongside me for all of it, but now a terrible new idea struck me. Had I been simply a puppet, playing into Valin's hands all along? Had my ideas really been André's manipulation?

André watched my face, the glint in his eyes sharpening as realization dawned on me.

"How long has Valin known?" I asked through gritted teeth.

He sneered at the question. "You think you are so clever. Did you really think your forgery would go unnoticed by a man like Valin? Why do you think you've had such a luxury of time?"

"From the beginning you meant for us to do the work, so he could take the credit?" I filled my words with scorn, but it did not faze him. He had no shame.

He shook his head. "I meant to learn the skill, but you denied me that! It doesn't matter. You know it, and I can learn it from you after we are married."

"As if I would ever marry you," I spat. Again I tried to pull free of his grip, but he closed his fingers around my arm so tightly that his nails bit into my skin.

"I think you will," he taunted. "Because if you don't, your father will hang, and your Jewish friends will be burned alive."

I clenched my fists to try to hold back the tremors of rage and fear, but they were in my voice as I spoke. "And how do I know they will be safe if I marry you?"

"That's all been worked out. The Jews will be given safe

passage back to Portugal, where they belong. As for your father, Valin has found a modest position for him in Bavaria, where he can work out the rest of his days with an ample supply of wine to keep him happy."

"After all he has done for you," I started, but André interrupted with an unexpected torrent of resentment.

"All he has done? He kept me enslaved for eight years by refusing to pass me out of apprenticeship! It is Master Valin to whom I owe gratitude, not Pitau. But marry me, Juliette, and I will be merciful to you and your father. And as my wife, you will regain your honor with the guild."

I spat at his feet. "I've met dogs with more honor! I'd rather marry one of them than have anything to do with you."

At that, he shook me so hard my teeth rattled in my head. "Marry me or you will burn with them," he hissed into my ear, like the snake he is. Hatred surged through me along with a rush of panic, remembering that night in Fouquet's cell.

With new strength I twisted in his grip, and jammed my knee hard into his groin, giving him the answer he deserved.

With a grunt, he loosened his grip on my arm and crumpled to his knees.

I turned and ran.

"You'll be sorry, Juliette," he gasped after me. "You'll be sorry!"

I flew back to Abraão's workshop. Papa was pouring molten gold into the mold Abraão had crafted for the setting, and when I came exploding into the room, he spilled it onto the floor.

"Juliette! What—" Isaac began, but then he saw my face. They all did. The room went as silent as the grave.

"You must flee!" I managed to breathe out. "We have been betrayed."

Papa only stared at me. "Betrayed? But how?"

Tears were streaming down my face, but I forced out the words. "I lied, Papa," I said, heaving a heavy sigh. "We never had the commission. I stole the diamond."

Blood drained from Papa's face and he reached a hand to the bench to steady himself. I turned to Abraão. "André is bringing soldiers. He knows you are Jews. You must flee, all of you. I am sorry. I am so very sorry."

Not a moment was lost after that. Miriam ran down the alley, raising the alarm among their Jewish neighbors, and soon people were scattering, carrying what they could on their backs.

It took us longer to gather Abraão's possessions in the workshop. We had the gold in the mold, and the diamond. Abraão did not want to leave his apparatus either, his most precious secret that allowed him to make precise cuts, but in the end, he had to, as we could find no way for them to carry it. His daughter, now frantic, pulled him away into the dark streets of Paris.

That left only Papa and me in the workshop. I looked again at Papa, his head in his hands, collapsing in on himself. I had repeated the same mistake again. I see it now: I was, as you have said, blinded by my ambition, and mistaking that for love, I ruined the very people I was trying to save. This time, though, I would not make things worse by trying to make amends. This time, I would take the blame, and the punishment. I would not let it fall on Papa's shoulders.

André meant to show Colbert the forgery as proof that we had taken the diamond. If we all fled, it would only confirm our guilt. The king would stop at nothing to find us. My father needed a little more time to polish the stone and finish the setting. He couldn't do that if he was running. There was only one slim chance for him to redeem himself now.

"You must go, Papa. You must find a place of refuge where you can finish the jewel, so that you can deliver it as planned."

"But where can we go?" he asked.

"Not we," I said. "You. I can buy you some time. Finish the diamond and deliver it to the king."

"You are all I have left, Juliette. I can't lose you," he said, pulling me to him.

I ached to cling to him and never let him go. So long I had striven for his approval, and now at last, when I had truly destroyed us all, to have him give it was more than I deserved. Reluctantly, I drew myself out of his embrace and wiped the tears I had not meant to cry.

I put the diamond into his pocket and gently pushed him toward the door. "You won't lose me, if you finish the diamond and take it to the king," I assured him. "They will pardon me when they see its beauty. They will see that we have worked in secret for the great glory of Louis, our *Roi-Soleil*."

He hesitated, his eyes searching my face, beseeching me to come with him. He reached again for my hand.

I gave him a confident smile, one more lie upon so many

others, and another nudge toward the door. "Finish the jewel and take it to the king, Papa. It will be exactly as we planned."

He took a deep, shaky breath and glanced around the workshop. "I could use a drink," he said.

"Go, Papa! Don't stop for anything!" I gave him a quick embrace and whispered an idea of where he might take shelter and not be discovered. Then I pushed him from the workshop and latched the door behind him, so he was forced to flee.

I retreated to the workshop, where I pulled Abraão's secret tool from the grinder, and threw it into the hot forge. The wood of the arm caught and burned at once. I pumped the bellows until the heat was enough to warp and twist the remaining metal beyond recognition. André would not have it.

When that was done, I brushed the dust from my skirts and my hair as best I could, and I returned to the receiving room, where I sat down in the fine old chairs of Abraão's front hall.

I dried my tears. And I waited—for André. For the king's soldiers. For my doom.

I close my eyes and breathe out a long sigh. I feel exhausted beyond words, like I've poured out all my strength with my story, and maybe even a part of my soul.

"The king knows the rest," I say quietly. "André brought the soldiers to the workshop. They searched but did not find the diamond. Nor did they find the apparatus we had used to cut it, to André's frustration. They demanded I tell them where the others had taken the diamond, but I refused to speak. They beat me and kicked me. They even held my hand in the forge, but I said noth-ing. Neither did André, who stood by watching. André, who had claimed to want me for a wife. When Monsieur Colbert arrived, he put a stop to the torture, insisting I should be brought before the king."

I shrug helplessly. "And here we are."

THIRTY-FIVE

"I will *kill* André!" The words burst from René's throat in a feral growl of rage. "I will tear the bastard apart with my bare hands! I will cut him down and grind him under my boot like the filthy cockroach he is!"

I've never seen René like this. His face is nearly purple, and he clenches the quill in his hand so hard it snaps. Even his anger when he first came into my cell this morning was mild in comparison. I flinch away from him. My sudden alarm seems to clear his head, and his expression instantly transforms into one of such contrite tenderness that my knees go weak beneath me.

"My dear Juliette," he says, and standing, he opens his arms to me. I press into him, and as his arms enfold me, I crumble into tears. Not a gentle weeping, but deep, wracking sobs. A torrent of all the pain and loss and struggle that I have endured these past two years. After holding up Papa for so long, having someone to hold me is such a sweet relief, and I find myself leaning heavily into him, savoring his strong support. He nuzzles his nose to mine, and his soft lips give me a tender kiss. Of course, he means for it to comfort me, but I am overcome once again with a wave of regret. Why couldn't I have accepted Papa's fate, and gone quietly from court? This—this love, this sanctuary—is enough for me, and yet I couldn't see it until now, when it is all too late.

I pull away a little, not wanting to leave the haven of his arms, but knowing I don't deserve it.

"I am no better than André," I hiccup through my tears. "I sacrificed everything—risked my father's life, the Benzacar family—and for what?"

"You are *not* like André!" René says, his grip tightening around me, drawing me back to his heart. "You risked flying close to the sun for the people you loved, not for yourself."

"But if I had accepted our fate after Twelfth Night . . ." I can't finish the sentence. The precious life I might have had with René, all squandered. It is too much loss to express with the simplicity of words.

René holds me, stroking my hair until my tears subside. Then, moving gently, he helps me to the cot, and I sit down on the edge. I expect him to sit beside me, but instead he kneels on the floor before me, taking my unburned hand in his.

"René, you will ruin your clothes," I protest.

"Forget my clothes, Juliette. Forget this foul cell." I look into his eyes, warm as honeyed sunshine, and I do. I forget everything but me and him, and the fathomless sea of love in those eyes.

"Juliette, I thought I'd lost you when your father fell from grace, and again when the king stole your father's design."

I open my mouth, wanting to reassure him that that's all behind us, but he shushes me, determined to finish what he has to say.

"I've nearly lost you so many times, I won't risk losing you again," he says. "So I'm asking you, Juliette, will you marry me?"

Everything that I am, that I have ever been, wants him. Before my lips can form words, my body is saying yes, my face beaming and my arms around his neck. But then the reality of the bare stone walls crashes over me again.

"But . . . I'm to die tomorrow." The words choke me as I say them, not just for the terror they hold, but because they stand between me and the one thing I want more than anything.

"I will marry you here," he whispers.

"Here?"

"Now," he says.

"Now?" I look around me at the barren cell. "René, there is no priest."

He shrugs. "God sees all. If we make our vows before him, we have no need of a priest. Will you have me, Juliette?"

My answer bursts from my mouth amid a torrent of laughter and kisses. I cannot resist the pull his body has on mine, and I don't even try.

René's face glows with happiness. Louis thinks himself the sun, but René outshines him, even without diamonds or gold embroidery or the treasury of France.

His step now buoyant as any bridegroom's, he pulls me back to the table. With the penknife, he strips the feathers from a quill, then cuts a length and curls it into a ring, tucking one end into the other. He takes my left hand, and slips the simple ring onto my finger.

"Are you ready?" he asks, needlessly. I've never been more ready for anything in my life, and I tell him so. He lifts my un-damaged left hand in his own and looks solemnly into my eyes.

"With this ring, I take you as my wife, Juliette Pitau, to honor and cherish." He pauses, then adds, "As my little mouse, who will do nothing dangerous ever again, all the days of our lives."

I laugh, even as I sniff to hold back tears of joy. "Fashion an-other," I say, and he creates another quill ring, which I slip onto his finger. "I take you, René Relieur, to be my husband, to honor, cherish, and obey, even if you were a ragpicker and not the son of a gentleman, all the days of our lives," I reply, my voice catching at the end, fearful that this vow will be dissolved on the king's scaffold tomorrow.

The corners of René's eyes crinkle. "I don't think you should vow to obey, Juliette. We both know that is beyond you once you get an idea in your head."

I give him a secretive grin and an upward flick of my eye-brows. Let him make of that what he will.

He pours us each a cup of wine, and entwining our arms, we drink together, our own makeshift cup of Communion.

"Then let us be declared man and wife in the eyes of God," René says, and in agreement, I press my lips to his, tasting the sweetness of wine and the victory of love over all things. He kisses me back, full and sweet, and the longing that pours from him rapidly lights my own. I pull at the hem of his shirt, eager to get my hands beneath it. When it is loose, he raises his arms, inviting me to pull it off over his head, which I do, then step back to admire my work. I have seen men stripped to the waist before—blacksmiths, and wool dyers, and my father's apprentices sweating at the grinder—but this clean, unscarred young body before me is a whole new glory. I bite my lip and contemplate how to start on his breeches. He obliges me by leading my hand to the buttons, though my fingers fumble through the task, distracted as I am by the hot kisses he presses along my neck and shoulder.

He kicks the pants from around his ankles, then grins as he begins loosening the laces of my bodice, releasing the tight stays that hold my figure rigid. It takes him longer to get through the layers of my petticoats. I am hit by a sudden wave of shyness as he lifts my shift over my head at last and the cool prison air splashes over my bare body. I am bruised and dirty, hardly the fair feast for his eyes that a bridegroom desires, and I worry that he is disappointed, but he reassures me with soft caresses, and soon we are in each other's arms on the bed, my shyness giving way to more urgent desires. He moves on top of me, but pain pierces my side as his weight settles against me, and I cry out. He pulls back, his eyes full of worry.

"My ribs," I say, pressing a hand to my side and gasping for breath. "It's where they kicked me. I am sorry." I can't look at him, embarrassed for undermining the passion of the moment.

"Oh, my love," he says. "I should have thought—" Gently he lifts me upward and repositions me in his arms, so that my body does not bear the weight of him, and more gently still, he holds and kisses me until the pain subsides and the passion returns. Only then, moving slowly to ensure my comfort, do we once again entwine in a slow-rhythm love, completing each other as we consummate our marriage.

Dark night has claimed the Bastille. In the glow of the guttering candle, we lie still in each other's arms, savoring each fragile second left to us.

"It's not enough, is it?" I say into the silence. My head is upon his chest, his arm around me. I can hear the strong, steady beating of his heart, and wish that my own could match it.

"Enough?" he asks, his fingers playing idly among my curls.

"The confession," I say. "It's not enough for the king to pardon me."

His hand tenses at the back of my head. I can tell he's trying to stay calm for my sake. "We have been careful in our wording. Surely the king will see that what you did was entirely in his service. He will see how much he needs you."

"But I've broken so many of his laws, and I challenged him before his whole court. He cannot let that stand."

René unwinds his arm and sits up at the edge of the bed. Then he stands, and begins searching for his clothes. "Then we must flee."

"We are in the king's prison," I remind him. "You can walk out of here, but I cannot."

"I will tell the guard we have finished, and when he comes to let me out, we will overpower him. I will take his weapons and we will fight our way out if we have to. We will run too far for the king to find us."

I put a hand on his arm to still his frantic preparation. "It will never work, René. If we lived long enough to escape the Bastille, they would find us. All roads from Paris are watched."

"Your father has not been caught, nor the Jews," he says, pulling on his boots.

"René, stop!" I insist, and he finally pauses long enough to meet my gaze. "I will not go."

"But you have said yourself, the king will not pardon you. It is your best chance, Juliette."

I shake my head. "I have risked the lives of too many people already. I will not let you become a fugitive on my account."

I lay my hand on his cheek, and he puts his own over it, holding it to him, turning his face just enough to kiss my fingers. His eyes are squeezed shut, but I can see the tears on his lashes.

"If the diamond is really as beautiful as you say—"

"It is," I say. "You've never seen anything like it."

"The king is a great lover of beauty, especially when it enhances his own. Surely when he sees the diamond, and learns how diligently you strived in his honor, he will relent."

"*If* he sees the diamond," I say, daring to raise a fear I haven't spoken until now.

René's eyes open wide. "Your father knows to bring it to court tomorrow, doesn't he? He wouldn't try to escape with it."

"Papa would never steal a jewel. But what if he's drunk, René? What if he's fallen apart again, as he did after Maman's death, and has forgotten everything?"

René is back on his feet, tightening the belt at his waist. "Tell me where he is, Juliette. I will bring him to court."

I hesitate. "Do you think the confession is enough to convince the king to spare my father? I will not send him to deliver the diamond if it means he goes to his death as well."

"The king is no fool. He will not kill the only man who can create such glories in his name. Valin has failed. André has failed. The Jews are missing. He will have to spare your father."

I want to believe him, but I remember the fury in the king's eyes, burning like a thousand suns. I cannot let my father risk it.

"Will you do something for me, René?"

"Anything, *mon coeur.*"

I, too, rise from the cot. I can't bear to be parted from René, but if there is any hope for salvation, any at all, I must send him away now. "Go to the Monastery of Saint-Éloi. Tell them I have sent you."

I go to the table and take up the last clean sheet of paper left. Quickly, I compose a letter to Papa, though the pain in my hand is excruciating and blood is soaking through the bandages before I am done. I have told Papa to give the diamond to René and to stay in the sanctuary of the church. I fold the note and pass it to René.

"Retrieve the stone. Take it and my account to Colbert. Convince him first. The king respects Colbert; perhaps he can be persuaded to argue for clemency for Papa."

"And for you," René says.

"And for me," I agree, though I know this is too much to hope for. "Do not tell them where Papa is. Not until the king has agreed to pardon him."

René puts the letter into his breast pocket, then gathers me once again into his arms, and I rest my cheek against his chest. I do not know how long we stay like that—perhaps minutes, perhaps more. Then he kisses me, long and deep, a kiss for holding and parting all at once.

"I will not let them take you from me," he whispers, when our lips part at last.

"Go, René, quickly. You will need time to convince Colbert."

He hesitates, his eyes pleading with me. "How can I leave you here?" he says, his lips dipping to mine again.

I pull away. "Please, René, go! You must!"

He releases me from his arms and nods, an expression of torment on his face.

"*Au revoir, mon coeur,*" he says. "This is not goodbye."

Then he gathers the pages of my confession from the table and strides to the door. Three crisp knocks bring the guard to open it, and he is gone, into the night.

The candle dies in René's wake. I return to my cot, chilled by the emptiness of it. Never have I felt so alone. The night passes in a blackness so complete it seems to stretch from God's heaven to the very core of my soul. I try to comfort myself with the memory of René's touch, or the feel of the stiff quill ring on my finger, but this only makes me feel his absence like an open wound. I try to draw sleep over me, but I know it is useless. I am all alone with only darkness stretching before me.

Thirty-Six

I feel like I've been lying in the dark for an eternity, and yet it is all too soon when the key turns in the lock and the door opens, as I know it signals that my judgment is at hand. It is still dark, so I can't be sure if it is very late, or very early.

"On your feet," the guard says from the doorway, and I struggle up with difficulty, every muscle and bone stiff and sore. With a guard at either elbow, I once again enter the prison's courtyard, where a shuttered carriage awaits. To the east, a band of gray on the horizon suggests dawn is only a few hours away.

As before, the carriage takes me to a tradesmen's doorway at the back of the palace, where I enter unseen from the street. Wagons unload crates of vegetables and boxes of candles in the predawn hours. I enter the king's house behind a slaughtered pig, and I cannot keep my gaze from the horror of its lolling head and vacant eyes.

One guard before me and one behind, I climb flight after flight of narrow stairs. It is a difficult climb—not because the stairs are steep, but because my final sentence lies at the top. Why am I being brought here so secretively, at such an early hour? I want to believe there is some plot afoot to see me spared, but other horrible possibilities send an uncontrollable shudder through my legs, and the guards have to hoist me up the last few steps.

Around a corner, along a corridor, and through a large, elaborate door, and we enter the brightly lit boudoir of the king. It is exactly as I remember it from that fateful night when he commanded the Violet be cut, except without the crowd of bystanders. Louis is seated in an ornate chair, wearing a long, heavy dressing gown of dark-blue velvet, golden suns embroidered a thousand times across its expanse. As if anyone could possibly forget his chosen moniker. The robe drapes around him and pools at his feet, so that only the toes of his golden slippers show. Jean-Baptiste Colbert stands to his right, the pages of my confession in his hand. They are the only people in the room, outside of my guards and me.

The king raises an eyebrow. I don't take his meaning until my guard presses hard on my shoulder, forcing me to kneel before him. Quickly, albeit too late, I lower my eyes and take on an attitude of abject humility. I wait for the king to address me, but he does not, and the long silence stretches, thin and tight. I do not dare to look at him, but I sneak a glance at Colbert. He is watching the door.

We continue this way, the cold stones threatening to buckle my aching knees. At last, the door opens again and booted feet enter behind where I kneel.

"Juliette!" Papa cries.

My hope drains away as Papa sinks to his knees beside me. René has not been successful in keeping him away. Papa drops the rosewood box he carries and gathers me in his arms. "Juliette, *mon petit bijou*, what have they done to you?"

"Nothing, Papa," I assure him, but I am looking at the rosewood box where it lies, knowing what it holds, and knowing that our last chance is slipping away. The king now has it all—me, Papa, and the diamond. He can do what he will without consequence. As if he reads my thought, the king now interjects himself into our meeting.

"Monsieur Pitau," the king says in a cool voice. "I hope I haven't been roused at this hour merely to see this touching reunion. I believe you have something of mine?"

Papa looks me hard in the eye. His breath smells of wine, and his eyes are red-rimmed and watery. He has been drinking, but he still has his wits about him. There is a determination in his gaze that harkens back to the old days, when he was the master of his destiny.

He picks up the box and stands, then drops into a deep bow before the king.

"Your Majesty, I present you with the Blue of the Crown. The work of my daughter, as much as anyone. If you are pleased with it, I pray you will find it within your infinite wisdom and mercy to spare her life," he says, and holds out the box.

Louis snatches it away before Papa's plea is done, assuring everyone in the room that he is making no bargains. He throws open the lid to reveal the finished stone. Then he freezes, his lips slightly parted, his face illuminated with his greed, his amazement, and a pale-blue reflection off the stone. I hold my breath, watch his eyes dilate. It is a full minute before he speaks, and then it is only a whispered "*Incroyable!*"

Reverently, Louis lifts the diamond from its cushion. Suspended from a blue velvet ribbon, it turns and dances and winks and laughs, the captured sun a flash of gold amid a glittering blue fire. A murmur of admiration shifts through the room as the diamond sparkles, a thing so bright and beautiful that even I forget for a moment that death awaits me.

At last, the king lowers the ribbon around his neck, and the great blue diamond, the golden sun at its heart, comes to rest in its true home over the heart of *le Roi-Soleil*. His lips curl with satisfaction and his eyes lift to Papa.

"Jean Pitau, you have done the impossible at last."

"I have done only what was asked of me, Your Majesty. I have done only what will serve you."

"And how have you achieved it?"

"Through the grace of God, Your Majesty," Papa says, his voice solemn and earnest. "And through Juliette's great sacrifice."

"Hmm." The king's fingers stroke the jewel as he shifts this way and that on his chair, admiring his reflection in a large looking glass. "No glass this time? No trickery?"

"Only diamond and gold, Your Majesty."

The king nods, his eyes still on himself and his magnificent prize. "And you now have the means to cut other diamonds this way?" he asks. I have a moment of panic, remembering that I destroyed the apparatus to keep André from it, but then I see the confident light in Papa's eyes and relax. He remembers it well enough to re-create it.

To the king, he simply inclines his head in a gesture of assent. "I await your command."

There is a long silence before the king can finally pull his eyes away from his reflection. He gestures toward the papers in Colbert's hand. "It takes great devotion to duty to take such risks to see my command met. I admire that devotion. And I am willing, under the circumstances, to forgive your lapse in judgment at Twelfth Night, for which I believe you have been adequately punished," he says, addressing Papa and ignoring me entirely. Still, his words awaken a flicker of hope in my heart. If he will forgive my father for a great public embarrassment, perhaps he will do the same for me.

"I trust that such devotion and loyalty will continue to guide you if you are reinstated to your position as crown jeweler, and that you will put the sun into gems only for me and at my command?"

"Of course, Your Majesty," Papa says, bowing again. "I thank you for the privilege of serving you."

"Very well then. See it done, Colbert. And you, Monsieur Pitau, you will make a formal presentation of the Blue to me in front of the full court this afternoon. Be sure Master Valin is in attendance."

"Yes, Your Majesty," both Colbert and my father say. Then, at last, the king turns his eyes to me, and my heart hammers so hard I think I might faint.

"Juliette Pitau," he says, drawing my name out much as he did the day before, this time savoring the suspense in which he holds me. "There is one thing, at least, that you did not lie about." He holds the diamond aloft, admiring it again. "It *nearly* exceeds my imagination."

"Thank you, Your Majesty," I whisper, as one of the guards jabs me to elicit a response.

"I am told you went to great effort to see it made so."

"Yes, Your Majesty," I say again, the tiny flame of hope in me growing stronger. Then he turns his full gaze on me, and the flame is snuffed out.

"But you have confessed to conspiracy and theft against the crown, and that remains punishable by death."

Despite everything, the pronouncement sends a shock through me, and I must put my hand to the cold stones to keep from collapsing.

"No!" Papa cries, and falls again to his knees at my side, wrapping a protective arm around me.

"In deference to your father, I will grant you a private execution by hanging," he says, his tone gracious, as if he expects our thanks.

"Please, Your Majesty," Papa begs, "she is the only family left to me."

The king waves away his pleas with an airy sweep of his bejeweled hand. "You are not so old, Monsieur Pitau. You can still find a wife, I think. A daughter is not so hard to replace." The king nods toward the guards. They pull me to my feet and out of my father's grasp.

It is then that the king's eyes catch me. They carry equal parts admiration and distrust. The corner of his mouth twitches, amused, as if my fate is all a game and he has just made the winning move. "Perhaps, mademoiselle, Monsieur Fouquet forgot to tell you that Icarus was the child, not the father. You should have studied your Ovid more carefully."

"You see and acknowledge that I was the architect, then," I say. Under other circumstances I would never venture something so bold to the king, but I have nothing more to lose. His only answer is a very slight incline of his head, but it's enough.

"Then you will pardon the J— You will pardon all others involved?" I ask.

The king's glare silences me. I am only angering him. "Mademoiselle, there are no Jews in Paris. Do you suggest I do not even know my own city?" He nods toward Colbert, who tosses the pages of my confession into the fireplace. They curl and crackle as the flames take them. The only other sound in the chamber is my father weeping. There will be no acknowledgment of all the Benzacars have done for the king. There will be no safety for them either.

"Juliette, *mon petit bijou*," Papa says, reaching for me, but the guards pull me away from him.

"I did it for you, Papa." It is the only farewell I have time for before Colbert speaks the king's orders to the men at the door.

"René, see to it that a priest is sent to confess her. I will conclude matters with His Majesty."

I had not realized until now that René is in the room. He must have entered with Papa and stayed behind me, by the door. I can see as I turn to leave that he has not slept. He has spent his entire night meeting with Colbert and retrieving Papa, and somehow bringing about this clandestine predawn meeting. Now he stands stiffly by the door, struggling to keep all expression from his face, and I know myself for the selfish monster I have been, to have regained his affection only to have it break his heart now.

He follows quietly behind my guards as we leave the palace, back out to the black-curtained carriage at the back. I am thrust inside once again. René speaks quietly to the guards and to the coachmen before he climbs in next to me and closes the door.

I am going to hang. My stomach, though empty, roils with nausea, and I cannot think. For two years, I have come up with a way out of one disaster after another, but now I cannot stir a single useful thought in my brain.

René takes my hand and grips it hard. And I squeeze it back. It is the only solid thing in my collapsing world. If I look at him, I will collapse too.

As the carriage rolls away from the palace, René lowers his arm around me and tilts his head toward mine. He does not speak, knowing the coachman might hear us, but he pulls back the curtain a bit, directing my gaze out at Paris one last time. I look, too desolate to care—until I realize the driver is not returning to the Bastille. In fact, he is moving away from it. I sit up, suddenly alert. On the outskirts of the city, I finally turn to René. I can barely see him in the darkness, but he must see or sense the question in my gaze.

"You are not Icarus, Juliette," he says quietly. "Not yet."

"But . . ."

"The beauty of a private execution," he says, "is that no one will know if you aren't in attendance."

I had been afraid to die, but now a much greater fear grips me. "René, you can't! He will hang you in my place!"

René's arm draws me tighter to him, and he gives me a wink and a secretive smile, waiting for me to put the pieces together. The coachman and guards are with us, so either René has found massive sums of money for bribes, or there is a greater conspiracy afoot here. Apparently, I am not the only one capable of schemes and plans. I look up into René's face with a new appreciation.

"The king cannot openly pardon you, Juliette, just as you predicted. Not when the whole court was watching. But Colbert was able to convince him of the risk in executing one of the few people in the world who knows the secret of putting fire in a diamond, when your father has proven so fragile. And there is the matter of the Jews."

"What about them?"

"They seem to have fled Paris and as yet have not been found. Colbert thinks they may be headed for Amsterdam. Another reason to commute your sentence to banishment."

Banishment. It should be a terrible word, but given that, only a moment ago, I thought I was bound for the gallows, a wave of relief engulfs me.

"You will be taken to Amsterdam," René continues. "You will have a letter of introduction to the house of Madame de Klerk, the wife of an associate of Colbert's, who will report to him if you do not comply, do you understand?"

I nod, still overwhelmed and rendered silent.

"In exchange for your freedom, you are to look for the Jews in Amsterdam—there is a large community of Jewish craftsmen there. You are to report your findings to de Klerk, who will report them to Colbert."

"I cannot turn them in, René," I protest.

He presses his fingers to my lips to silence me. "It is the agreement you will accept in exchange for your life," he says, tipping his head toward the front of the coach, where the driver and the guard may well be hearing us.

"I will look for them," I agree. Looking and finding, after all, are not the same thing.

I press my cheek against his. It is rough with stubble, as he has had no time to attend to his own needs since yesterday morning. "I know this is your doing, René. However can I thank you?"

"I wish I was as clever as you," he says, looking down at our clasped hands and stroking my fingers. "I wish I had secured a future for us."

"What do you mean?" It hadn't occurred to me, amid this unexpected revelation, that he had no place in the plan.

"The banishment is for life, Juliette. You are not to return to France or have communications with anyone in the country. The penalty for doing so will be death."

"And you?" I ask, barely able to form the words. I trace my fingers along the crisp line of his cheek, the narrow ridge of his nose, the soft, high curve of his upper lip, trying to commit them to memory.

His gaze falters and falls to his lap. "I am bound to Colbert's service, to staying with your father and assuring that he holds to his deal and is able to cut more stones in the same style for the king. That was the deal I had to make with Colbert before he would agree to argue for your life with Louis. I am sorry, Juliette. It was the only way."

I press myself now into his arms, my head against his chest, to hear that strong, steady heart once more. He holds me for a moment, then tucks his fingers under my chin to lift my lips to his. This time, our lips press together in a kiss that must last a lifetime.

All too soon, the driver turns off the road and comes to a stop. René releases me from his arms as the coachman jumps down from his seat.

The sun breaks over the horizon as he opens the door. It glows through the branches of an apple orchard, white petals swirling like snow on a gentle morning breeze. Paris lies away to the east; we are on the road to the sea.

Beside the carriage sits a hay wagon, with a tall farmer on the seat, holding the reins as if impatient to depart.

René reaches into his pocket and pulls out an envelope. "*Le Renard* sails for Amsterdam from Le Havre in three days' time. Your passage is here. She is a merchant ship. You should be comfortable. You will also find letters of introduction for you at the house of de Klerk."

"Will I never see you again?" I say, pressing my hand to his cheek, not caring what the coachman sees or thinks. He moves my hand to his lips and kisses each finger with an expression of such tenderness that I think I might break.

"I am sorry, Juliette."

"Then I release you," I say, though I have to fight down the tears to say it. "I release you from the pact we made last night."

"No, Juliette—"

"Yes. You must find another to marry and be happy."

The coachman clears his throat with a dry cough. "Mademoiselle, it is time to go," he says.

Tearing my eyes from René's face, I take the coachman's offered hand and step down from the coach. René follows, and we walk to the hay wagon. We face each other one last time beside it.

"Promise me, Juliette, you will not attempt to return to France," René says, gripping my good hand till the bones ache. "The king will be merciless if you do. Promise you will stay safely in Amsterdam."

"I promise," I whisper, wondering how I will bear staying away when I can't bear to leave.

The coachman clears his throat a second time.

René offers a hand to help me into the wagon bed.

"No one is to know of your leaving. You must conceal yourself in the hay until you are far from Paris," René says.

I nod, but I stay as I am, perched on the back of the wagon, still gripping René's hand.

"*Adieu, mon coeur,*" René says, and I begin to weep, for it is *adieu* in all its finality, and not *au revoir.* Still I do not release his hand. The coachman gives an annoyed snort and shouts an order to the wagon master, who cracks the reins. The cart jolts forward, and only then do our fingers pull apart. The guards turn René back to the carriage, and we are carried away from each other. I watch the coach until it is only a spot of dust at the gates of Paris, then I curl into the hay and sink into a dreamless sleep despite the bumping cart.

THIRTY-SEVEN

AMSTERDAM, 1675

Time passes slowly in Amsterdam, a city with more water than land. The canals, the frozen winters, the dozens of languages spoken on the street—all are foreign and baffling, and two years drag by in a dull repetition of chores.

I am not exactly a prisoner in the de Klerk household, but I am watched, and I know Colbert receives reports of my behavior. Not that there is much to report. I serve as a lady's companion for the eldest daughter, and seldom have a moment of my own. Adrienne de Klerk is a pleasant young lady, utterly unable to extend her curiosity or imagination beyond the quest for a suitable husband. She helps me learn Dutch, and I teach her French, carry her shopping, and accompany her to balls and picnics. Other attendants flirt on such occasions, but no one courts me, and I don't wish them to. I do not want any of the men here. My heart still belongs to René, even though I released him from our union. Even though I doubt, as I look back on it, that he would have joined with me in that impromptu marriage if he had thought I would survive past the next day.

For many months after arriving in Amsterdam, I expected to hear something from him. I could not quite believe that my banishment was real—that I would remain utterly cut off from all those I loved in France. In the moment when I had expected death, I had felt like I was being spared entirely. But as the months passed in silence, I began to realize that I am isolated and alone. I don't even know if my father knows I'm alive. Did they tell him the truth of my banishment, or was he led to believe, along with the rest of court, that I was hanged that day in the courtyard of the Bastille?

After a year in Amsterdam, I committed myself to thinking of it as home. Even so, I cannot make it feel like home, and I mourn the loss of France, Papa, and especially René every night when I retire to my lonely bed.

At first, I did not set about the task Colbert had given me, to seek out the Benzacar family. Not in any official capacity, anyway. I did not know what Colbert intended to do should he find them. Louis had spared me only to ensure that the secret of the Mazarin cut was not lost, but that didn't mean he wanted others to access it. He could be ruthless in his quest to outshine his rivals, and he had no love for Jews.

I used my duties as Adrienne's companion to keep me in the house and avoid searching the city, but Colbert apparently urged Madame de Klerk to release me from those duties for his task, so she began sending me daily to one market or another, with a reminder to keep an eye open.

It was easy enough to learn where the Jewish district could be found. Though Amsterdam is part of a Spanish colony, the Jews have not yet been expelled, and many Spanish and Portuguese Jews live openly in the Jodenbuurt, the Jewish quarter, where they ply their trades as moneylenders, goldsmiths, and gem-cutters.

I did not seek out the Benzacars for the sake of France, but I could not stay away from the Jodenbuurt, even when my duties did not have to take me there. I told myself it was because I was drawn to the sounds and smells of the many workshops. The busy Jodenbuurt felt like home, but I knew it was more than that. I was looking for familiar faces. I was looking for Isaac.

Nearly a year after my arrival, I finally saw him. I was walking aimlessly through the quarter when I spied him, standing in the doorway of a gem-cutter's workshop, taking the evening air. He wore an apprentice's apron, and his lanky body had filled out, his chest and arms grown broad with hard work and the onset of manhood.

I stopped suddenly, frozen in place by surprise and joy. Others on the street bumped into me, toppling eggs from my marketing basket and spitting rude remarks in Dutch and Spanish.

The commotion caught Isaac's attention, and he craned his neck to see what had caused it. For the briefest of moments our eyes met, and he held my gaze. Isaac's face filled with surprise. Then his eyes narrowed and his jaw clenched. He turned abruptly and disappeared back into his workshop. I knew not to follow. I knew I had not been forgiven for all I had cost them, nor would I be.

With a heavy heart, I fled the Jodenbuurt. Had I not disobeyed his grandfather and brought André to the workshop, they would not have had to flee their home. They would have received the payment and the honor they deserved. Isaac had no doubt lost his sweetheart at the bakery, and perhaps much more. Had old Abraão and his wife even survived their flight from France? Whatever had happened, I knew I had done enough damage to their lives, and I vowed to leave them alone.

That night, and for many nights thereafter, I prayed that Isaac would have a better life in Amsterdam, where he could be a true apprentice in a true workshop. I prayed, too, that they might someday forgive me. I did not tell Colbert I had found them, and I did not return to the Jodenbuurt.

Another year has passed since then. I ply my needle and give French instruction to Adrienne, under the watchful eye of her mother. The dull obedience of my life here has soaked into my bones, so I have no curiosity at all when Adrienne comes skipping into the parlor waving a letter, thinking it is the sweet, secret words of a paramour. I am dumbfounded when she holds the letter out to me.

"You have an admirer, I think," Adrienne sings in French. I have been teaching her French for two years, but her words still cling to their Dutch cadence and come out like a song.

"How could I have an admirer?" I answer in Dutch, which must in turn sound flat to Adrienne.

"Open it," Adrienne prods, pushing the letter into my hands and hovering where she can read over my shoulder.

The letter is written on an expensive, heavy paper. I don't recognize the seal, but when I spy the handwriting, my heart stops dead in my chest.

I cannot tear the seal open fast enough. It is a simple message, written in perfect, looping script that flows cleanly across the page. Written in French, it reads,

> *Mademoiselle Juliette Pitau,*
>
> *Your order is ready at Elzevier's Print Shop and Bindery. Kindly pick it up at your convenience.*
>
> *The proprietor*

"What did you order?" Adrienne asks. Like most rich girls, she is enraptured by any hint of a secret not her own that might be passed around. Sometimes, I let her "discover" my secrets, but this time, I will not. Instead, I arrange my face to imply boredom, even though my heart has been transformed into a captive dove, beating against my rib cage.

"It is a copy of Ovid, to help us improve our Latin," I say, surprising myself with my excuse. I haven't thought of Ovid in years. Two years.

Adrienne sighs heavily and turns away, utterly uninterested now, as I knew she would be. She complains constantly of her

Latin lessons. She would much rather study the latest styles at her dressmaker's.

That afternoon, while she is practicing harp with the music maestro, I hurry from the house and along the canals and avenues to the Elzevier Print Shop. I have never been there, but I find it quickly, my heart dragging me to it like an impatient dog on a leash.

Little bells announce my arrival as, with a shaking hand, I push the door open and step inside, into the pleasant aromas of leather and parchment. Shelves of books and pamphlets line the walls, but my eyes skim past them, hungry for only one sight. Then a figure steps through the curtain that conceals the back room, and it is as if my soul is flooded with light. My heart beats faster, needlessly. The swell of love within me is enough to push the blood through my veins.

He wears none of the finery of court. The sleeves of his rough linen shirt are rolled to the elbow, and a heavy leather apron covers his shirt and plain woolen breeches. He is the most beautiful sight I have ever seen. I want to run my hands through his smooth brown hair, and kiss each one of his long, beautiful, ink-stained fingers. My body wants to do things that make me blush.

He is wiping his hands on a rag as he enters, but then he looks up and our eyes meet. The last vestiges of my reason drown in the warm honey of his eyes.

I step forward, hungry for his embrace, but though he is smiling, he gives a quick shake of his head, glancing back over his shoulder to indicate we are not alone.

I step back, and force myself to speak calmly, though my voice breaks with my eager joy. "How are you here?"

"I left Colbert's service," he says, still beaming.

"He let you go?" I cannot believe it, and yet here he is.

He nods. "Your father works like a man on fire since the king reinstated him. It is rumored that he will take a new wife soon."

My joy falters a little at this news. I can't help feeling regret, and betrayal, that Papa has forgotten his old family.

"He misses you still," René says quickly, reading my expression. "But he is strong and healthy, and his work keeps him from the bottle."

I nod and remind myself, I want what is best for Papa. And as I think it, my jealousy evaporates and I feel only happiness for him. René goes on recounting what has happened in Paris since I left: Master Valin has fallen into disgrace, and André is gone, rumored to be seeking a position in Austria or Russia. I smile at the idea of André in frozen Saint Petersburg, trying to worm his way into the ruthless Russian court. I like the idea that all of Europe stretches between me and him.

René continues, but I am hearing less and less. One question burns above all the others. There is only one thing on which all my happiness rests, and so I interrupt him.

"René, why are you here?"

"Colbert only required me to stay because he feared what would happen with your father in the wake of the cutting of the Blue. When he saw he no longer needed me, he released me from service. With my saved wages, I purchased an apprenticeship in the bookbinders' guild, and in my evenings, I studied Dutch so that I could seek a position here when my apprenticeship was complete. I've been here nearly a month now. I have a job, and a place to stay, though it's not much."

"But why here? In Amsterdam?" I persist. I need to hear confirmation of what every fiber is yearning for.

"Why do you think, Juliette?"

I grasp his hand then and press it to my heart, not caring about the damp ink on his fingers.

The master of the shop calls from the back room, and René's smile fades a little.

"I have to go," he says. "Meet me the day after tomorrow at lunchtime by the weighhouse in Dam Square?" He gives me a quick, furtive kiss that leaves me hungrier than ever.

I have no time to answer before he disappears through the doorway, but it scarcely matters. There is nothing in all the world that can keep me from that meeting.

It is not easy to get away from the de Klerk household but Adrienne proves an excellent ally when it comes to matters of romance, and so she convinces her mother to let us walk in the square that afternoon. We arrive together, but Adrienne happily skips off to a café scandalously unaccompanied, while I cross to the weighhouse to meet René.

He is already waiting, pacing nervously beside the squat stone structure. He carries a parcel under one arm and wears plain brown woolen breeches and coat—not the elegant silk and embroidery of court, nor the solemn black of a clerk in the king's service. I watch him for a moment before he sees me, and I wonder how I ever thought him a gentleman's son. He is far too kind and honest. He's never looked more handsome than he does now in simple, honest wool.

He turns, and when our eyes meet, his face shines with a reserved smile. He offers me an elbow, and I force myself to take it demurely, though I would rather dive into his embrace. Together, we begin a leisurely circuit around the square.

After a moment, he speaks. "When we parted, Juliette, you told me you released me from our marriage."

Is he trying to tell me he has married another in the ensuing years? I swallow hard and nod. "It wasn't really a marriage anyway."

He bristles. "I believed it so," he says. "In the eyes of God. In my heart."

I nod again, but cannot speak for the fear that's clenching my heart. Why has he come here, if he means only to ensure that our connection is severed? Why didn't he just leave me in my dull loneliness?

"So I have to ask now." He stops walking and turns to face me, his expression serious and his voice brimming with emotion. "Do you still want me?"

His question makes me want to slap him and kiss him all at once. "Of course I want you, René!" I burst out, tears stinging in my eyes now. Several passersby glance in our direction with expressions of curiosity or surprise, and I lower my voice. "I thought I would never see you again. I released you so you could have a happy life."

"Would you allow me, then, to have that happy life with you?" he asks, and I think my heart will burst.

I throw my arms around him, though this brings more disapproving glances from those around us. He unwinds my arms and holds me back to look into my eyes. "Is that a yes?"

I laugh, despite myself. "It's a yes."

"Good," he says. "So it's settled then."

"Settled," I agree, glowing with delight. He offers his elbow again so we can resume our stroll, but I am floating more than walking.

"Louis kept his promise to knight your father, by the way," René says. "He is Sieur Pitau, which makes you the daughter of a gentleman. Can you still settle for a lowly bookbinder? We will be poor at first, and even if I rise, we will not be wealthy. And I will need your assistance, at least until I can establish myself."

I flex the fingers on my right hand. They are stiff, from the burn scars and from lack of use in anything more challenging than penmanship and needlework, which they will now do, though clumsily. The idea of trying them in a craft again makes them tingle.

"I know nothing of bookbinding. Will you teach me?" I ask.

"It will be my delight," he says.

"Then it shall be mine too," I say, drawing myself tighter against him on his arm.

We continue to walk, and I know that the glow of love I feel must be radiating around us, because people passing give us indulgent smiles. I smile back, proud to be on René's arm. But one worry still won't let me go. I only want truth between us from now on, so I speak.

"It is impossible for me to return to France, you know," I remind him. "If you marry me, it will be impossible to go home."

"I think France is a small thing to give up for a girl who has captured the sun," he says. By now, we find ourselves back at our starting point, and here, quite suddenly, René drops to a knee before me, and holds out a ring. All around us, people pause to watch.

"Shall we do it right this time?" he asks, smiling. "Juliette Pitau, will you marry me . . . again?"

I can barely stand still as I stretch out my hand and let him slip the ring onto my finger. But when I see the ring itself, my mouth falls open in shock.

Six rubies fan out like the corona of the sun in an ornate setting of swirling gold. I would recognize the craftsmanship anywhere, and I know the stones too. They are the rubies from Maman's brooch—the one Papa melted down to set the Blue. The only part of her jewelry I didn't sell. And the goldwork—only one master jeweler has such skill.

I clutch the ring to my heart, unable to speak. René rises and puts a supporting arm around me, which is good, since my knees have gone watery.

"I have kept a correspondence with your father, Juliette, as two who loved you and mourned your loss. You were his favorite, you know."

I shake my head. "I am only a daughter."

"You were his *petit bijou*. His most precious jewel. Do you know, he buried you beside your mother and brother, and in the months when I was still in Paris, he visited the graves often. He left many remembrances on your grave."

It gives me a queasy feeling to think of Papa visiting my empty grave, so I return his attention back to the ring. "But how did you get this?"

"I told him I hoped to marry, and I told him something of the lovely French girl who worked in the house of the de Klerk family."

I draw in a sharp breath. "He knows?" This has been a lasting sadness of my exile, worrying that my father believes me dead.

"I didn't tell him that. That was prohibited. I only told him I had found a girl I wished to marry here in Amsterdam. That she was beautiful, and enterprising, and loyal to a fault. That she was French by birth, but unable to return to France due to unfortunate circumstances. It has been a long correspondence, you understand. So many details have passed between us. In the end, he gave me this ring, in a letter noting that even a household servant should have a dowry."

I can scarcely breathe, I'm so overwhelmed with joy. So much restored to me. So much I never expected.

"You know that you still cannot write your father," he continues. "But I do intend to keep up my correspondence. Perhaps someday, he will visit me and I can introduce him to my wife."

I am weeping uncontrollably into René's handkerchief when

Adrienne crosses the square to us. She is concerned until she sees the ring on my finger. Then she whoops with joy and squeezes us both in an embrace that elicits laughter and applause from onlookers.

"I should go," René says. His cheeks are pink. I can feel a blush rising on my face too. He begins to turn, but then remembering the package he has been carrying the whole time, he hands it to me.

"I meant for you to have this when you came to the shop," he says, handing me the parcel. "*Au revoir*, mesdemoiselles." He bows, first to me and then to Adrienne, before striding away, a distinct bounce in his step.

"Open it! Open it!" Adrienne demands, hopping from one foot to the other in excitement.

I untie the string and pull away the brown paper. Inside is a thin book, bound in fine red leather, a pair of golden wings tooled on the cover. I am sure it is the work he presented to graduate from apprenticeship.

We admire the cover together before I open it to the first page to see what story lies within.

Adrienne wrinkles her dainty, freckled nose. "It is only the Ovid you bought," she grumbles.

It is the story of Icarus, from Ovid's *Metamorphoses*. I laugh that he has redeemed my lie to Adrienne.

The sun is shining as we walk back to the de Klerk house, where I will give the mistress my notice. I must start planning for the days and weeks ahead—preparing linens and setting up a new household with what little money I have—but all I can think of is Icarus, his wings of goose feather and wax spread wide in that expansive sky.

Ovid got the story wrong. Because I am flying high, burning with passion for life, and I do not think that this time I will fall. In this moment, in this world, beneath the golden sun in its brilliant blue sky, nothing seems impossible.

Author's Note

This book is first and foremost a work of fiction. My fiction is, however, built upon a framework of historical facts:

1. In 1668, Jean-Baptiste Tavernier returned to France from India with an array of diamonds as well as tales of adventure. Soon after, he appeared before Louis XIV, and sold him a large number of diamonds, including the Tavernier Violet, which weighed around 114–117 carats (the numbers vary slightly in different accounts).

2. In 1671, Louis ordered the Tavernier cut. Though history tells us little more about him, the crown jeweler who cut the stone was named Sieur Jean Pitau.

3. It took Pitau two years to cut the stone. It became known as the Blue of the Crown, or, more commonly in English, the French Blue.

4. The French Blue was cut in an early form of the brilliant cut, which was a novel way of cutting diamonds

at the time. The Tavernier Violet's shape, however, did not lend itself to a true brilliant cut, and so the dimensions of the cut had to be modified to adjust for the stone.

5. The invention of the brilliant cut is attributed to Cardinal Mazarin, who, along with Dowager Queen Anne, ruled France during the regency of the child king Louis XIV. Mazarin's magnificent collection of eighteen diamonds passed to the French crown at his death in 1661. At that time, Louis XIV gained full control of his throne at the age of twenty-two.

Upon these thin historical facts, I have built my story. I was fascinated by the premise of a man being ordered to cut the largest diamond owned by the French crown (and possibly the largest blue diamond in all of Europe at the time) in a style that was brand-new, that had only been achieved a handful of times, and that was not appropriate to the shape of the stone. At once, I began to wonder what such a seemingly impossible task might do to a person, and how it might be achieved. From that simple thought the grand fiction of my story arose.

Jean-Baptiste Colbert, Jean Pitau, Suzanne du Plessis-Bellière, Nicolas Fouquet, and (of course) Louis XIV were all real people. Louis XIV, at the time this story takes place, lived in the Louvre Palace in Paris, as the magnificent Palace of Versailles was not completed until 1682, seven years after the conclusion of my story. Nicolas Fouquet, however, would not have been in Paris; he was imprisoned in Pinerolo, Italy, before the time of this story, and so his presence in the Bastille is a fiction. Juliette, René, and André are purely fictional as well. History (at least the history that has made its way into English) tells us nothing of Sieur Pitau's family or workshop life. The last major plague to hit Paris did so in 1668, so the fevers that killed Juliette's family in the summer of 1671 are only a small fictional stretch, as historian Vanessa Harding notes that plague epidemics in Paris often persisted for as long as three years.

The Jewish Benzacar family is purely fictional as well; however, the circumstances of their lives are based in fact. Jews were very active in the gem, gold, and diamond trade throughout Western Europe. In Spain and Portugal, they suffered expulsion, forced conversion, torture, and death at the hands of the Inquisition, and many fled those countries. The Low Countries were experiencing an economic boom and were tolerant of religious differences, and therefore became a haven for many Sephardic Jews (the Jews of the Iberian Peninsula), who brought their trades with them. This migration led to the thriving diamond industries of cities like Amsterdam and Antwerp that persist to the present day.

As for Jews in France, they had been expelled and recalled at various times through the course of history. In the early 1600s, Jews began to reenter France and were marginally tolerated, but an edict of 1615 made it illegal for Christians to shelter or converse with them. Jews were barred from living in Paris and were charged insulting "head taxes" (the same tax levied on cattle) to enter the city during the day. With the annexation of Alsace and

Lorraine and the migration of Jews out of Spain, the number of Jews in France rose during the reign of Louis XIV, mostly in the form of communities of *conversos* in outlying areas. These groups were nominally Christian but kept Jewish traditions alive in the privacy of their homes. They were tolerated because of their wealth and great skill as craftsmen, and because their secrets made them easily exploited. They could not, however, legally settle in Paris, and historians estimate that no more than three to five hundred Jews lived a precarious, secret life in or around the city in the mid-1600s.

The history of gem cutting, as well as that of specific gemstones, is sketchy, and conflicting accounts of both technologies and pedigrees exist. Some sources suggest Mazarin's diamonds were cut in the brilliant style, while others argue that few or none of them were. Some sources suggest that at least two of his stones were acquired and/or cut in Portugal, including a fine diamond called the Mirror of Portugal. Unfortunately, diamonds have been prone to both theft and recutting over the centuries, and stones like the Mirror of Portugal have disappeared from record.

As for the French Blue, it, too, disappeared when the crown jewels of France were stolen in 1792, during the French Revolution. It was never recovered. However, just a few days after the statute of limitations for the theft ended, the Hope Diamond appeared in Britain. The French Blue was heart-shaped and weighed 67–69 carats. The Hope is rectangular, with a weight of around 45 carats. Today, the Hope Diamond is housed at the Smithsonian Institution.

It had long been assumed that the Hope was the French Blue,

recut to disguise it. This assumption was finally confirmed beyond reasonable doubt in 2009, when a lead model of the French Blue was found in a museum in France, allowing the facets of the two stones to be compared. The model also allowed for other research on the long-gone French Blue, including the discovery that the sunburst cut around the culet at the heart of the diamond would have appeared nearly colorless from certain angles, so that if the stone had been mounted over a backdrop of gold, a golden sun would have appeared in the heart of the stone. A fine diamond, indeed, to symbolize France's self-declared Sun King, Louis XIV.

Acknowledgments

Novels, like children, often take a village to raise, and *The Jewel Thief* is no exception. So many readers and fellow writers have offered critique and advice, including Tara Dairman, Claudia Mills, Betty Mobley, Leah Tanaka, Anne Braden, Elaine Vickers, Jennifer J. Stewart, Heather Alexander, Ida Olson, Sarah Schantz, and Kristen Nitz. I am so deeply grateful for the community of writers on the Colorado Front Range and beyond that has supported me through the high and low points with open arms, warm hearts, and the occasional glass of sangria.

My agent, Jennifer Weltz, knew just what to do to get the manuscript into the hands of the right editor, Dana Leydig. As for Dana, wow. She has stretched me in ways that have taken both Juliette's story and my skill set to new heights. How does one say thank you enough for all of that?

And of course, I cannot neglect to thank the team at Viking that has cut, shaped, and polished my rough pages into the gem you now hold in your hands. Thank you, thank you, thank you. You are all quite brilliant.